'We kissed and... me. I want to...'

Brodie said. 'It was ....joy it. That much I do k.....

Chey glared at him. 'What is that supposed to mean?'

'It means you liked it as much as I did. So what's your problem?'

'I *never* get involved with clients.'

'Then I'll have to cancel your contract.'

She immediately launched to her feet. 'You can't do that!'

He rose smoothly and brought his hands to his hips. 'The contract that cannot be broken has never been devised.'

'I'll sue you!'

'Before or after we make love?' he returned smoothly.

Chey folded her arms. 'I don't sleep around.'

'I don't want you to sleep around,' Brodie retorted. 'I want you to sleep with *me*.'

Available in December 2003 from Silhouette Special Edition

Her Secret Affair
ARLENE JAMES

SILHOUETTE®
SPECIAL EDITION™

*First published in Great Britain 2003
Silhouette Books, Eton House, 18-24 Paradise Road,
Richmond, Surrey TW9 1SR*

© Deborah Rather 2001

ISBN 0 373 24421 5

23-1203

*Printed and bound in Spain
by Litografia Rosés S.A., Barcelona*

ARLENE JAMES

grew up in Oklahoma and has lived all over the South of the USA. In 1976 she married 'the most romantic man in the world.' The author enjoys travelling with her husband, but writing has always been her chief pastime.

SILHOUETTE®

Desire™ 2 in 1

are proud to introduce

DYNASTIES: THE BARONES

Meet the wealthy Barones—caught in a web of danger, deceit and…desire!

Twelve exciting stories in six 2-in-1 volumes:

0104/SH/LC78

SILHOUETTE®

Desire ™ 2 in 1

is proud to introduce

DYNASTIES: THE DANFORTHS

Meet the Danforths—a family of prominence...
tested by scandal, sustained by passion!

Coming Soon!
Twelve thrilling stories in six 2-in-1 volumes:

0105/SH/LC96

SILHOUETTE®

*Super*ROMANCE™

proudly presents
a brand-new series from

KATHRYN SHAY

Serenity House

They'd grown up at Serenity House—a home for girls.
Now they're coming together for the first time as
adults. Childhood friends who'd shared difficult times,
who'd shared hopes and fears, laughter and tears—
and perhaps most important of all...secrets.

Practice Makes Perfect
October 2004

A Place to Belong
November 2004

Against the Odds
January 2005

1004/SH/LC94

was screened from general view by an overgrown tangle of greenery, but a small army of gardeners were at work taming the jungle that had been allowed to grow rampant. Already the yard was shaping up nicely, and she could see workers in the distance replacing a section of fencing that had been removed for some reason. She wondered if Brodie Todd was building a pool and hoped intensely that he wasn't slapping some garishly modern cement job into the backyard of this graceful old antebellum mansion.

She left the car parked to one side of the wide brick drive that arced in front of the house, gazing sadly at a magnificent marble birdbath which had been toppled onto its side in the grassy center of the looping drive. Measuring at least three feet across, the bowl would require several able bodies to lift it back into place. Chey sincerely hoped that Brodie Todd meant to do just that, and promised herself that she would mention it to him at the first opportunity. Leaving everything but her keys behind in the car, she climbed the steps and crossed the front porch.

For this meeting she had chosen from her spring wardrobe a pale pink designer suit trimmed in light gray with a narrow, knee-length skirt and a brief, tailored, asymmetrical jacket. Pale gray stockings and smoke-gray shoes with high, fashionably wide heels completed the ensemble. With her long blond hair coiled into a tight roll against the back of her head and her makeup sparingly but expertly applied, she presented a sleek, neat business persona.

A small brass bell suspended from a wrought-iron arm hung by the door, and Chey gave the clapper a vigorous shake. The resulting peal echoed loudly all over the estate, causing the gardeners to pause at their labors and raise their heads and Chey to grab the bell with both hands in order to quell it. The door emitted a rusty crack and squeaked open. A small, pale woman greeted Chey.

"Miss Simmons? I'm Kate, the housekeeper. Won't you come in?"

"Thank you."

Perhaps five feet tall and thin to the point of emaciation, Kate wore her medium-brown hair pulled back in a pony-tail. She seemed both bursting with energy and dangerously frail. Turning, she said, ''The family is in the garden room at the back of the house.'' Indicating with a glance over one shoulder that Chey should follow, she set off briskly, bouncing up onto her toes with every step, arms swinging at her sides. No wonder she was so thin, Chey mused, the woman could burn more energy just walking than Chey could at a mad dash. She led Chey down the broad central hall, past the elegant, curving staircase and all the way across the big house in mere seconds, only to abandon her after brusquely announcing, ''She's here.''

Chey had the impression of glass and greenery and cob-blestoned floor in the heartbeat before a husky, cultured female voice made her head turn to one side. ''Hello, again. It's Chey, isn't it? Or would you prefer Miss Simmons?''

Chey smiled at the long, patrician face of the woman who approached her, her long, sleek body dressed in light-weight, pale green bouclé knit with a bright scarf looped loosely about a long, swanlike neck. ''Mrs. Todd. Nice to see you again, and Chey is perfect.''

''Then you must call me Viola.'' Long, slender, slightly gnarled fingers curled around Chey's hand. ''Let me intro-duce you to my grandson and great-grandson.'' She whirled away, and her chin-length, ruthlessly bobbed silver and white hair whirled with her. ''They're over here, on the other side of this jungle, wrestling with a weight bench, whatever that is.''

Chey followed, thankful for the sedate pace as she wound her way through a virtual forest in pots and wooden boxes. She heard a clang and muttering, followed by a screeching little voice that insisted, ''Wet me, Daddy! Wet me!''

Just ahead of her, Viola came to a stop and said urgently, ''Seth, don't!''

At the same instant, a deeper, gruffer voice barked, "Son, no! You'll—" a wail interrupted, followed by more clanks and a gusty sigh, "—smash your finger," the man finished resignedly. "Here, let me look at it."

The wails were already subsiding as Chey stepped up beside Viola Todd. The man was on his bare knees, his dark head bent over the small body in his likewise bare arms, a shambles of pipe and padded board beside them.

"It's not bleeding," he said, examining the tiny finger. "The nail looks okay. Just a pinch on the end." He lifted the little fist and lavishly kissed the uplifted finger. "Some strawberry jam ought to fix it. Let Grandmama see to it." He gave the affectionate title a French pronunciation. *Grahn-ma-ma* stooped and opened her arms. Chey was shocked at the bright red head that hurtled into those outstretched arms.

"Gramuma, I poke my fingder in the jam jar?"

"If you please," Viola assented, grunting as she lifted the child off his feet.

"Pwease," he intoned solemnly, squeezing his grandmother's face between two chubby palms, the injured finger sticking out.

Viola laughed and carried him away, saying only, "Brodie, get up and speak to this woman." Over her shoulder, the red-headed imp stared at Chey curiously and waggled his fingers in a hello wave. She smiled in reply before turning her attention back to the man now rising slowly to his feet.

Something about him made her step back in shocked awareness. Perhaps it was his height, for he stood easily six inches taller than she. Or perhaps it was all that bare, bronze skin, as he wore only jogging shorts, a loose muscle shirt and running shoes without socks. Then again, it might have been the contrast between his pale blue eyes and the coarse, ink-black hair mowed flat across the top of his head and precisely groomed into the neat, meticulous mustache and goatee which framed his sculpted mouth and squarish chin. Or perhaps it was the face itself, which, while all sharp angles and flat planes, was unabashedly handsome. Or it might have been the frankly curious, blatantly appreciative manner in which that pale blue gaze leisurely traveled over her and came to rest, finally, on her face.

Chey was aware suddenly of the thudding heaviness of her heartbeat, and in the next instant a pair of pictures flashed before her mind's eye: Brodie Todd handsomely turned out in tux and black tie, and Brodie Todd stretched out in bed, drowsing sleepily, his unshaven beard a bluish shadow on his jaw. She blinked, and found herself staring into a pale blue mirror of her own thoughts. She backed up another step, once again taking in the whole of his face. A lazy smile slowly lifted one corner of his mouth, a knowing, challenging, promising smile that made her heart plummet straight to her toes. It terrified her, that smile, triggered a primal instinct for survival, so that her only thought was to turn tail and run, fast and far, the project and everything else be damned. Then he reached for her, and even that thought dissolved.

He clapped one palm onto her shoulder and grasped her fingers with the other as if he meant to shake her hand even if he had to hold her in place to do it. Lightning shot down her arm and sizzled in her chest. She barely suppressed a gasp. He just stood there, staring at her until she looked away in self-defense.

"Brodie Todd," he said coaxingly, his voice pitched low and intimate. "You must be the designer, Chey Simmons."

She lifted a brow, willing her speedy heartbeat to normalcy, and corrected him tartly, "Architect, refurbisher and interior designer."

"All right." He chuckled and went on softly, "Interesting name, Chey."

They stood in silence for several seconds after that. His hands felt heavy and hot. Finally, she forced herself to look at him. The first words out of her mouth were a complete surprise to her. "It's Mary Chey, actually."

His smile dazzled. "Mary Chey. I like that. It's nice to meet you, Mary Chey. You've been very highly recommended, your talent much praised. No one bothered to say that you are also quite beautiful."

Panic surged up in her, and she looked away again. Much belatedly she managed to murmur, "Thank you."

"You're welcome," he said, sliding his hand down her arm from her shoulder. "Let's have some coffee." Her feet felt welded to the floor, but he turned her and literally propelled her toward a small, round, glass table off to one side. Viola was there, sitting on the edge of her chair and holding a jam pot for the child, who sat, legs splayed, facing her, his finger in jam all the way to the last knuckle. He pulled it out, curling it at the end, and plunged it into his mouth.

Brodie sat her next to his grandmother, across from the boy, pushing Chey down quite firmly into the slatted iron chair. "How do you take yours?" he asked.

She blinked up at him.

"Coffee," he said. "How do you take yours."

"Uh, black."

He grinned, fully aware of her confusion, and moved to the cart standing next to the glass wall, where he poured coffee from a silver pot into a china cup. Chey followed his every move with her eyes, even as she began to feel more herself. She didn't register the view beyond until Viola asked, "Do you like our pool?"

Chey abruptly, guiltily, switched her gaze, first to Viola's face, then to the vista beyond the glass wall. It was magnificent. The pool had been built to mammoth proportions and was flanked with no less than four Grecian fountains. Gazebos with louvered sides had been built at both ends and surrounded with plants. A chin-high, black wrought-iron fence with impressive scroll work had been erected around the entire area. Chey was relieved to see no slide, not even a diving board, nor could she imagine the typical plastic or aluminum lawn chair in this very classical setting. Apparently neither could the designer, for many stone tables and benches had been grouped among the greenery and beneath the trees. To one side, nearest the house and outside the pool gate in a cool, shady spot, stood an elaborate playground surrounded by several inches of dark pine mulch; a little boy's paradise. "It's wonderful," she said succinctly.

"The gazebos serve as bathhouse and bar," Brodie told her. Bringing her cup and saucer to the table, he dropped a thick linen napkin in her lap. "Have a pineapple tart," he said, placing that plate before her as well. It wasn't a question or even a suggestion, and she bristled slightly at the tone of command, but when she lifted her gaze to his, she found his lips twitching against a smile, and her indignation immediately wilted. "They're one of Marcel's specialties," Brodie went on, "and you know how temperamental chefs can be. You'll offend him deeply if you don't eat."

With that, he presented her a fork. She snatched it from his hand, and he walked around her chair and dropped into the one next to her, mouth quirking with that smile he still strove to suppress. He knew how he affected her, blast him, and she didn't doubt that he was somehow doing it on purpose. Leaning back, he prepared to enjoy his coffee at leisure while watching her steadily over the rim of his cup.

In pure defensiveness, Chey broke the crust of the tart with her fork, anything to distract her from Brodie Todd's sultry perusal. Still warm, the tart exuded a piquant, sharp-sweet aroma that made her mouth water. She cut off a bite and shoved her fork beneath it, lifting it toward her mouth even as she blurted, quite without meaning to, "You're not eating."

He chuckled and sipped from his cup before saying with mock severity, "I'm being disciplined."

Chey closed her lips around the flaky confection at that moment, and the full flavor of the cooked pineapple burst within her mouth. She widened her eyes, savoring the incredible taste as she chewed and swallowed. "Oh, my," she said.

"Which is why Brodie's already had four of those this morning," his grandmother revealed with a chortle.

Chey lifted an eyebrow at his version of "disciplined," but she could understand why he'd stuffed himself. The thing was pure heaven. She began to eat with genuine gusto.

Brodie sipped from his cup again and admitted unrepentantly, "I could eat the whole plate of them. And I will, too, unless some kind soul does it for me."

"In that case," Chey said, swallowing another delicious bite, "I just may have another."

He laughed at that, sliding down in his chair and putting back his head so the sound could roll up from his throat. "I love a woman with healthy appetites!"

"If she eats like you," Viola said, placing the jam pot between her great-grandson's legs, "she'll have to work out like you." She grimaced and confided to Chey, "All that sweating and grunting. I don't understand why a person doesn't just eat less."

"Grandmama is the queen of self-denial," Brodie said affectionately. "She won't even *taste* one of Marcel's tarts."

"Of course not," Viola sniffed. "I won't try crack cocaine, either, or tobacco or any number of harmful things."

"Her list of harmful things, however, does not include mint juleps," Brodie divulged, and Chey laughed around a bite of tart.

Viola feigned shock. "The mint julep is the most efficacious concoction ever invented by man."

Brodie smirked. "The mint julep is nothing more or less

than crushed ice, a sprig of mint, some sugar and a glass full of hard liquor.''

Chey wiped her mouth with her napkin and reached for her coffee, while Viola lifted her chin and primly announced that a little hard liquor never hurt anyone. Brodie winked at Chey and said, ''Lest you think that Grandmama overindulges, I should tell you that she strictly confines her alcohol consumption to two mint juleps a day, one at lunch and one as a night cap.''

''That's right,'' Viola confirmed, ''and I'm as healthy at eighty as you are at thirty-six.''

Chey's jaw dropped along with her coffee cup, which she barely managed to direct back to its saucer. ''You're *eighty?*''

''Eighty-two, to be exact,'' Brodie answered for his grandmother, who preened blatantly—until a blob of strawberry jam hit her smack in the chest. All eyes turned to the child, who looked as surprised as everyone else. Having buried his hand in the jam pot up to the thumb joint, he obviously hadn't foreseen the difficulties of trying to clean it by shaking.

''Seth!'' Viola exclaimed, while Brodie just groaned and put his head in his hands. Wide-eyed, Seth stuck his entire hand in his mouth, while Viola wet a napkin in her water glass and dabbed at the stain on her dress.

''You'll have to forgive my son,'' Brodie said with a sigh, lifting his head and looking at Chey. ''He's only three.'' While speaking, he reached over and removed the jam pot from his son's lap. ''I suppose he really needs a nanny.''

''What he needs is a mother,'' Viola retorted.

Brodie sent her a direct look and said carefully, ''He has a mother.''

''Humph.'' Abandoning the stain, Viola rewet the napkin and reached for the boy, who yelped, scooted out of the chair and ran in a wide loop around his father, right to

Chey, reaching for her with both hands. It apparently never even occurred to the little imp that he might not be welcome, and she reacted completely without forethought, as she had done any number of times with her numerous nieces and nephews. Grabbing up her own napkin, she caught that small sticky hand before it caught her. As he was already climbing over the arm of the chair, she quickly guided his feet away from her skirt and, for lack of any better option, settled him in her lap. He laid his head back against her chest, looked up at her and exclaimed loudly, "You pwetty like Mommy!"

Chey smiled limply. Suddenly she wondered why the newspapers hadn't mentioned Brodie Todd's wife. The next instant she pushed the thought away as insignificant and said politely, "Thank you. Now if you're going to sit in my lap, young man, you have to have that hand washed."

He acted as if he didn't hear her, but when Viola leaned forward and began cleaning his hand with the damp napkin, he sat still—as still as a three-year-old can sit, anyway. Brodie said, entirely too lightly, "You obviously have experience, Mary Chey. Do you have a child of your own perhaps?"

She lifted her gaze to his and said purposefully, "No. But I do have thirty-one nieces and nephews."

His cup rattled in his saucer. *"Thirty-one?"*

"It'll be thirty-two before long."

"How many brothers and sisters do you have?"

"Nine."

When he didn't immediately reply to that, she looked up at him. His mouth was hanging open. *"Ten* kids?" He sat back in his chair with a plop. "Holy cow. This one runs me absolutely ragged."

"I can imagine."

"I'm sure you can." He sat forward again. "Don't misunderstand me. I love this little terror." He smoothed a hand over the top of the boy's bright red head. "I wouldn't trade what I have with him for anything in this world, but I just couldn't do it *ten* times.''

''Not many people can,'' she said. ''The most any of my brothers and sisters have is five. That would be Frank, he's the oldest, and Mary Kay. Bay and Thomas and their wives each have four. Johnny—he's the baby—Mary May, Matt and Anthony have three apiece, and Mary Fay has one and is expecting one.''

Brodie was smiling. ''Are all the women in your family named Mary?''

''Each and every one,'' she confirmed, ''including my mother, who is Mary Louise, and both of my grandmothers. I guess my mother's something of a poet at heart because she rhymed us all. Mary May, Kay, Fay and Chey. I think she ran out of the standard options by the time she had me. Did I mention that my brother Bailey is called Bay?'' she asked rhetorically. ''And me, they call Mary. I guess Chey was just too much for everyone.''

For some reason he was grinning very broadly. ''But you prefer Chey.''

''Well,'' she admitted, ''Mary is awfully common, especially in my family.''

''There is nothing at all common about you,'' he told her blatantly.

''I should hope not,'' she quipped, ignoring a shiver of delight.

He reached across the table then, and covered her hand with his, and suddenly the comfortable, chummy atmosphere evaporated. ''I think it's time I showed you the house,'' he said silkily, ''unless you were serious about that second tart.''

''Regretfully not,'' she said, pulling free her hand and scooting back her chair. ''Like your grandmother, I prefer to exercise a little more self-control.''

''Don't be fooled by Grandmama,'' he said, getting to

his feet. "As if Seth doesn't provide her with enough exercise, she works very hard out in the garden."

"Gardening isn't work," Viola protested ardently. "It's pure relaxation."

"For you," he said, bending down again to pluck the boy off Chey's lap so she could rise. "It's pure torture for me."

Viola pointed toward the weight bench. "That would be torture for me."

"To each his own," Chey said brightly.

"An excellent theory," Brodie commented, passing the boy to his grandmother. "I have a theory about self-control," he went on, reaching out an arm to bring Chey to his side. "General restraint makes occasionally losing it quite enjoyable. Don't you agree?" he asked in an intimate voice that stopped her heart and closed her throat.

Chey coughed and muttered, "I, um, prefer not to lose mine at all."

"Maybe you just haven't found the indulgence you can't resist yet," he suggested softly.

She couldn't have answered that if she'd wanted to, and he knew it. She saw it in his eyes. Abruptly, he dropped his arm and looked to his son. "Don't wear out Grandmama. Understand?" The boy nodded, two fingers in his mouth. Brodie bent and took his son's small face into his hands, turning it toward Chey. "Tell Miss Chey, 'Good to meet you.'"

"Goo to mwee oo," the boy said around his fingers.

Viola pulled his hand from his mouth and instructed him to try again. He managed it better this time.

"It was nice to meet you, too," Chey said. She widened her gaze to include Viola. "It was especially nice to see you again, ma'am."

"I know you'll do well for us, dear," Viola Todd said. Then she looked to her grandson and a silent communication passed between them.

He bent and kissed first the boy and then his grandmother on the cheek. Straightening once more, he moved toward Chey, lifting a hand to take her arm. Automatically, she shied from his touch. It was a foolish thing to do, foolish and telling, and it brought a flush of embarrassment to her cheeks. Brodie just smiled knowingly and clasped his hands behind him, the hunger in his pale blue eyes as blatant as any declaration. Well, Chey mused as she strode off in front of him, she now knew what it felt like to be a pineapple tart on that man's plate.

Chapter Two

"We'll start down here on the first floor and work our way up," Brodie said in a brisk, businesslike tone.

Chey nodded at that and folded her arms tightly as they passed through the doorway into the central hall side by side. "How many rooms are there?"

"Twenty-eight rooms on the first two floors, counting the butler's pantry and linen storage. The third is made up of the laundry, an apartment belonging to Marcel and Kate, the couple who cook and keep house for us, and the attics, which are a virtual warren of irregular cubicles crammed with furniture and junk. Kate and Marcel have just finished renovating their own space, so that need not concern you, and I don't foresee using the attics for anything other than storage, but you're welcome to take a look. Much of the furniture appears usable to me, but you would be the better judge."

Chey nodded with interest. "These old houses often turn

out to be hiding valuable antiques. It's possible we'll find some of the original furnishings.''

"That's good. I like the idea of authenticity—within reason, of course.'' He opened the first door they came to. "This is one of the worst,'' he said, "the breakfast room.''

She peeked inside, leaning past him to do so. The room was indeed a shambles. A plumbing leak had caused the ceiling to fall in and the wallpaper to peel. The carpet had rotted away and left the wood planking beneath exposed. A swinging door, now off the hinges, leaned against one wall. Large, multipaned, ceiling-to-floor windows looked out into the garden room, and like those of many homes of the period, which were taxed according to the number of rooms and doors they contained, the bottom section could be raised to create a direct pass-through. "I assume that doorway leads to the kitchens,'' she said, pointing to the vacant space next to the unhinged door.

"Yes, via the butler's pantry, which also opens into the formal dining room. We could go through that way since the floorboards are sound, but it's such a mess I'd rather not take a chance on ruining that pretty suit you're wearing.''

She ignored the compliment, quickly withdrawing from the room. "I have to come back and take measurements, anyway.''

Thereafter, she kept her distance. They made a thorough survey of the entire first floor, which, in addition to the breakfast room and kitchens, included an actual ballroom, a large formal parlor, a formal dining room capable of seating two dozen comfortably, a cloakroom, a billiards room, a "smoking" room, an informal family room, two rest rooms, a "ladies withdrawing room" now claimed by Viola as a type of office, and an antiquated elevator from the 1930s. The kitchen had been completely renovated with modern, restaurant-quality appliances and fixtures, but Chey was relieved to see that the original brick floors, exposed beams and fire ovens had been left alone. The formal rooms were dingy and unattractive, having been last redecorated in the 1950s. The billiards room had been gutted; some of the floor had rotted. The cloakroom and smoking room had been relegated to storage, while the family rooms were shabby and horribly "updated" with shag carpets and cheap paneling. The two rest rooms were barely adequate, and the library, with falling shelves and a fireplace that undoubtedly leaked, was in deplorable shape.

The second floor had fared better and boasted a long, wide landing that ran the length of the back of the house and opened onto a balcony that overhung the garden room. Two smaller hallways branched off the wider, central one, allowing access to fourteen separate chambers. As in so many older homes, some rooms could only be reached by traveling through others and several doorways had been blocked by previous renovation. A cramped, rickety servants' stairway plunged straight down into the butler's pantry, its lower access blocked by a locked door and table. Chey noted that the shaft, which ran all the way to the third floor, provided perfect access for a central air-conditioning system, which had to be a prime consideration, given the hot, sticky Louisiana summer now rapidly approaching. Chey decided to make it a priority issue.

Brodie had set up a temporary office in a room at the front of the house that opened onto his personal bedchamber, and he'd had special electrical and telephone lines installed there to protect the several computers that he had up and running. The electrician he had employed had done a cursory inspection of the remainder of the house and had reported that some sections had been rewired as recently as twenty years previously, while some rooms utilized wires much older and some were without electricity altogether. Brodie, therefore, had engaged the man to draw up a rewiring schematic and present a proposal, which he now plucked from the metal table that he was using as a desk and handed over to Chey, much to her delight.

"Thank you," she told him, tucking the rolled schematic

under one arm. "This will make it easier to put together my bid."

He seemed amused by her choice of words. "What bid?"

"I thought you wanted me to bid on the project," she told him, confused.

"I want you to *oversee* the project," he said flatly.

"You mean, you've already made a decision?" she asked, astounded.

"I made the decision before I wrote the letter," he said matter-of-factly.

"Before you even met me?"

He folded his arms and perched on the corner of the metal table. "There are better ways to judge a person when it comes to business, Mary Chey. I assumed you'd know that. Besides, my grandmother met you at the tea, went there for that express purpose, in fact, as soon as my investigation confirmed you were the best person for the job."

"You had me investigated?" she demanded.

"Thoroughly, your business dealings anyway. I never pry into a person's private life."

Chey was temporarily dumbfounded. She tried to be offended, but he'd picked her for the job, after all. Still, it rankled somewhat, knowing that someone had delved into her past. "That's an odd way to conduct business, isn't it?" she asked with some asperity.

"On the contrary," he said calmly, "it's an efficient way of doing business."

She couldn't argue with that. Chey glanced around, a purely defensive gesture, and realized that art objects and other items from all over the world comprised much of the clutter. "What about personalities?" she asked. "Clashes happen, you know."

"The way I look at it," Brodie said, bringing her attention back to him, "it's easier in the long run to work with someone who does a good job even if you don't particularly like the individual, than to discover that someone you genuinely like is going to shaft you with shoddy work."

"That's one way of looking at it," she said coolly.

"My way," he retorted succinctly. "So, do we have a deal or not?"

"That depends," she said smoothly, though in truth she had no intention of turning down the job. "Exactly what is the deal? I mean, if you don't want me to bid on the project, then I can only assume you're offering a salary?"

He shook his head. "Not at all. I know exactly how much this job is worth to me, how much it will probably cost and what a reasonable profit on it would be for you. I propose to deposit everything I'm willing to spend into a special bank account to which you will have unlimited access. I expect fully three-fourths of the sum will go into the house. The rest is yours. If you overspend, you diminish your own earnings. If you underspend…well, I'm warning you here and now that I expect quality for every penny and I'll be personally inspecting the work and the invoices."

It was eminently fair, provided he put up enough money. "What if I'm not satisfied with the sum you're willing to spend?"

"Then I'll look elsewhere," he said simply. "But I think you'll approve. And just for the record, the way I see it, I'm buying your expertise. That means you are in charge of everything that has to do with refurbishing, repairing and redecorating the house. Everything."

"Except you'll be checking up on me," she pointed out.

"Just to be sure I'm getting my money's worth," he clarified. "I won't be second-guessing you. You are the expert here, aren't you?"

His directness, like everything else about him, unsettled her. She was used to tiptoeing around certain issues, to employing great diplomacy and tact in swaying her clients to allow her to act for them. She said, with a little more asperity than she intended, "You bet I am."

He grinned, the wretch. "I'm banking on it, not that it's

much of a gamble. I happen to know that, in addition to your degree in architecture and design, you have a good deal of experience in restoration and the attendant construction disciplines. In fact, I'm told that you have actual on-the-job experience in trim carpentry, plumbing and masonry.''

He actually knew about the summers she'd spent working in the trades with her brothers! She didn't know whether to be offended or impressed. The former felt safer. "Then why did you ask?" she snapped.

He chuckled unrepentantly. "Just to see how you'd respond. I dislike false modesty.''

"And I dislike arrogance.''

He laughed outright. "Is it arrogant to do your homework? To be sure someone's up to the job?''

She couldn't really argue with that, but she didn't have to like it. Folding her arms huffily, she said with heavy sarcasm, "I suppose you think you're a better business person than I am, because I've never gone to such lengths to check out anyone I've contracted with.''

"But then you aren't the one ponying up a million dollars.''

Her mouth fell open. It was almost twice what she'd expected, and she'd been prepared to fight, wheedle, beg and wrangle for that! She swallowed her mental exclamations and got her mouth wrapped around a sensible reply. Eventually. "Uh, that…I can definitely work with that.''

He chuckled. "I should hope so.'' He straightened and extended a hand toward her. "So then, are we agreed?''

She'd have been insane to balk at that point. "Absolutely.'' She put her hand in his. Lightning shot up her arm and down her spine. What was it about him that did this to her?

"I'll have the contract in your office tomorrow morning,'' he said, then, releasing her, he rose smoothly from the corner of the desk and swept his arm toward the door. "Now, shall we finish our inspection?''

She slipped by him untouched, but she was well aware that he was amused by her reluctance to come into physical contact with him again. She only wished that she could be amused about it. The fact was, it troubled her greatly. Men did not affect her this way; she didn't allow it, and she didn't like it one bit that she seemed to have no control over the matter where Brodie Todd was concerned. It left her little recourse except to restrict her attentions solely to the business at hand and ignore everything else.

He took her through his own Spartan, dreary bedchamber, several empty ones, three cramped, outmoded bathrooms, and Viola's slightly more personable suite. He pointed out every element of Seth's rooms, from the corner cabinet filled with toys in the playroom to the narrow bookcase crammed with reading material in the bedchamber. Brodie was especially concerned about the lack of amenities available for guests, explaining that he often entertained influential people, even foreign dignitaries on occasion, but he emphasized that the family rooms must come first. They were just leaving another nondescript room when a small body hurtled around the corner and flung itself at Brodie's knees, exclaiming, "Daddy, I see Mama!"

Brodie looked up as Viola came into view, huffing slightly from trying to keep up with the boy. "How is she?" he asked. "Anything new?"

Viola shook her head. "She seems completely unchanged to me, and Brown says she's seen nothing beyond the usual eye flutters and twitches."

Brodie sighed and nodded. Viola stroked his arm consolingly. "Poor thing," she said. "I know you want her to improve."

"I want her to damned well wake up," he muttered fiercely, but before anything else could be said, Seth loudly demanded, "Twucks now, Gramuma!"

A duet of voices, Viola's and Brodie's, instantly instructed the child in the art of courtesy, and he rewarded them with compliance, changing his demand to a plea. "We pway twucks now pwease?"

When Chey and Brodie left the room, Viola was on her hands and knees on the floor unrolling a mat with a scale drawing of a highway system on it while Seth pulled out an entire carton full of toy trucks.

"I really should hire a nanny," Brodie said once the door was closed. "Caring for a small child is too much for Grandmama."

"Why don't you then?" Chey asked, curious despite her better judgment. Silently she was wondering why the child's mother didn't just step in.

Brodie grimaced. "I don't want my son raised by servants. It might be different if his mother could devote a little attention to him."

"Why can't she?" Chey heard herself asking.

For the first time, Brodie's control seemed to slip. His handsome face hardened, and his hands tightened into fists. "See for yourself." Abruptly, he led Chey down a hallway toward the last of the rooms, saying, "I don't want her disturbed any more than necessary, for reasons you'll understand, I'm sure. I've already seen to her needs as best I can. In fact, I doubt it's necessary or even desirable that you do much with her suite, but I thought you ought to see it, at least." With that he opened the door of what seemed a combination sitting and hospital room. The walls had been plastered and painted coral pink. A ruffled sofa and chair stood around a plush rug and a delicate table overflowing with a large vase of fresh flowers. The rest of the furnishings were strictly utilitarian, however, from the hospital bed to the monitors and intravenous pole. A small metal cart bearing a tabletop television and stereo was parked at the foot of the bed. Music played softly.

A tall, husky woman with short, tightly curled gray hair stood up from a comfortable chair as they entered the room. Chey nodded, but Brodie ignored the other woman, moving instead to the bed. The big woman's mouth turned down at both ends, but it struck Chey as her usual expression rather than one of present disapproval. Chey approached the bed more out of curiosity than anything else and watched silently as Brodie sat down beside the small figure lying there. He picked up a slender, manicured hand and held it cupped in his own, speaking softly, telling the other person who Chey was and why she was there. Carefully, Chey sidled toward the foot of the bed, desperately wanting to see the person to whom he was speaking. What she saw shocked her deeply for two reasons.

The first was that the woman appeared to be comatose. The second was that hers was the face of an angel framed by bright, strawberry blond hair flowing over her shoulders and frilly white lace nightgown. Someone had made up her face, adding subtle color and shadow, but the angel herself slept on unaware. Indeed, only the gentle rise and fall of her chest gave any indication at all that she actually lived. Chey felt slightly sick to her stomach and told herself that it was compassion for the poor thing upon the bed, as well as her husband and son. It was at least partly that, but it was also more, and Chey was, at bottom, honest enough to admit to herself that she felt a twinge of pure envy as she watched Brodie reach up and gently cup, then pat one rosy, angelic cheek before rising to his feet once more and joining her at the foot of the bed.

"The doctors say it's best to keep familiar things around her, so we brought her own furniture with us. We painted the walls her favorite color and set up the room exactly as it was in Dallas." He nodded at the large woman standing to one side. "As her nurse, Brown came with us." Finally, he addressed the older woman. "This is Miss Simmons, Brown. She's going to transform the house, bring it all up to form for us. If you or Janey have need of changes in your rooms, Miss Simmons is the one to consult."

"I could use some fresh paint on my walls," Brown stated matter-of-factly, "and the toilet in the bathroom runs all the time. I don't need nothing else."

"And Janey?" Brodie asked. "What about her?"

Nurse Brown bristled. "I take care of her needs."

A muscle flexed in Brodie's jaw. "I realize that," he said tightly. "I meant, do you need any changes to make your job easier?" The woman shook her head. Chey couldn't help noticing that her eyes were as cold and steely a gray as her hair. Brodie tilted his head. "Fine. If you think of anything later, just let me know." With that he turned toward the hall door, motioning for Chey to follow. He pulled the door closed behind them, muttering, "Hateful old sow." He glanced at Chey and said, "Sorry. But that woman rubs me the wrong way."

"Then why keep her on?"

He grimaced. "Because she's devoted to Janey. They knew each other before, you see. Brown was, is, a friend of the family. Janey's mother died when she was small, and I guess for that reason Janey's always depended on Brown. After the accident, Brown wouldn't leave her side, and since the doctors think that if Janey wakes up again, it will help to have familiar faces and things around, I've kept her on." He sighed, fingered his short, thick goatee and said, "I wouldn't have moved Janey at all, frankly, but my grandfather died six months ago, and Seth and I are all the family my grandmother has left, so I decided to move everyone home to New Orleans, and that meant bringing Janey, and therefore, Brown with us."

Chey nodded her understanding, then ventured carefully, "Exactly what is Janey's condition, if you don't mind my asking?"

He shook his head and moved once more down the hall-way toward the stairs. Chey fell in beside him as he spoke. "She's in a coma, obviously. The doctors don't know ex-actly why, some sort of trauma to the brain. She was drink-ing that night. It was March, Seth's first birthday, as a mat-ter of fact. Anyway, she fell into a nearly empty swimming pool. It's a miracle she didn't drown, but I sometimes won-der if that wouldn't have been kinder."

Chey stopped and waited for him to turn to face her. "I'm sorry," she told him sincerely. "Two years of watching your wife languish in a coma must have been very difficult."

"Ex-wife," he corrected.

Chey blinked at him, the air fixed in her lungs. He wasn't married! Not that she should care. Better if he were. But surely he hadn't divorced his wife *after* she'd been injured. In Chey's opinion, that would have been despicable. It wasn't, however, any of her business.

He folded his arms and tucked in his chin, looking down at her, his blue eyes holding hers as surely as any physical touch. "We should get up to the third floor now," he said, changing the subject.

She nodded, and he moved down the hallway once more. As he led her toward the upper and final story of the house, he talked about the changes he had made to accommodate the couple who cooked and cleaned for him. He'd had everything updated to their personal specifications, including the plumbing and wiring. Obviously, he considered it their private domain. The attics, however, were of prime interest to her, and she was right about the treasures hiding there.

Though dusty and disorganized, the place was crammed with enough antiques to keep an antique-lover happily busy for days just cataloging and investigating, exactly what she determined to do. At first glance it looked as if she could furnish the entire house with what she found there. It was an absolute treasure trove, and though she wasn't dressed for it, Chey could not resist digging through the most easily accessible portion. Before she realized it, she was absorbed in her discovery. She forgot about the pristine condition of her suit and everything else. It was one magnificent find after another, and the next thing she knew, Brodie was pushing hair out of her face, hair that should have been confined in its usual sleek twist. She looked up at him, shocked speechless to find him so close. He wound a golden-blond strand around his forefinger and tugged gently. She felt it all the way to the soles of her feet.

"I thought Wonderland was the temples of Malaysia or the rivers of India," he told her softly, "but I see that for you it's a musty old room full of used furniture."

Her heart, which seemed to have leapt up and lodged in her throat, was beating so hard she could barely speak, but somehow she managed to form the words, "Not used, antique."

His smile spread all the way across his face. "Antique," he conceded. Then she realized that his face was descending toward hers, that he meant to kiss her. She tilted her chin up, but at the first electric brush of his lips against hers, she yelped and hopped away, bumping her upper thigh on a sharp corner. Dumbly, she looked down and recognized a walnut sugar chest, probably built about 1840. One part of her mind spun out an assessment. A plantation piece from the days when sugar was a precious commodity kept under lock and key, it was not found much north of the Mason-Dixon line and would make an excellent occasional table. Another inner voice screamed that she should run before something awful happened, something that would change her life forever, something for which she was not prepared.

Defensively, she grabbed a lamp and cradled it in front of her as a shield, babbling, "I have to get back to the office, but if you don't mind I'd like to take some of these things with me for appraisal."

He looked at her for a long moment as if trying to decide whether or not to remove the impediment and press the advance, but then one corner of his mouth kicked up in a wry smile and he nodded. "Just show me what you want, and I'll carry it downstairs."

Inwardly, she breathed a sigh of relief—and tried her best to ignore the underlying disappointment.

Brodie stood leaning against a pillar on the front porch, thoughtfully stroking his goatee as he watched Chey's flashy little car roll down his drive toward the street, the almost nonexistent back seat crammed with several items he'd lugged down from the attics for her, among them the lamp she'd latched onto when he'd tried to kiss her. The lamp might be a priceless, once-in-a-lifetime find, but it was more likely that she'd latched onto it in pure self-defense, because he'd definitely scared her with that attempted kiss. What he didn't understand is why the hell he'd done it.

Oh, she was a spectacularly attractive woman, and he'd fully meant to kiss her from the instant he'd laid eyes on her—starting with those small, slender feet and those long, slender legs and ending with that long, slender neck, pretty oval face and sleek, pale golden hair. He wanted to ruffle her cool exterior, pull down that hair, kiss off that pink lipstick, rip the buttons from that neat, tailored suit, watch those light green eyes darken with unregulated passion. He wanted to strip her naked and lay her down. But Brodie Todd was a pragmatic, if sometimes emotional, man, and he'd realized from the beginning that she wasn't likely just to topple over and invite him to join her.

Unlike so very many women of his acquaintance, this one was going to take finesse. He accepted that as part of the challenge, a sort of enhancement. In her enthusiasm over the contents of the attic, she'd given him proof of the passion he'd suspected all along, and he'd lost sight of the big picture, the ultimate goal. She had gotten so caught up in her dusty, jumbled finds that she hadn't even noticed when her stockings shredded and her bright hair began sliding free of its confinement. He had become so caught up in her that he'd forgotten to go slowly, to move cautiously—until she'd literally leapt away from him, and then it had taken all his control not to drag her back to him. He was surprised that she hadn't bolted in that very instant, but she'd taken her time, pretended indifference by concentrating her attention and her enthusiasm on the things in the attic. Then she had run, and she was running still.

He wondered how far he would have to let her go before he could coax her back to him. He did not wonder why he was so damned certain that he was going to do it, not that he was at all certain that he should. It would be complicated. Chey Simmons was not some casual conquest to enjoy one night and forget the next morning. She was going to be around for a while, beginning Monday morning when she had promised to fax the formal designs for his approval. Unfortunately, his fax was going to be down on Monday morning. Yes, continued interaction with his family was guaranteed. Luckily, they had liked her. True, she hadn't seemed particularly taken with Seth, but she'd handled him well. Then again, she ought to have, considering the size of her family.

Nine siblings. He was still surprised and a little awed by that. He wouldn't have thought it would, but somehow the size of her family added a complex cachet to her persona. His only frame of reference was the closeness that he had shared with his younger brother. The idea of multiplying that by nine boggled the mind. For the first time, the thought occurred that if he'd had more siblings, he wouldn't be so alone now. Then again, people couldn't be replaced. His brother would still be gone, still be missed. He would still have a hole in his life and heart that could not be filled.

Pushing thoughts of his brother and the accident that had ended his life from mind, Brodie turned back into the house. He was relieved to find that, despite its dilapidation, the place was really starting to feel like home. Mostly it was his family, of course, and part of it was the city—the old queen had lost none of her allure—but a lot of it was the house itself. It spoke to him in the quiet, wordless whispers that only the heart could hear and understand. It fairly begged to be restored to its original and rightful splendor. Nevertheless, he'd dreaded the refurbishment—until now.

Now he was actually looking forward to it, thanks to sweet, aloof Chey Simmons.

Stopping at one end of the staircase in the wide, bisecting hall, he placed one hand on the graceful, curved banister and looked upward. Her concern for Janey had been as genuine as his own, though not for the same reasons, of course. He shook his head and began to climb the stairs toward his son's room. Along the way, he allowed himself to feel the disappointment of diminished hope for Janey's condition. The doctors had warned him not to put too much stock in what had happened, but he'd been there, and the impact of the moment remained with him still. It had occurred as they were moving her, when the medical personnel were putting her into the ambulance for the trip to Louisiana from Dallas. After more than two years of unknowing, unseeing, nearly immobile silence, she had opened her eyes, looked at the young man holding the door and said quite distinctly, "Hello."

Brodie, who had just come out of the house, had stopped dead in his tracks. Then he had rushed to her side, but her eyes were rolling, as they often did, and she had not responded to his attempts to elicit further response. In that instant, she had seemed, sounded, perfectly lucid, but to his knowledge she had not been so since. He had so hoped, had prayed, that she was going to come back to herself and go about her life as they'd planned. He wanted that. He wanted Seth to have a real mother. He wanted her not to suffer. He wanted to be free of the unexpected, unbargained-for responsibility. And now, he wanted Chey Simmons. And he was determined to get some part of what he wanted.

As he moved toward Seth's room, he made a mental note to call the new doctors again before getting back to work on his exercise equipment. They might not have anything to offer him, but at least it would keep his mind off Chey Simmons. For a while.

Chapter Three

She didn't even glance away from the computer when her assistant Georges came into the office from the shop. "What is it now?"

"You have an important visitor," he announced with a flourish, "and I took the liberty of bringing her back."

Chey looked up with a practiced smile in place. Her mother moved gingerly through the doorway, the strap of her scuffed patent-leather purse clutched tightly in one gloved hand. Sighing inwardly at the sight of the small, warped, straw hat perched atop her mother's usual coil of smoke-gray hair, Chey pushed back from the desk and got up to kiss the other woman's cheek. It wasn't the fact that her mother's hat was decades out of fashion and that the sprig of honeysuckle which had been pinned to it was wilted and browning that pained Chey, but that she had purchased for the woman any number of stylish new hats which were never worn. As far as Louise Simmons was concerned, nice things were an unconscionable waste. It was as if she simply could not stop being the selfless mother who dared not dream of anything beyond the basics for her children and never of anything for herself. Chey wondered if her mother ever even thought of herself as anything other than just that, a mother. And while Chey was deeply grateful for, even in awe of, that kind of dedication, she had never wanted it for herself, precisely because it seemed so very limiting.

Louise allowed Chey to steer her to the lyre-backed chair in front of the French Provincial desk and sat down, drawing off her gloves. She laid them atop the little pie-crust table at her elbow and said chattily, "I once gave five dollars for a table just like that at a second-hand store. Do you remember that table, Mary?"

Chey pressed her pink, professionally manicured nails to one smooth, golden-blond temple and tamped down her impatience. "I do, but that old pie-crust table is not why you're here, Mama. What's going on?"

Louise went straight to the point. "Kay and Sylvester are wondering if you're going to attend their little *fais-do-do* for Melanie's graduation. I told her of course you would, but she said you said something about not being sure of your plans, but it's only April, and that's plenty of time to arrange your calendar, so I was sure it wouldn't be a problem. Still, I thought I'd ask and have a little visit with you at the same time. We don't see you often enough, you know."

Chey sat down during this cheery speech and busied herself straightening the already neat desktop as a familiar sense of guilt stole over her. She would, of course, attend the graduation party. She wanted to. And yet, these family celebrations often left her unhappy and resentful.

"The term *little fais-do-do* is a contradiction in terms, Mama," she said smoothly, "especially in this family."

With nine siblings, all married and all with families of their own, Chey sometimes felt like the lone member of a large tribe who just didn't get it. They were all content to carry on in the time-honored traditions of their clan, marrying young and birthing babies with the same casual joy with which they might play the accordion or fiddle for an impromptu dance in the backyard. Only Chey had resisted the mold. Only Chey had other plans, dreams. Only Chey had remained determinedly single and childless, reserving her dedication for her career. Only Chey did not fit in.

"Kay says that the kids stay out all night long and get into trouble when left to themselves," Louise went on, ignoring Chey's comment. "She wants to keep Melanie well occupied with family that night. I thought she was overdoing it a bit, but Frank says she has the right of it, and—"

"Frank would know," Chey said for her.

"Since his five have turned out so well," Louise finished with satisfaction.

If by "well" one meant that they'd all gotten through high school before they'd started having babies, Chey mused silently. Only she and a few of her nieces and nephews had gone on to college.

"By the way," Louise said, changing the subject. "Fay went for her ultrasound yesterday, and the doctor says it's almost surely a girl. Isn't that perfect? Now they'll have one of each."

"Any hope they'll stop at one of each?" Chey asked acerbically.

Louise rolled her eyes in apparent exasperation. "For heaven's sake, Mary Chey, most people like babies!"

"I like babies," Chey said. "I just think the Simmons clan has enough. I mean, am I the only one who thinks that life is about more than making babies?"

Louise answered that with a deep sigh. "It's about more than making money, too, you know."

Chey rolled her eyes and spread her arms. "This isn't about money, Mother. It's about accomplishment and quality of life. It's about doing something meaningful and being someone admirable."

"It's about you, dear," Louise Simmons said softly.

"You've accomplished a great deal professionally, and I'm very proud of you. But don't you see that not everyone is fixated on their profession?"

"I'm not fixated, Mother," Chey retorted defensively.

"You have no life apart from this business. You don't even date," Louise pointed out. "How will you ever meet a man if you don't even date?"

An image of Brodie Todd flashed across her mind's eye. She banished it immediately, snapping, "I don't care about meeting men."

"But don't you grow tired of being alone, dear?" her mother asked, going on when Chey merely shrugged. "I know you don't want children, and that's fine. Parenthood isn't for everyone, and goodness knows I've no reason to complain with thirty-one, almost thirty-two, grandchildren and eleven great-grandchildren, but I do worry about you being alone."

"Mom, I have just as much family as you do," Chey pointed out.

"But you don't have anyone of your *own*," Louise said gently.

"You should talk. Daddy's been gone for twenty years, and in all that time, you've never even looked at another man."

"When you've had the best—" Louise began a familiar litany.

"I know that you loved him," Chey interrupted, "and it just proves my point. That kind of love is very rare."

"All your brothers and sisters are happily married," Louise pointed out, "and here you are, thirty years old without even a steady boyfriend. A woman as pretty and bright as you ought to have a husband."

"Mother, please, not now," Chey pleaded impatiently.

Georges appeared just then, a sheet of paper in his hand. "Sugar, would you look at this invoice? I can't make heads or tails of it, I swear."

Louise subsided immediately, grasped the handle of her

purse with both hands and looked down. "You have work to do," she said softly, rising to her feet. "What shall I tell Kay and Sylvester, dear?"

Chey managed a smile. "Tell them I'll be there, of course."

Louise beamed. "Of course you will." She reached across the desk and cupped Chey's cheek in one worn hand. "Come for dinner soon, will you?"

Chey nodded, warmed despite her irritation. "Soon, Mama." She placed her hand over her mother's and hugged it briefly between her own palm and her cheek. She stood and smiled her mother through the door, then braced her hands flat against the desktop and bowed her head. "Thank you, Georges."

He wadded the piece of paper in his beefy fist, not at all to her surprise. The invoice had never been written that Georges Phillips could not decipher. It was part of what made him so valuable to her.

Solidly middle-aged and decidedly rotund, he was an odd combination of flamboyance and distinguished style. At the moment he wore a vanilla white suit and matching silk ascot with a flame-red shirt on his stocky, yet graceful body. His thinning, dark blond hair was combed back ruthlessly, allowing the silver of his temples and winged brows to challenge his blunt nose and plump mouth for dominance of his round face. His physical appearance and droll manner of speaking always put Chey in mind of a slightly slimmer, fitter Alfred Hitchcock, albeit one given to sometimes absurd sartorial splendors. Unfortunately, he was as astute with people as with billing invoices.

"Don't thank me," he told her snippily. "I didn't do it for you. I did it to spare that old dear's feelings. She's concerned about you."

"Well, she has no reason to be," Chey protested. "Why can't she understand that I'm perfectly happy just as I am?"

"Perhaps because your lifestyle is completely foreign to

her," he suggested, "and just possibly because you aren't as happy as you want everyone to think."

"I am so!" Chey refuted hotly.

"Sugar, this is Georges you're talking to. I know you better than you know yourself—and so does your mother, I suspect."

"You wish," Chey retorted sourly. "Just because you've been married countless times doesn't mean that everyone has to trip down the aisle after you."

"Four," he corrected primly. "You have more fingers than that on each dainty hand, and don't change the subject. Honestly, Chey, if you weren't married to this business, you'd have a personal life like your mama wants. You'd have a man, a husband."

"Maybe I should just marry you," she retorted. "That would be good for business and get my family off my back, too."

He made a face. "Not my style, darling. It'd be like marrying my sister."

"Georges! Do you have a sister?" she teased, knowing perfectly well that he was one of three brothers.

"Don't be cute. And if you want your family off your back, then find a man and fall in love!"

"You should know better than anyone that it's not that easy," she insisted.

"At least I try," Georges said huffily, putting his round chin into the air.

"And you'll keep on trying," Chey said drolly.

"We're not talking about me," he said, pursing his cherry-red mouth.

"No, we're talking about your boss," Chey pointed out dryly, "the person who signs your paycheck."

"The person who would be lost without me," Georges added confidently.

He was right, darn him. She'd be lost without him as her assistant and friend, but he was wrong about the other. She had no intention of ever marrying. It would be unfair. Her career was much too important to her and left no room for the depth of dedication necessary for marriage and especially parenthood. Her family and friends didn't understand that, however.

Chey sighed and slumped back in her chair. The position gave her a new perspective on the picture on her screen, and she immediately leaned forward again to tweak the placement of a certain element in the room design. For days now she had done little else but work on the Fair Havens project, and this was the final preliminary design.

"What do you think of this layout for the master suite?" she asked Georges, who walked around to lean over and study the computer screen.

"From a decorator's perspective," he finally said, "I love the claw-foot tub. From a man's perspective, give me a real shower stall."

"But the whole room is effectively a shower stall," she explained. "It uses special waterproofing so curtains and stalls aren't necessary."

"He's still standing in a bathtub to take a shower," Georges pointed out. "I wouldn't like it. Okay, so the shower stall is not a period piece, but we can make it *look* period."

Chey sighed and reached for the mouse. "You're right. Let's try this." She deleted the claw-foot tub and quickly inserted a partially sunken, built-in tub-and-shower combination of faux marble.

"Oh, that's good," Georges commented. "The faux marble keeps it lightweight for a second-story installation, and this particular design eliminates the need for curtains and doors. And it has the right look."

A chime sounded, alerting them that someone had opened the front door. "I'll go," Georges said, turning away from the desk.

Chey nodded absently, muttering, "Thanks. I want to get this faxed over to Fair Havens."

She manipulated the computer mouse and clicked. The

expensive, photo-quality printer spooled up and began to spit out a black-and-white, computer-generated sketch. The ink wasn't even dry before Chey spun her chair and loaded the first sketch into the fax machine. She had added Brodie Todd's fax number to her computerized telephone book days earlier, and she called it up now. The fax machine was dialing even as the printer was spitting out the second sketch. Unfortunately, before the printer finished disgorging sketches, the fax machine reported that no connection could be negotiated with the dial-up number.

Drat. She would just have to take the drawings over herself then. After quickly making copies, she stuffed them into a folder, grabbed her briefcase and swept from the room. Georges was showing a unique brass-and-wrought-iron chandelier to an off-the-street customer, probably a tourist.

"I have to go to Fair Havens," she announced, moving swiftly to the door. "Won't be long. I'm just going to drop off the preliminary designs."

Georges nodded and focused again on the customer. Chey walked out onto the banquette, or sidewalk, and turned left, then left again into the narrow, tunnel-like passage that led to her courtyard and tiny garage. It was only a few hundred square feet walled off from the rest of the old city block, but it was her own personal haven away from the world. She often sat here in the evenings, nursing a glass of wine, the scent of honeysuckle so thick that the sounds of the old city seemed to float on it. But she hadn't done so lately and, she admitted, probably would not anytime soon. She tended to immerse herself in every project, and the bigger the project, the deeper that immersion. With Fair Havens, she couldn't even see sky.

She opened the garage door and let herself into the driver's seat of the car. Moments later she eased the car through the passage and paused level with the banquette until a break in traffic allowed her to pull out onto the narrow street. A quarter-hour later, she turned the small coupe onto the Fair Havens drive, marveling at the newly restored view from the street. Gone were the scrubby undergrowth and wild vines that had hidden a six-foot-tall, black wrought-iron fence, not to mention the house, from the view of passersby. The grounds were immaculately groomed, and the massive birdbath in the circle in front of the house had been restored to a balanced, upright position. A stone bench and three marble garden angels of different sizes and styles had been added. Even with the exterior of the house still in a sorry state, the effect was simply stunning.

Suddenly, she was uncertain that her designs were up to the challenge. Perhaps she should return to the office and take another look at what she'd done, think it all through a little better. Yet, even as she considered the notion, she knew that her designs were not the root of her sudden reluctance to march up those steps and ring that loud brass bell. Her heart was racing for another, entirely different reason. Brodie Todd.

He unnerved her, intrigued her, disturbed her in ways she just hadn't expected. It was humbling to be so intensely physically aware of someone. She'd been telling herself for days now that the man could not be as wildly attractive as she remembered, and even if he were, the man was not for her. He was a client, and she never got involved with clients. It was unprofessional. Besides, the man had divorced his comatose wife! And he was a father.

Closing her eyes, she told herself sternly that it wasn't Todd as much as the job. She hadn't had a challenge like this in far too long, but it was a challenge to which she could, would, rise. She put the car in Park, shut off the engine and got out, grabbing her briefcase from the passenger seat. She couldn't deny an alarming quiver in the pit of her belly as she climbed those steps, however, and when the door opened, her self-lies died abruptly and ignominiously.

Her mouth dried up at the very sight of him, standing

there in crisply pleated, pale linen slacks and a loose, deep blue silk shirt that made his darkly lashed eyes glow like sapphires. The top three buttons of the collarless shirt were undone and the long sleeves were rolled up, exposing a small portion of smooth, bronze chest and strongly corded forearms. His smile flashed warmly.

"Hello."

She found it difficult to be pleasant simply because she so desperately wanted to be. "Your fax is not receiving," she said, embarrassed that her voice sounded breathless rather than brisk.

"Yes, I know," he said simply. "Sorry about that."

She lifted one knee slightly and attempted to balance her briefcase against it while extracting the file folder. "I'll just drop off these sketches."

She held up the file, but he didn't take it. Instead, he stepped aside and drew the door wide. "Come in."

She thought wildly of tossing the file inside and running. Instead, she stepped decorously over the threshold, letting him know that she didn't intend to stay. "I'll just leave them. You can look them over at your leisure and let me know what you think."

He didn't reply directly to that, just closed the door and instructed, "This way," before turning and walking down the hall.

She wanted to throw something at his back, but she took a deep, calming breath and followed reluctantly. He took her all the way through to the garden room again, where everything had been rearranged. The fully assembled exercise equipment now occupied one end of the room, with the small forest of plants forming a privacy barrier of sorts. The table and chairs had been placed as close to the glass wall as possible, and a pair of small dry-sink bases had been brought down from the attic and arranged in such a manner that they did not block any portion of the view even while standing handy for service. One now held a pitcher full of iced tea and several slender tumblers. A marble plant stand held an old-fashioned oscillating fan, and a pair of oil lamps hung from two crooked lamp stands that flanked the table. Chey could almost see the room by the soft glow of lamplight, the table laid with china and silver and white linen. A table laid for two. She shook away the vision, commenting, "Someone's been busy."

"Do you approve?" he asked, lifting both arms wide.

"Very much," she answered, placing her briefcase atop the table.

"I won't mind if you make changes."

The way he said it told her a great deal, and she looked at him in a new light. "You did this."

He tilted his head in acknowledgment. "Grandmama really only has a care for the gardens." He pushed a hand through his hair, admitting sheepishly, "And I'm getting a little impatient with the house."

"Well, maybe these will help," she said, placing the folder flat on the table.

He immediately turned away. "Care for some tea?"

"Oh, no. I have to get back to the shop."

"I'd rather just go over them now, together. It'll save time in the long run."

It sounded like an order. Biting back an outright refusal, she pulled out a chair. "In that case, iced tea would be fine."

He got busy pouring the tea then carried the drinks to the table and took the chair closest to her. After sipping from his glass, he sat forward and pulled the folder around to flip open its cover. The sketch of his grandmother's suite was on top of the stack of renderings. He looked at the floor plan carefully, tracing the traffic pattern with his fingertip, then switched to the artistic conception.

"Oh, she'll like this. Didn't I see this sofa in the attic?"

Chey swallowed the mellow tea in her mouth and said, "Absolutely." She leaned forward, intending to elucidate, but he laid aside that sheet and picked up the next, which was a rendering of the nursery. Brodie laughed aloud and leaned back in his chair. "This is wonderful!"

A delicious warmth spread through Chey. "I'm glad you approve."

"Very much," he said, setting aside that one and picking up the next, which was his own. He tilted his head, studying the sketch. Chey found that she was holding her breath, and she literally flinched when he picked up the next sheet with his free hand, that of his office suite. "This is almost perfect," he finally said.

She felt an irrational stab of disappointment and immediately scolded herself. *Almost perfect* was practically unheard of in her business, especially at this stage. "What's the problem?" she asked anxiously.

He waved a hand. "Nothing important. It completely has to do with the office. I have my own system, and the office arrangement has to facilitate that. We'll fix it. Otherwise, I like what you've done. Very much." She smiled, and he smiled back. Then, instead of picking up the next drawing, he leaned toward her suddenly and asked, "Are you hungry? Because I'm starving, and it is almost lunch time."

She immediately began to disengage. "Oh, I—"

"Grandmama has taken Seth on an excursion," he interrupted, "and I find I'm not crazy about eating alone anymore." He reached for her hand and folded his own around it, his gaze holding hers. "Have lunch with me? Marcel will be thrilled. He constantly complains that he doesn't have enough to do."

She knew without doubt that she shouldn't, though she'd had lunch with clients before, of course. Yet, this was different. Staying would definitely be foolish, so she smiled, shook her head and *intended* to say, *No, thank you.* What came out was simply, "Thank you."

"Excellent!" He was up and moving before she could correct herself. He disappeared into the house, and returned again moments later. "I hope you like seafood salad in pita bread with yam chips. Marcel is a genius with yams." He sat down and leaned close once more. "Marcel is a genius with food, period. Now let's have a look at the rest of these." She smiled wanly and watched in silence, puzzled by her own acquiescence, as he went over the renderings of the downstairs rooms.

He made a few suggestions about the game room, saying that he'd found among the articles in the attic a sideboard which would make a marvelous wet bar and a classic old billiards table for which he'd ordered new slate. She took out a pencil and lightly sketched in the changes, barely noticing how closely together their heads were bent until he took the pencil out of her hand. Looking up, she sat back and watched as he made a few changes himself, her heart suddenly pounding with awareness.

"Will that work, do you think?" he asked, leaning his shoulder against hers.

She barely glanced at the paper. "Appears workable to me."

He looked up, something dark and intense shadowing his blue, blue eyes. Just then, a tall man dressed all in white wheeled a cart into the room. Having already met his wife, small, pale Kate, Chey was somehow unprepared for big, black Marcel with his round, shaved head and hands the size of small hams.

"Ah, company at last!" he exclaimed, flashing her a smile.

"I promised Marcel that he would get to cook for a great many people," Brodie explained indulgently, "and he's growing impatient." The big man chuckled as he prepared the table with the previously imagined china, silver and white linen. All that was missing, Chey mused wryly to herself, was the lamplight, and thank God for that!

Marcel took his leave the moment the food was on the table. Brodie hadn't exaggerated the big man's talent, and it only took one bite to know it. The flavors of diced shrimp, crab, clams, celery, brown rice, pecans, onion, bell pepper and mayonnaise flavored with chili powder and other spices mingled on her tongue. When she followed it with a cinnamony sweet yam chip, the effect was exquisite.

"Coconut cream cake for dessert," Brodie announced before taking a huge bite of his own pita.

Chey rolled her eyes and shook her head, but her traitorous gaze strayed to the second tier of the serving cart where an old-fashioned shortcake had been piled high with custard, whipped cream and toasted coconut.

"I'd get fat if I lived in this house," she blurted.

His blue gaze swept over her. "I don't think so. You seem to have a naturally svelte figure. I'd lay odds you don't even work out."

"I'd have to if I ate like this all the time," she retorted, tacitly admitting that he was correct and purposefully ignoring what felt very much like a compliment.

"Some workouts are hugely satisfying," he said softly, then looked away before she could determine what exactly he meant by that. He went on, admitting, "I love good food. It's one of the great luxuries of life, don't you think?"

With her mouth full of the most scrumptious seafood salad she'd ever eaten, she could do nothing more than nod her head in agreement. He smiled at her, a slow, lazy, speculative smile that set her insides to quaking. Determinedly, she fixed her mind on work, specifically this very room. What a lovely place it was with its view of the gardens and pool. The potted plants seemed to bring the outside indoors. She looked up, thinking that two or three ceiling fans would be welcome additions. She imagined strings of twinkling lights, tables scattered among the plants for an informal dinner party. How charming it would be.

"You know," she said absently, "since you expect to entertain a good deal, we may want to rethink how you're using this room."

"What do you have in mind?" he asked, leaning on one elbow. She told him and could see the approval building in his eyes. "Okay, sounds good, but you didn't say where the workout equipment would go."

She thought about it, winnowing through her ideas aloud. "We could use the old smoking room, turn it into a regular gym, but it's right in the middle of the formal rooms downstairs, and I don't like the feel of that."

"No one will use the equipment other than me, anyway," he commented.

"Then we should dedicate a space for it in your suite," she said, reaching for the folder that had been pushed to one side. She flipped open the cover and removed the drawing she wanted, then shoved aside her plate and plucked the pencil from behind her ear. Swiftly, she began sketching again. Brodie shifted his chair closer and watched, munching his pita idly. "If we removed this wall," she muttered, marking it out, "and opened the dressing room this way, we could put in an exercise room. We could make the bathroom a little smaller if needed."

"Uh-uh," he said. "I like that bathroom. I *love* that bathroom."

"Okay, leave the bathroom," she said, putting back what she'd been removing. She tilted her head, studying the drawing again, and tapped an area of it with two fingers. "I wonder which of these rooms is the largest. I plugged the data into the computer, of course, but I didn't put the figures on the print out, and naturally I can't remember now."

Brodie popped the last of his pita into his mouth and pushed back his chair. "If you've had enough to eat, why don't we just go look? I have a measuring tape around here somewhere."

"Good idea."

He got up and pulled her chair out for her as she followed suit. Marcel appeared as they were moving away from the table. "You can remove the lunch plates," Brodie said genially, "but leave the dessert. We'll be back for it."

"That seafood salad was luscious," Chey told the chef, and he beamed.

"Now you've done it," Brodie told her, pulling her arm through his.

"What?"

"He'll meet you at the door with a plate of food the next time you arrive," Brodie warned, only half joking. "Marcel lives to cook. Feeding people wonderful food is his primary mission in life. I sometimes worry that if I don't get some empty bellies in here for him to fill he'll leave and go back to restaurant work."

"No wonder you're impatient to get the house into shape," she said.

"The satisfaction of my stomach depends upon it," he quipped dryly.

She shook her head, laughing, and only later, as he escorted her upstairs, did she reflect that this man's charm was lethal. They went into his office, where he searched out a small, flimsy measuring tape that did not exceed ten feet in length. Just to complicate matters, the silly thing would retract without warning, snapping right out of her fingers, which meant they often had to start all over again. It took several tries to get two measurements in the outer chamber, and by the time they managed it, Chey was holding on to the end of that tape measure for dear life, reluctant to let go for any reason, so when it retracted again and it seemed she couldn't stop it, she stupidly followed it—right into Brodie Todd.

She bumped against his chest and, startled, looked up, the tape measure and their hands trapped between them. For an instant, he seemed as shocked as she was, but then he let go of the measuring tape case, and it hit the floor between her feet with a clunk, leaving her with the end of the tape still clamped between her fingertips and her wide gaze trapped by his own rapidly darkening one. He moved his hand, dropping it slightly and opening it to slide his palm across her ribs, just beneath her breast. The other hand he clamped around the nape of her neck. She couldn't seem to look away or move.

He bent his head, then brought her mouth to his with the gentle pressure of his hand at the back of her head. Sensation swamped her, radiating from his hands and mouth into her skin, muscles and bones, suffusing her with a trembling warmth that sent her good sense begging and pooled heavily in her breasts and belly. At first the kiss was light, tender, easy, just a simple meeting of lips. Then, entirely of their own accord, her eyelids fluttered shut, and everything changed.

He wrapped his arms around her, tilted his head, and opened her mouth with his, sliding his tongue inside. She heard a hiss and was dimly aware that it must have been the tape sliding into the case, which meant, of course, that she had let go of the end, which would explain how her hands came to be sliding up his chest and around his neck. He made a sound of acute pleasure and tightened his arms, plastering her body to his as his tongue delved deeper.

She forgot why this was a bad idea. She forgot everything but the desire for more. She wanted to be closer, to feel more, to do more. She needed more from his mouth, more from the hard, sculpted planes of his body, more from the hands now kneading her flesh with mounting urgency as she moved against him. As if he knew exactly what she needed most, he dropped a hand to her bottom, cupping and lifting her against him even as he wedged a knee between hers, shoving her skirt indecently high. She melted from the inside out, undulating instinctively against him.

Suddenly they were two wild things, grabbing and grinding, trying to devour each other. She was so lost that she didn't even hear the little voice that shattered it. All she knew was that one moment she wanted to tear his skin open and crawl beneath it, and the next instant he was shoving her away. She blinked up into his face, astonished to be doing so and then more astonished by all that had just happened. She didn't have time to be embarrassed, thankfully, because Seth hurtled past her and threw himself at Brodie.

"Daddy, I saw pishes!" He held out his arms. "Gweat big pishes!"

Brodie finally looked away from her and smiled down at his son. "That's great!" Chey became aware of another person entering the room then, and heat bloomed in her cheeks. She turned away, folding her arms, and pretended to be studying the far wall. "Did you go to the aquarium?" she heard Brodie ask.

Viola answered him. "No. We were walking along the street and…"

Chey barely listened to the story, something about a truck delivering fish to a local restaurant and a broken crate, ice going everywhere. Chey became aware, belatedly, that everyone was laughing, but she couldn't manage more than a smile as the full realization of what she'd done finally settled over her.

Kiss seemed too small a word for what they'd shared. A mere kiss didn't make your insides tremble and clench long after the fact. It didn't make you curl your hands into fists just to keep from reaching out for more. Even her throat was trembling so badly that she could barely swallow. Suddenly she had to get out of there.

"I think I have everything I need for now," she announced abruptly, turning and heading toward the door. "I'll show myself out." He said something to Viola, then Chey heard him coming after her and picked up the pace.

He caught her at the top of the stairs, hauled her around easily, his big, exquisite hands with those long, tapered fingers and wide palms encircling her upper arms. His blue gaze plumbed hers. "Chey, we haven't even had dessert."

She managed to look away. "None for me, thank you. I really have to go."

"When will you be back?"

"Soon."

"Very soon, I hope." His voice was rough, husky. "As soon as possible."

"As soon as possible," she agreed, which wouldn't be

soon at all. He slid his hands up and down her arms, and then he finally let her go.

She was in the car before she remembered that she'd left her designs and briefcase in the garden room. She didn't go back for them. She didn't dare.

Chapter Four

Brodie strangled the telephone receiver with both hands, then closed his eyes and tamped down his temper before calmly going back to the conversation.

"Will you please give Ms. Simmons *another* message," he said, keeping his tone light and breezy, until the end when he allowed the underlying steel to show through. "Tell her that if she doesn't present herself on my doorstep within the next twenty-four hours I will personally hunt her down and drag her here!"

He rolled his eyes, allowing her prissy assistant to nervously rattle on and on about how busy she'd been and how hard she was working and how he was personally sure that she'd be back in touch as soon as possible. He'd heard it all before and was no closer to buying it now than the first time. The little coward was avoiding him, but no longer. He wasn't above using any of the weapons in his arsenal, which was formidable, and she might as well learn it now.

''Twenty-four hours,'' he interrupted flatly and turned off the phone.

It had been more than a week since that kiss. He'd called repeatedly, even dropped by her shop to return her briefcase and sketches, but the only face he'd seen, the only voice he'd heard, belonged to that fashionable fireplug of an assistant of hers. George, he thought the name was.

Brodie personally hated assistants. He'd tried to work with them, but they invariably got in his way. It was easier just to do what had to be done himself than to delegate everything. Besides, the business pretty much ran itself from the corporate offices in Dallas. He had a lean, efficient staff operating a mere dozen offices around the world and a state-of-the-art web site. It was a neat, tight operation and a lucrative one. Oh, he knew he could make some fast bucks in a big way if he'd go public, put a BMT Travel Agency on every other street corner, but he knew instinctively that in the long run it would be the death of the thing.

BMT's success was built on personal service to exotic locales. Part of the allure had to do with the fact that not just anyone could get in on the deal. Spaces were limited and prices high, satisfaction an absolute guarantee. His customers were upscale and demanding, just like him, and he personally negotiated every service contract with every nation that sponsored a tour package, which often resulted in travel visas not available to the general public. He also had the final say on every package that was designed and put together by his team, and he always took the first tour himself before any customer was allowed to buy space. Otherwise, he spent most of his time with Seth and Viola.

It was a good life, but he was mature enough to admit that lately it seemed to lack something, something about five-feet-six-inches tall and deliciously curved. He pondered that kiss again. The sizzle was still with him. Every time he looked in the mirror he half expected to find his eyebrows singed off. It had been a long while since a kiss had so affected him. Who was he kidding? No kiss had ever affected him like that one, and he knew darn well that she'd felt the same thing, so why was she avoiding him?

She could be involved with someone else. He disliked competition, but he could handle it—given the chance. Then again, he firmly believed that a man made his own chances, and so he would see her tomorrow. One way or another.

The bell rang at precisely ten o'clock in the morning, too late for breakfast and too early for lunch but well within the twenty-four-hour deadline. Brodie got up from his desk and started downstairs, aware that someone else within the household would likely beat him to the door.

When Brodie arrived on the scene, it was Viola who stood to one side of the closed door, beaming affectionately as Seth regaled "Mish Chey" with the latest episode of his morning television program, complete with extravagant gestures and sound effects. Chey stood, staring down at him politely as he spoke. Her assistant stood next to her, a familiar briefcase tucked beneath one arm as if to justify his presence. Not even bothering to pretend interest in the prattle of a little boy, he craned his neck to see what could be seen of the house. It was he who spotted Brodie and sent a discreet elbow to his employer's ribs.

Chey straightened as Brodie strode near, and for an instant he thought he saw a flash of heat in her eyes, but it was followed so quickly by wariness that he couldn't be certain. He didn't smile, though the impulse was strong. She looked like a confection ready to be devoured, all ivory and pale blue and yellow hair twisted into an elaborate knot that begged to be unwound.

He placed a quelling hand on top of Seth's head; otherwise, the monologue could have gone on indefinitely as Seth tended to get caught up in these recitals and embellish them, imagination blending seamlessly with actuality. Seth looked up, caught Brodie's wrist with both hands and tried to climb him like a tree, announcing unnecessarily, "Mish Chey an' some guy come see us, Daddy."

Brodie ignored Chey and concentrated on the assistant, sticking out his hand. "I believe the name is George?"

"It's *Zhorzh*," the man sniffed, emphasizing the pronunciation with a decidedly French accent. Brodie mumbled an ill-natured apology, and only then did *Zhorzh* grace him with a handshake.

"This is my son Seth," Brodie said by way of introduction, "and this is my grandmother, Viola Todd."

"How do you do?" Georges said, bowing slightly over Viola's hand.

To Brodie's everlasting amazement, Viola actually blushed and batted her lashes. "A pleasure to meet you, Georges."

Brodie barely restrained himself from rolling his eyes. Georges literally shoved past Chey, saying, "You don't need me, do you, dear?" Before Chey could answer him, he addressed himself meaningfully to Viola. "I only came to get a look at this beautiful old house."

Taking the bait, Viola insisted, "Well, I must show it to you, then. Come along, Seth."

Georges handed the briefcase to Chey and followed Viola and Seth down the hall. Chey stared after them with such barely concealed disgust that Brodie had to discipline a smile. He was perfectly aware why Georges was there, and it wasn't to see the house. He had to wonder just how much buffer she'd thought Georges would be.

"Let's do this in my office," he said, knowing that it would afford the greatest privacy of any room in the house, aside from his bedroom. The business setting apparently appealed to her, for she nodded and started briskly for the stairs. He let her pass him, wondering if she realized how much her hips swayed with her consternation. Grinning to himself, he slid his hands into his pants pockets to quell the urge to put his hands on her.

He followed her up the stairs, admiring the way her slender skirt pulled neatly across her rounded bottom with each step. By the time they reached the landing, his hands had made fists inside his pockets. Counting prudence the better part of valor, he went ahead of her and opened the door to his office. She stepped inside as if expecting to find a trap. He closed the door behind them and went to remove a crate of files from a chair at the end of the desk for her, then slid around to his own chair. She sat down gingerly, crossed her long lean legs and placed the briefcase on her lap. He took his seat and rolled the chair as close to the corner of the desk, and her, as he could. She was already spreading out the designs. A glance showed him that they were quite detailed this time and many more in number than before. She had been busy, and he gave that industry the respect it was due, studying each design carefully.

The family rooms were much as they'd discussed before, only the designs were fully realized this time. The guest rooms were the big surprise. She had employed specific themes here, each one designed to show off his personal collection of artifacts and art objects. One room was labeled Oriental, another European and a third Polynesian. The big surprise was the room labeled Western Americana. All of the designs, though specific in theme, showed an underlying period fashion in line with that of the rest of the house. He might have been an antebellum planter who had managed to see the world and even the future and bring back pieces of it to decorate his lovely home.

He tossed the last of the renderings onto the top of the pile he had made of the others and sat back in his chair, contemplating the woman who had made them. "These are," he said deliberately, "incredible."

She sat a little straighter, her personal guard lowered by the long minutes concentrated on business. "You approve then?"

"Wholeheartedly."

She smiled for the first time and dove back into her briefcase. "You'll need to look at these lists and schedules then.'' Eagerly, she brought them out, lists of contractors, supplies, tasks to be completed, schedules for the same. He looked over everything carefully, nodding his approval.

"How soon can we get started?"

"I thought we'd start with the air-conditioning," she said delightedly. "I can meet the contractor here tomorrow. He ought to have men on the job in the next day or so."

He tossed the papers aside. "Do it."

She seemed surprised. "Just like that? No quibbling over details?"

"We've been at least a week longer at this than I would have liked," he drawled meaningfully.

She immediately bounced up to her feet and began stuffing the papers into the briefcase. "Fine. We'll be here tomorrow."

He recognized a bolt when he saw it and sat forward abruptly, clamping a hand around her wrist. "Sit down."

He meant it as an order, and she took it that way, slowly sinking down into her chair, the briefcase balanced on the corner of his desk.

"I fail to see what else we have to talk about," she said crisply, her gaze targeted on her lap.

He almost laughed at that. Instead, he got up and walked around his chair to the end of the desk. He parked himself on the corner and folded his arms, intending to be firm. "You know perfectly well what we have to talk about."

She said nothing.

"I'm not going to let you pretend it didn't happen," he told her patiently. She lifted her chin, neither answering him nor looking at him. He sighed and leaned forward, spelling it out. "We kissed. We were interrupted. You ran, and now you're avoiding me. I want to know why." She looked down but didn't say a word. He straightened and folded his arms again, insisting, "It wasn't because you didn't enjoy it. That much I do know."

Finally a response. She glared at him. "What is that supposed to mean?"

"It means, you were as heated up as I was." She looked away again. "You liked it as much as I did," he insisted doggedly. "So what is your problem?"

"I don't have a problem," she said with a shrug. "I just prefer not to repeat the experience."

"Why?"

"Why should I?"

He chuckled mirthlessly at that. "Oh, I don't know, maybe because I melted your underwear." She shot him an affronted look. "Mine was smoking, too," he assured her bluntly, noting the flare of satisfaction in her eyes, "which adds up to plenty of reason to repeat the experience as far as I'm concerned."

"It means just the opposite to me," she said, smoothing her hands down the narrow wood arms of the chair, "because I *never* get involved with clients."

"Until now," he corrected coaxingly.

"Sure of yourself, aren't you?" she snapped.

He went down on his haunches beside her chair. "Is it someone else? Are you involved with someone else?"

She bit her lip, looked down, then admitted, "No."

"So it's strictly a business decision?"

"That's right."

"Then I'll have to cancel your contract."

She immediately launched to her feet. "You can't do that!"

He rose smoothly and brought his hands to his hips. "The contract that cannot be broken has never been devised."

"I'll sue you!"

"Before or after we make love?" he returned smoothly.

She glared at him and folded her arms. "I do not indulge in casual affairs."

"Good, because this is a long way from a casual attraction."

"I'm certainly not interested in anything serious, either!"

"Look," he said bluntly, a little desperate now, "I'm not rushing you to the altar, I'm just trying to get you into bed!"

She went immediately frosty. "I don't sleep around."

"I don't want you to sleep around," he retorted. "I want you to sleep with *me!*"

She grabbed up her briefcase and began stuffing renderings into it. "That's not going to happen."

He leaned close and said softly into her ear, "No? You really have no inclination to explore this thing between us, this incredible attraction?"

"Don't even go there," she said dismissively, snapping her briefcase shut.

"Oh, I'm going there," he promised, leaning even closer and speaking softly into her ear. "And so are you. Because this thing has a strong grip on both of us, and you know it as well as I do."

"That's some ego you've got," she retorted, sliding away to put the chair between them.

"Yeah, right, it's my ego that's got you heaving and shaking like a creaky bellows, I suppose. Or is it just that you've been close to me?"

She opened her mouth, then closed it again and lifted her chin. "Forget the job. I don't need this." She shoved the briefcase under one arm and headed toward the door.

He leaned casually on the corner of his desk and asked smoothly, "And what about our contract?"

She stopped then turned and glared at him. "You said yourself that the contract was never written that couldn't be broken."

"Ah, yes, that's true. However, I'll tell you something they probably don't teach in business school. When it comes to things like this, the one with the most lawyers and the deepest pockets generally determines just what a contract does or doesn't say and when or *if* it gets canceled. And my pockets are definitely deepest."

She gaped and took her briefcase from beneath her arm

by the handle. "So now you're saying you won't let me out of the contract?"

"Do you really want out?" he countered. "This is the kind of job that a career hangs on, and if you're as serious about your career as you say you are, you won't walk away from it."

The chin went up a notch higher. "You can't use career considerations to force me to sleep with you."

Laughter burst out of him. "You think that's what this is, coercion?"

"Isn't it?"

He tamed his grin and shook his head. "Not at all my style. Seduction's much more my thing."

"Well, that's not going to happen," she insisted.

"Then why walk away from a career-maker?"

He knew he had her when that chin went down. "If I stay it's strictly business." Instead of replying to that, he merely bowed his head. Could he help it if she took that for acquiescence? "So long as you know that," she went on. He just looked up at her and sighed, letting her assign whatever she wanted to it. "Fine, then we understand one another," she announced crisply and turned again to the door.

"I'll expect you tomorrow morning," he said.

She paused a moment, then nodded crisply and went out. He shook his head. Did she really think that was it? If so, then she had a thing or two to learn about Brodie Todd. He wasn't about to ignore the strongest attraction he'd felt for a woman in…well, he just wasn't going to ignore it. And she wasn't going to, either. Because he wasn't about to let her.

Chey adjusted her clear plastic safety goggles, hitched up the legs of her khaki pants, crouched and braced her hands, carefully lowering herself into the narrow opening of the crawl space. She went onto all fours and looked around. Matt's flashlight illuminated the pathway ahead, and she crawled after him, ignoring the cobwebs and dust. Matt muttered curse words in Cajun French. Remembering that his little sister was present, he glanced at her sheepishly and explained, "Tore my pants on a nail. Gail's gonna shriek."

"I'll replace them for you," Chey told him.

"That's not the point, Mary," he mumbled, shining his light around the narrow, empty space. "These're still gonna be torn. My Gail's still gonna bust my eardrums." He targeted a clump of wires with his light. "Yeah, right there. Looks easy enough to run new wires in here. We'll closet the main unit in the corner of that room to the right, open it to the hall, run the ducts through here to the other floors." He shone the light up and down a black shaft, illuminating the brick on the outside wall in spots. "Job's gonna take minimum ten days with a full crew, that's every man we got, and putting off all the other work."

"Can you do it?"

"Sure enough. Cost a pretty penny, though. I'm sayin' that up front."

"How much?"

"Twenty, maybe thirty thousand," he said pointedly. "I'll have to figure it."

"Do that," she told him, backing out the way she'd come. "Then get to work." He followed, chuckling.

"That's our Mary. Get things done."

She positioned herself below the opening in the floor, stood, and hauled herself up out of the space. After getting to her feet, she removed the goggles and began to beat the knees of her pants clean.

Matt climbed up after her and began brushing cobwebs out of his curly light brown hair. He turned her around and dusted off her backside.

"And who do we have here?" asked a disturbingly familiar voice. Chey sent a censorious glance over one shoulder, achingly aware of Matt's broad, white smile and the discerning blue eyes of Brodie Todd. Everywhere she went lately, Brodie Todd was there, brushing against her, murmuring into her ear, prodding her to say more and react more than she intended. She could never relax, knowing that he might appear at any moment, sending her nerves into spasms of awareness and loosening her tongue. Deliberately, she stiffened her spine and made the necessary reply, reminding herself that the man had a right to know who was working on his house.

"This is my brother."

Brodie lifted an eyebrow and stuck out his hand. "Brodie Todd. How do you do?"

"Matthew Paul Simmons," Matt said in that funny, formal way of so many native Louisianans. "Everyone, they call me Matt."

"Nice to meet you, Matt. I take it you're on the job?"

"Yes, sir, and a good job we're gonna do for you, too, Mr. Todd."

"It's Brodie, please."

"All right, Brodie." Matt beamed his approval at this informality.

"And what is it that you do, Matt?"

"Me, I'm the heat and air man. I'm gonna keep these Louisiana summers outside of this big old Fair Havens house and warm up your bones in the winter. That's my job."

"And I'm sure you're good at it or you wouldn't be here," Brodie commented, glancing at Chey.

"Hoo, now there's the truth. Our Mary, she don't stand for nothing but the finest work. Sometime I don't even like to do for her," he confided, "'cause she's so particular."

Brodie chuckled. "That's why she's the best," he said, smiling down at her so intimately that she gulped.

"Yeah, she sure is," Matt admitted, squeezing her shoulder. "She don't hardly have time for nothing but work. That's how come she's still single, pretty girl like her."

"Hardly a girl," Chey gritted out, her cheeks heating with embarrassment.

"Sure 'nough, she's right about an old maid," Matt teased, "but she's still my baby sister. You by chance have you a sister, Brodie?"

Brodie shook his head, his smile faltering. "No. I had a brother."

Matt might be oblivious to his own sister's distress, but he picked up on the other man's verb tense correctly. "Oh, I'm sure sorry for your loss."

Chey looked up sharply, shocked that she had almost missed the implication herself. To her surprise, naked pain swam the surface of Brodie's blue eyes. He nodded and murmured, "Thank you. I miss him." He renewed his smile. "You're lucky, you Simmonses, having so much family."

"Yeah, we sure do," Matt agreed heartily. "Whenever you need somethin' you got to go no further than family. You take Mary, now, she's got all the help she needs right at her fingertips. Frank, that's Francis Delaney, the eldest— me and him, we got the same birthday, May 6, only seven years apart. Well, anyway, Frank, he's the mason. Anything you do with a brick or a stone or a tile, that's him. Now, Thomas—that's Thomas Ducian, not Tommy, his son, or Tom Beltran, the brother-in-law, husband to May, who's the third oldest—anyway, Thomas, he's the electrician. We work together a lot, me and Thomas." Brodie nodded as if he was actually following all this, while Chey grimaced inwardly and tried to distract Matt with a shake of her head.

"Anthony Sherman," Matt went on heedlessly. "We call him Anthony on account of Thomas, he's got a boy named Tony, you know, after Anthony, and Anthony, he's got his own boy. We call him Tony-Tony, on account of him being a Tony junior."

"Matt," Chey put in quickly. "I'm sure Mr. Todd has a lot to do and is uninterested in our family peculiarities."

"No, no," Brodie interrupted. He looked at Matt. "Go on, please. It's fascinating."

Matt stroked his lean, square chin. "Well, let's see, Anthony, he's a carpenter, a genius with them tools of his. An artist, that's what he is. He'n build furniture as fine as anything you can find in any store, old or new.''

"A talented family," Brodie said, smiling down at Chey, who was tapping her toe impatiently.

"Bay, that's Bailey Michael," Matt rattled on, "his thing is floors. You know, carpet and vinyl and them beautiful inlaid woods and all. And Johnny—he's the baby of us all—Johnny is roofs, any kind of roofs. Clay, shakes, shingles, tin, even gravel, it don't matter, Johnny does 'em all." Matt shuddered. "Me, I got no tolerance for heights. Give me a cubbyhole anytime."

Brodie peered into the crawl space and shook his head. "Too claustrophobic for me."

Matt just grinned. "Yeah, that's what Johnny says." He stroked his chin again and went back to his original subject matter. "I almost forgot the brothers-in-law." Chey rolled her eyes and huffed an impatient breath, but Matt kept talking, sure of his audience. "Tom Beltran, he's appliances. Got a shop over in Metairie. And Sylvester Gilroy—he's husband to Kay, the middle sister—now, he's foundations and concrete." He glanced down at Chey, a puzzled look on his face. "Who'm I leavin' out there, Mary?"

"Carter," she answered with a resigned sigh.

Matt snapped his finger. "Carter Dupre! That's Fay's husband." He grinned unrepentantly. "They're expectin' the nex' one most anytime now. And Carter, he's not in any of the building trades, you know. He's a car mechanic, and not one of them shade-tree boys, neither. Real handy to have around, Carter."

Brodie laughed. "I can imagine. Sounds like the whole family's handy."

Matt nodded proudly. "Yeah, even Mary. She can't just stay home an' have babies like the rest of the gals. She's gotta go crawlin' in dusty old holes and plannin' everything down to the millisecond."

He patted her on the cheek as he spoke, failing to see,

apparently, that she was steaming. Stay home and have babies like the rest of the gals, indeed!

"I think you've said enough, Matt," she said through a smile that exposed her clamped teeth.

He just chuckled and dragged her to his side in a hug, saying to Brodie, "She'll do you a good job. Yessir, you can trust our Mary. Nothing but the best for her."

Brodie slid his hands into the pockets of his pleated chinos and fastened heated eyes on her. "That's what I'm counting on," he said smoothly. "That's exactly what I'm counting on."

Arrogant flirt. Chey narrowed her eyes at him, letting him know that she didn't consider him the best at anything, certainly not what he was implying. He was implying that he was the best at making love, wasn't he? Or was it just that she couldn't get the idea out of her mind? She shook her head, the ponytail at the nape of her neck flopping back and forth between her shoulder blades.

"Uh, I need," she said, to cover her actions, "that written estimate today."

Matt wrinkled his nose in distaste. "Yeah, okay. I'll get right on it." He looked at Brodie and explained, "Have to do this myself. My Gail, she'll type it up for me and get one of the kids to take it on over, but she can't do the figures. Got no head for numbers. Not that I mind. You know?" He winked at Brodie and added wryly, "Her figure's okay without the numbers."

Brodie laughed in understanding, and Matt thumped Chey on the tip of her chin with his fist before sauntering off, the flashlight stuck in the back pocket of his jeans. Chey sent Brodie a limp smile and started off after Matt, only to be drawn up short by Brodie's hand on her forearm. She backed up a few steps to break the contact and glared up at him.

"It's not nepotism," she hastened to assure him. "Matt really is the best man for the job."

"I don't doubt it."

She frowned at that. "Then what do you want?"

He leaned close, ostensibly to adjust the collar of the simple white camp shirt she had donned for the occasion. He tugged on the points, then brushed his hands lightly across her shoulders. "It's you, Mary Chey," he told her softly, leaning close, his head bent near hers. "I just wanted to touch you." And he did, smoothing his hands down her arms, then lifting them to gently massage her shoulders. She stood rigid, frozen, pretending that her every nerve ending did not suddenly tingle with delight. Finally, she found her voice and her indignation.

"I thought we agreed to keep this strictly business."

He cocked his head. "Did we? Funny, I don't remember agreeing to any such thing."

"Now that's a blatant lie! I remember clearly...." That bowed head, that blank look and resigned sigh. Outrage and embarrassment suffused her. She didn't know which one of them she was more upset with, him for letting her think he'd agreed or her for thinking it. The only one she could lash out at, however, happened to be him.

"I ought to smack you," she huffed.

His gaze dropped blatantly to her mouth. "Oh, baby, please. Right here." He tapped his pursed lips with a forefinger.

She turned on her heel. Laughter followed her down the hallway as she strode away, but more than once that day she found herself wondering what would have happened if she'd accepted his challenge. One part of her wished she'd slapped him, and yet she couldn't help thinking of that kiss in his suite. Smack him, indeed. She'd be better off smacking some sense into her own head—if only she could figure out how to do that.

Chapter Five

Crouching, Anthony tapped the thick wooden beam overhead. "No problem here," he announced. "All the cross beams are sound. I'll replace the subfloor, then you can get Bay in to do his thing."

Chey breathed a sigh of relief. "That's good news. Probably save us a solid two weeks." At five feet and six inches, she could stand upright beneath the old house, but the six-foot-high space felt uncomfortably low, so she invariably caught herself ducking her head.

His investigation done, Anthony turned toward the short, narrow ladder that led up to the ground, his booted feet crunching across the gravel liberally sprinkled with tiny seashells and even some small pieces of animal bone. Chey followed, climbing up the trio of steps behind him. It was the second time in the last few weeks that she'd made this trip, the first time with her brother-in-law Sylvester, who had inspected the foundations and pronounced them generally sound. Two corners of the south end of the big old building had been jacked up and reinforced just to make everything level and plumb. For days Kate had been exclaiming how easily all the doors were opening and closing on that end of the house. Next the plumber had come to make his assessment. A full week of pipe replacement had followed, but even that had not been as extensive as Chey had feared it might have been. Now, even though the plumber was still on site and would be periodically for some time to come, it was Anthony's turn to ascertain the true condition of the floors.

Anthony climbed up out of the opening, then reached down to help her do the same. Once they were both standing on the grass in the sun again, he closed and bolted the small, plank door that gave access to the underside of the house. Together they walked around the corner, climbed a narrow set of concrete steps and entered the kitchen through a storage-room door. Seth was sitting on the butcher-block island next to a metal mixing bowl beneath a rack of gleaming pans suspended from the bead-plank ceiling. His face was dirty, and he popped a chocolatey finger from his mouth and cried loudly, "Hewo, Chey-Chey!"

He'd been calling her Chey-Chey ever since Georges had tried to explain what they did and had told him the name of her business. She smiled uncertainly and moved closer, asking, "Are you supposed to be up there?"

He nodded just as a frazzled Marcel rose from cleaning the floor, a messy spoon and damp cloth in hand. "We had a little accident," Marcel explained.

"I dwop a 'poon," Seth confessed, swiping his finger around the bowl and holding it out to her. "Wanna licked?"

Anthony laughed, and Chey had to smile, too. "No, thank you."

The boy next offered the finger to Anthony. "Wanna licked?"

Anthony shook his head, long blond hair ruffling, and

patted his flat middle. "Better not. We girls have to watch our figures, you know."

Seth put the finger in his mouth, screwing up his face at the same time. "Woo nod ah gwir," he exclaimed around his finger.

Anthony looked down in mock surprise. "I'm not a girl? You sure?"

Seth went off into giggles, nodding so violently that Marcel reached out and steadied him. Chey elbowed Anthony in his slender ribs. "Stop teasing him before he falls off there and hurts himself."

At thirty-six and a father himself, Anthony was still a big kid at heart. He was also vain about his good looks. The only one of her brothers over six feet tall, Anthony was blessed with a fine physique, blue eyes and straight golden hair almost as long as Chey's. He was also the only member of the family to have married more than once. After his first short, volatile marriage, he seemed genuinely happy now with Mikki, her two kids and their own little Tony-Tony. The divorce had been a major upheaval for the family, though, especially for their deeply religious mother.

"I need you to take a look at the library," Chey said to him.

Seth immediately tried to wiggle off the edge of the island, exclaiming, "I show woo!"

To keep the boy from falling, Marcel quickly set him off the counter top, saying, "Now, now, Seth. I told Miss Viola you'd be here with me."

"Marce, I show Chey-Chey," he insisted, running over to her and slipping his gooey hand into hers.

Chey could tell that Marcel would welcome a reprieve. The man was a marvel in the kitchen, but he only had two hands. It seemed unfair to expect him to baby-sit while beginning lunch preparations. What could it possibly hurt to walk the boy out to his grandmother? Chey asked, "Where is Viola?"

"She went to answer the door," Marcel answered.

Chey vaguely remembered hearing a bell before they'd crawled up from beneath the house. She looked down at Seth and decided aloud, "We'll take the boy with us and see if we can find her." Seth gripped her hand and jumped up and down. Anthony lifted an eyebrow. "It's on our way," she told him curtly.

"Whatever," he replied lightly, but she knew what he was thinking, that it was unusual for her to cater to a child. "Cute little guy," he murmured as they pushed through the kitchen door into the butler's pantry. Well aware that he was being discussed, Seth turned up a cherubic face. Chey glared at her mouthy brother and pushed on into the hallway, the boy's hand held firmly in hers.

They skirted the curving base of the main staircase and found Viola on the other side of it talking animatedly with Georges. Spying Chey, he shifted smoothly into assistant gear, declaring, "There you are! I've been trying to call you on your cell phone all morning."

Chey winced. "It's in my bag, which I did not take with me to inspect the underside of the house. Sorry. What's so important that you drove out here?"

"The marble tiles that you wanted for the ballroom floor are not available in sufficient quantity. The supplier says he's found some used ones in Baton Rouge, though, and that they are an 'adequate' match, his word not mine. I didn't feel comfortable making a decision about them."

Chey sighed and considered for a moment before answering. "Tell him to go ahead and pick them up but not to send them here until I can get out to his warehouse and take a look at them. If we don't use them at Fair Havens, I'll buy them myself. Someone's bound to want them sometime."

"Tell him to send them straight here," countered another voice. Chey turned and looked up. Brodie was standing on the stairs just above them. "No need for you to take a financial risk," he told her. "I'll buy them. If the color and pattern don't meet with your approval, it'll be my problem.''

It was a generous offer, but she suspected that his motives went beyond mere thoughtfulness and she disliked having her decisions countermanded. ''That's not necessary.''

''I think it is,'' he said, coming down the stairs. She opened her mouth to argue, but he turned his attention to Seth. ''Someone needs his face washed.''

Knowing perfectly well who that someone was, Seth yanked free and scuttled behind Chey, crying, ''I show Chey-Chey!''

Glancing up at her, Brodie reached around and tugged Seth forward. ''What is it you want to show Ms. Chey?''

''I show Chey-Chey,'' Seth whined, trying to pull away again.

''He heard me tell Anthony that I wanted him to take a look at the woodwork in the library,'' Chey explained. ''That must be what he wants to show me.''

''Ah.'' Brodie nodded in comprehension, then bent over to bring his face to the level of the boy's. ''You know perfectly well, young man, that you've been forbidden to go anywhere near the library or the game room. Don't you?''

Seth nodded even as he whined around his finger, ''I show Chey-Chey.''

''You go straight upstairs to your room and stay there until lunch,'' Brodie said firmly, ''and if I catch you anywhere near the library or the game room, you're going to be in big trouble. Understand?''

Seth nodded mutely and ran to Viola, who whisked him off up the stairs.

''I didn't know he'd been forbidden to go to the library,'' Chey apologized.

''No reason you should,'' Brodie replied, ''as you weren't told. He was.''

''I should have realized that those rooms would be dangerous for a little boy, though,'' Chey admitted. ''The shelves and chimneys are coming off the walls, and the floorboards are weak. Not that I intended to take him there, actually. I was planning to drop him off with his great-grandmother.''

''Well, then, mission accomplished. No cause for concern. Now about those tiles....''

''I ought to get back to the shop,'' Georges announced abruptly.

They had a perfectly capable young woman who came in part-time to help out when Chey was away from the shop on one of these big projects. She was incapable of making design decisions, as Georges well knew, but she could handle customers off the street, and the matter of the tiles had yet to be settled. ''Wait just a minute,'' she said to Georges, then turned back to Brodie. ''There is no reason for you to buy tiles that you may not be able to use.''

''But I *can* use them,'' he said. ''If not in the house, then outside. Grandmama wants to lay pathways beneath the trees on the back of the property. If the tiles don't work for the ballroom floor, we'll use them out there.''

''You want to use expensive marble tiles to make pathways beneath the trees?'' she asked skeptically.

''Anything wrong with that?'' he countered.

She wanted to argue that if he was doing this just to get on her good side it wasn't working, but with Georges and Anthony standing there, she dared not open that can of worms. Nodding at Georges, she murmured that she'd see him back at the shop. His immediate departure brought Brodie's attention to Anthony.

''About those weak floors and falling shelves,'' her brother said. ''I'll take care of those first thing.''

''That must mean,'' Brodie mused, pointing a finger at him, ''that you're the carpenter.''

''Right. Anthony Sherman.''

''Not to be confused with Tony,'' Brodie said, ''who

would be your nephew or Tony-Tony, who would be your son.''

Anthony grinned, obviously impressed. ''He's just starting to walk, my boy.''

''Walk today, run tomorrow, scheme the next,'' Brodie commented wryly, offering his hand. ''I'm Brodie Todd, by the way.''

''I figured as much,'' Anthony said, giving that hand a firm grip and shake. ''Pleasure to meet you.''

''Likewise.''

''Grand old place you've got here. You'll be glad to know that the underpinning is sound.''

''Indeed, I am,'' Brodie told him. Then he glanced at Chey, leaned in close to Anthony and said, ''Tell me something. What's the deal with this Georges guy? He strike you as a little odd?''

''Odd?'' Anthony hooted. ''The man's a bona fide mystery. Did you know he's been married *four* times?''

''You're kidding!''

''Don't ask me to explain it.''

''All right, I'll explain it,'' Chey snapped indignantly, honor-bound to defend her friend and aide. Unfortunately she had to think a moment before she could come up with a good explanation for Georges's mysterious appeal. ''Women like a sensitive man,'' she finally said.

They both gaped at her. ''Sensitive?'' Anthony snorted, while Brodie ducked his head and coughed discreetly behind his fist. She glared at him to let him know he wasn't hiding his laughter from her.

''Not every woman wants a macho man,'' she informed them both haughtily.

''Most do,'' Anthony retorted, but Brodie made a more logical argument.

''Manly and sensitive are not mutually exclusive,'' he said, then stroked his chin and went on thoughtfully, ''but perhaps you wouldn't know that.''

''She ought to,'' Anthony said.

"Oh, right," Chey shot back. "Like any of my six brothers even knows the meaning of the word *sensitive*."

"Hey!"

"I wouldn't want get into the middle of a family argument," Brodie said mildly to Chey, "however, you must know plenty of men—other than your brothers—who are both manly and sensitive."

"You're talking to Virgin Mary Chey," Anthony quipped snidely, and Chey felt her face explode with heat. Anthony immediately realized he'd gone too far and tried to backpedal, saying to Brodie, "Uh, that is, Chey isn't interested in men."

"Could've fooled me," Brodie drawled. Chey gasped and glared murderously first at Anthony and then at Brodie.

Anthony, at least, realized he'd jumped from the fat into the fire and muttered weakly, "I mean, she works a lot."

"I've noticed that, too," Brodie said quietly, his gaze thoughtful as it rested on her blazing face. Then, clearly taking pity on her, he announced, "I have work to do myself. Nice to meet you, Anthony. Be seeing you around. Chey." With that he left them, moving off down the hall toward the back of the house.

Chey glared daggers at her sheepish-looking brother, then turned smartly and led the way toward the library.

Later that same evening, as Chey sat at the makeshift desk put up for her in the smoking room, she heard a shuffling of feet outside the door and then a light knock. Her heart climbed into her throat, but she told herself that she was being foolish and called out for whoever it was to come in. The door opened slightly, and Brodie leaned in past it. "Busy?"

Immediately her heart plummeted to her stomach. She glanced meaningfully at the laptop computer screen in front of her. "Yes, actually."

He came fully into the room and closed the door behind

him, saying, "I won't keep you long." She looked at the door and said nothing.

He slipped his hands into his pants pockets and looked down at his toes. "It's about those marble tiles."

Chey swivelled around in her armless, wheeled chair. "What about them?"

"I owe you an apology. I should have told you right up front what I was thinking instead of simply countermanding you like that. I realized later that it could have been construed as a challenge to your authority, and that wasn't my intent at all."

"It would've helped if you'd explained your thinking up front," she admitted.

"So we're clear on this?"

"If you're really intending to use them for a pathway beneath the trees, then we're clear."

"What else would I use them for?"

"Oh, I don't know. The thought did occur that you might be trying to impress me."

"By challenging your authority?"

She felt heat stain her face again as the foolishness of the argument hit home. Quickly turning back to the screen of the laptop computer, she began circling her finger on the mouse pad and said, "Right. Okay. We're clear." She used her thumb to click the mouse at a certain point in the list she was making and began typing in a new item, effectively dismissing him. To her annoyance, she felt his hand on the back of her chair.

"One more thing," he said, pulling her chair around.

She glared up at him, wary and uncertain. "What's that?"

"Stand up," he directed imperiously.

She blinked, puzzled. "I beg your pardon."

"I need you to stand up."

She studied his expression, but it told her nothing. Then his gaze dropped to the chair, and she decided that must be it. Perhaps something was wrong with it. She rose to her feet. The next instant he reached out with both arms, swept one around her shoulders and the other about her waist and yanked her against him. She made a surprised, gurgling sound just as his mouth covered hers. Too shocked to think intelligently, she obeyed her first impulse and attempted to ask what the devil he thought he was doing, but the instant she opened her mouth, his tongue plunged inside, and a liquid warmth filled her, swirling from her chest up into her head.

Instinct bade her close her eyes and hang on to him. Her eyelids went down, but when her hands encountered the warm, solid bulk of muscle that lay beneath his shirt, she jerked them away, shocked by the sudden pooling of warmth in the pit of her belly and the ease with which her body succumbed to temptation. She could not seem, however, to stiffen her spine sufficiently to keep him from molding her body to his. One hand moved down to splay between her shoulder blades, pressing her sensitized breasts to the firm wall of his chest, while the other cupped a buttock and brought them pelvis to pelvis.

A hot, thick haze enveloped them, blocking everything but the energy pulsing between them. Chey lifted up onto tiptoe and twined her arms around his neck, consumed with the sweep of his tongue and the heat of his hard body, particularly the rigid length that branded her belly right through the layers of their clothing.

She knew, vaguely, that this was a mistake, but she couldn't for the life of her remember why. Then suddenly she was stumbling slightly, arms aloft, heels on the floor. She opened her eyes and looked straight into pale blue ones rimmed with long, black lashes. Backing up a step, she blinked as if to clear her vision and realized that he was panting even as he smiled.

"Definitely likes men. Not virginal," he pronounced succinctly.

Suddenly she wanted to slap him, crack her palm hard

against his cheek. He must have seen it in her eyes, for he
flashed her an unrepentant smile.

"Go ahead," he said. "It was worth it."

She curled her fingers into her palm, determined not to
give him the satisfaction of knowing he'd read her mind.
"I didn't want that!"

"Not much you didn't," he scoffed. "No more than me,
I'd guess."

She turned away from him and folded her arms defensively. "What is it with you? Why can't you just take no
for an answer?"

"I'm not sure." The raw honesty of that made her turn
to face him again. He seemed as bemused as she. "I really
don't know what it is about you that feels so right," he
said, almost to himself, "and I don't understand why you
don't feel it, too." His blue eyes narrowed. "Or rather, why
you don't just give in to it."

Chey gulped surreptitiously and glanced into the corner,
saying caustically, "Don't flatter yourself."

He didn't answer for so long that she was forced to slide
a look at him. Finally he said thoughtfully, "I don't think
I am," as if he'd truly considered the possibility. Then
suddenly his gaze targeted hers, boring deep. "I think
you're afraid," he said.

She was appalled, insulted. Nervous. Lifting her chin,
she insisted haughtily, "I am *not* afraid of you."

He studied her a moment longer. "No," he said absently,
"not of me." He tilted his head to one side, as if listening
to some inner voice, and concluded, "Of life perhaps."

Her heart ceased to beat. Everything inside her froze. For
an instant, she was certain that he could see inside her to
the deep, yawning fissure that threatened constantly to
crack open and engulf her. Gasping in panic, she turned
away. Immediately she sensed movement, but she knew
without a doubt that if he touched her then she would shat-
ter. Stepping adroitly aside, she lifted a hand to ward him
off. He stopped in his tracks.

"I'm sorry," he told her. "I shouldn't have said that."

"Go away!" she demanded sharply. He lifted a hand toward her, but she flinched away. "Please," she added. He hesitated a moment longer, and she fought the urge to cover her ears with her hands, as if he might tell her something she couldn't bear to hear. Then he stepped back, hands falling to his sides.

"When you're ready to face this thing," he began as she folded her arms and bowed her head, "I'll be here," he finished softly. She neither spoke nor moved. An eternity seemed to tick away before she heard the sound of the door opening and gently closing once more.

Chey shielded her eyes from the blazing Louisiana sun and pointed to a spot some fifteen feet to the left of the second chimney about the level of the top of the second story. "There," she said, and Frank trained his binoculars.

"Oh, yeah. Sure enough. Missed that spot. Just needs pointing up, a little mortar in the grooves."

"Make sure the color of the new mortar matches the old."

"Land sakes alive, girl," Frank said, lowering the binoculars. "I been doing this since before you were even a gleam in our daddy's eye. You think you have to tell me my business?"

"I know, I know," Chey apologized immediately. "Habit, nothing more. Not everyone is as conscientious as you are, you know, and it's my job to worry about the details." Frank hunched a shoulder dismissively.

"Chey-Chey!" She turned in time to see Seth hurtling around the corner of the house toward her.

She bent instinctively and caught him up in her arms. He was a little chunk of lead. Before long she wouldn't be able to lift him at all, which meant he'd be knocking her down since he'd developed this disturbing tendency to throw himself at her. "What is it?" she asked.

"Swunch tie. Marce say so."

The translation took a moment. "Ah. Lunch time." Marcel insisted on laying out a spread for everyone on the place, day after day. Kate said having workmen crawling all over the place was the best thing that had happened to him since they'd hired on with the Todds.

"This here must be Brodie's boy," Frank said, ruffling the boy's bright hair. As a grandfather several times over, he was especially fond of children.

"He is, indeed," Brodie said from a few feet away.

Chey immediately put the boy onto his feet and backed up a step. Seth ran to Brodie, who picked him up and carried him over to Frank.

"Son, this is Frank Simmons. He's another of Chey's brothers." Brodie and Frank had met and had a long chat earlier that morning. Chey had pretended to be unconcerned, busily examining the brick face of the south end of the house. Her ears had burned at times, but she'd dared not get close enough to actually hear what was being said. Proximity to Brodie Todd was dangerous to her peace of mind.

"Mary Chey is my baby sister," Frank was explaining to the boy.

"Chey not a baby!" Seth exclaimed, and the men laughed.

"She is to me," Frank said. Then he looked at Brodie. "Hey, you know, my boy Spence has two kids about this age. We ought to get 'em together."

"Uh, Frank," Chey began. "I don't think—"

"Sounds great," Brodie interrupted. "Seth doesn't really have any friends his own age, yet. We've signed up for a neighborhood play date thing, and we're taking him to a story time at the library, but there seems to be a dearth of three-year-olds around here. Why don't you have your son call me?"

"Yeah, I'll do that, sure 'nough," Frank agreed.

"Meanwhile," Brodie said congenially, "join us for

lunch. Marcel sets a fine table. Your sister can attest to that.''

Before his sister could attest to anything, Frank politely refused. ''Oh, I thank you much, but my Genevive, she's expecting me home for lunch, and your Marcel could learn a thing or two 'bout gumbo from her, I reckon.''

Brodie chuckled. ''In that case, I'd say you're a very lucky man.''

''Oh, I got a good one,'' Frank said with a grin, ''but luck ain't got nothin' to do with it. A Simmons knows how to marry right.'' He waved a hand, warming to his subject. ''Even Anthony. He might've messed up the first time, but he sure nailed it the second. Shoot, we could give lessons, I reckon, on picking good ones. Except her.'' He pointed a finger at Chey, ignoring how she rolled her eyes and lifted her hands heavenward. Shaking his head he said to Brodie, ''That child is plumb backward. Won't even try.''

''My brother has a hard time imagining why any woman might prefer to remain single,'' Chey interjected sharply.

''Anyone,'' Frank corrected, ''man or woman. Seems to me the good Lord means us either to marry or enter His service, and you, Mary Chey, are no nun.''

Chey closed her eyes, mortified beyond words, while Brodie observed gently, ''Maybe she just hasn't found the right person yet.''

''Well, now, that's a cold fact,'' Frank agreed, ''but you know what the Good Book says, 'You don't look, you don't find.'''

''I believe that's, 'Seek and ye shall find,''' Chey corrected him smartly.

''Same difference,'' Frank insisted.

Chey sighed and shook her head. ''Do you really want to keep Genevive waiting just so you can criticize me?''

''Ain't criticism, little girl,'' he told her sternly. ''It's pure concern, for you and our mama, too. I swear, you are breaking that good woman's heart.''

Chey closed her eyes and began to count to ten. Brodie

cleared his throat and rescued her, asking Frank, "Are you sure you won't join us for lunch?"

"Naw, but I thank you, just the same."

"Another time then," Brodie said, shifting Seth in his arms.

"Sure enough," Frank replied. "We'll be on the job first thing Monday."

"I'll tell my chef Marcel to expect you," Brodie said.

"Oh, I don't know that," Frank demurred. "I got six guys on my crew."

"Not a problem," Brodie assured him. "Marcel will insist." He looked at Chey then and said, "Speaking of which, if we don't show up at the table soon, he'll come after the three of us with a hook."

"Chey-Chey, come on," Seth urged, whining a little and reaching out to wrap one arm around her neck and pull her close.

Frank chuckled and moved away, calling, "I'll see you all next week."

"Thanks, Frank," Brodie answered. "And don't forget to have your son call."

Frank lifted a hand in acknowledgment, his gaze moving speculatively between Brodie and Chey before he moved on. As Chey watched him go she felt strangely disoriented. Her life seemed to be careening out of her control. Brodie had moved himself right in and taken over. As proof, there went her eldest brother, dressed in his usual scruffy jeans and a plain white T-shirt from the local discount store, intent on setting up play dates for the three-year-old of a man with whom he wouldn't normally have even struck up a conversation.

The three-year-old in question was another part of the problem and not just because his small hand had latched onto the French braid at the back of her head. He seemed certain that she, like every other adult within his orbit—excluding Brown who spent all of her time with her patient—adored him. Short of being downright mean, Chey hadn't found any way to discourage the tyke. She'd look up and there he'd be, wanting to know why she was doing whatever she was doing at the moment. She'd learned early on not to try to fob him off with the platitudes that often satisfied her nieces and nephews at his age but to offer him, instead, honest simple answers and hope he'd go away. At the moment, he was urging her to come to the lunch table, proclaiming that he was "hungwy."

Knowing from experience that it was useless to argue, Chey allowed herself to be turned and escorted toward the back of the house. Brodie said nothing, but the twinkle in his sky-blue eyes clearly indicated that he was well aware she wouldn't disappoint or rebuff the boy. It hit her like a bolt of lightning, the realization that he was using the child to coerce her into keeping company with him. The fact that he was succeeding, despite her personal convictions, shocked and frightened her. The physical pull between them was strong, electric, even now with the child between them, and she ought to be running in the opposite direction. Instead, she was doing just what he wanted her to.

She gathered the child into her own arms just to put some distance between her and his father. Seth wrapped his legs around her waist and laid his head on her shoulder, his hand still clamped around her braid.

"He means well," Brodie said softly, walking at her side. At first she thought he meant Seth, but then she realized that he was referring to Frank.

"They all mean well," Chey acknowledged wryly. "That doesn't make it any easier to put up with their interference."

"I think they just want you to be happy," Brodie said.

She glanced at him sharply. "I'm happy."

"Are you?" he asked, reaching out to bring her to a halt, a hand clamped around her forearm. "Are you really happy?"

Why did everybody keep asking her that? The question was a trap. If she insisted that she was really deliriously happy, he would think she protested too much. If she admitted that there were times when the life she had structured for herself felt empty and hollow, he would surely make more of it than it was. Finally she lifted her chin and said calmly, "No one's happy all the time."

"That's true," he said. "Every life has at least one area that could benefit from change. When that area is a small one, easily ignored and endured, we are, generally speaking, happy. When it's dead center of who and what we are, then we have this aching emptiness inside us that won't go away. Sometimes it overlaps, and we're happy with part of our lives, unhappy with other parts. Isn't there part of your life that you're unhappy with?"

She could hear her heart beating in her ears, but it didn't drown out the small voice that shouted, "Yes!" She made a mental effort to put that rascally little voice right back into its box, however, and answered his question with one of her own, intending to turn the tables on him. "Is there a part of your life with which *you* are unhappy?"

"Absolutely," he said, his hand coming up to rest heavily on the top of her shoulder.

Chey swallowed, trapped by his gaze, until with a purposeful nod he pulled the boy from her arms and carried him around the corner of the house. She took a deep breath, suddenly realizing that she was oxygen-deprived, and gathered her wits about her. That man was not going to make her believe that she was somehow essential to his happiness, she vowed.

But what if it were true? What if, somehow, she could bring him—and herself—a measure of happiness? The depth of her own yearning caught her completely off guard, frightening her so that she resolutely, mechanically quelled it. She *was* happy, she told herself sternly, no matter what anyone said. But the what-ifs were piling up, and she wondered how long it would be before she couldn't see beyond them anymore.

Chapter Six

Chey added a touch of red to the gold in the computer palette, decided it was too orange and deleted it. *Perhaps a touch of green,* she mused, typing in a new code of numbers. The palette on her screen disappeared, then gradually reformed. Very nice. She enlarged the gold portion and studied the palette for a moment before dragging over a section of medium, mossy green and beginning to tinker with it. The door creaked open just then, and she looked over warily to find Seth hanging on the doorknob. Relief that it wasn't his father made her more friendly than she might have been otherwise, and she said cheerily, "Hello."

He came into the room, leaving the door open, and just stood there a moment with two fingers in his mouth. Then suddenly he ran toward her, threw himself at her lap and scrambled up, the hard rubber soles of his shoes connecting sharply with her shins and thighs. She helped him in order to protect herself, turning his back to her chest, pulling his legs out straight in front so that his feet stuck out past her knees. He tried to look up at her and bumped her chin with his head. Sliding his head over to her shoulder, he tilted it back and gazed up at her with perfectly guileless eyes of a clear, bright blue. "Hewo," he said.

"Where is everyone?" she asked, smiling to cover her irritation. He shrugged one little shoulder. She decided to be more specific. "Where is your father?"

"He workin'."

That was a relief. "And your great-grandmother?"

"Gwamuma in dhere," he said, pointing a finger at the wall. In that direction lay the elevator, restroom and Viola's office, in that order.

"You mean in her office?" she asked, and he nodded vigorously.

"Yeah, an' Marce cookin', an' Kate to da store, an' Mama sweeping," he added.

Chey felt an unwanted rush of sympathy. "Yes, I know that your Mama is sleeping."

He suddenly rocked forward and reached for the computer. "Pway game!"

She pushed her chair back out of reach, saying sternly, "That's not a game. I don't have any games on this computer."

He put his fingers in his mouth and said, "Da-ay pwa ga."

Automatically, without even thinking about it, she pulled his hand from his mouth and scolded gently, "It's rude to speak with something in your mouth, particularly your hand. Besides being unattractive, it makes it hard for people to understand you. Now what were you saying?"

He stared at her with huge eyes, swallowed and said quite clearly, "Daddy pways games wif his c'puter."

She couldn't help smiling. "I'm sure he does, but I don't have any games to play on this computer."

"What's dat?" he asked skeptically, pointing to the screen.

"That's a color palette," she explained patiently. "I'm putting together color schemes for your house."

"Okay," he said, and settled in to watch.

She could have put him down, of course. She *should* have put him down and sent him from the room, but he wasn't really in the way and seemed determined to be on his best behavior—for the moment. Soon enough, she reasoned, he would grow restless, and she would send him off with a small object lesson: behave and remain; misbehave and go. She rolled her chair a little closer to the table and began to work again. As she did so, she found herself explaining what was happening. In short order she'd put together a series of schemes built around gold and green. The small color printer brought in for her use was pushing out the first one when Viola and Brodie walked into the room.

"There you are!" Viola exclaimed, and Seth immediately slid off Chey's lap and onto her feet, which he trampled in his haste to get to the door.

"I'm sorry," she said to Chey, snagging the boy's hand. "Seems like every time I turn my back lately, he's gone."

Brodie smoothed a hand over the back of the boy's head, saying, "You worried us, son. Next time, be sure you have Grandmama's permission before you leave the room. Okay?"

"'Kay," Seth agreed, nodding affirmatively.

Brodie turned to Chey then. "I hope he didn't make a nuisance of himself,"

"No, not really," Chey said, surprised that it was so. Quickly, she changed the subject. "Come and look at what we've done here." On each sheet of paper were printed two large, overlapping circles of green and gold. Rectangles, triangles and squares of accent colors varied from page to page, depending upon the room to which they were assigned. "This is my favorite," she admitted, tapping a paper accented with a deep, muted violet. As Chey expected, Viola preferred the greens, singling out a paper printed with shades from light to dark. No doubt her love of the color was tied up with her love of her gardens. Brodie paid close attention to the blues, browns, greens and golds meant for his suite.

Chey pulled aside two papers accented with burgundies and mauves, explaining, "I thought we might use this scheme for the formal parlor and ballroom, gold as a primary in one, green in the other, same accents, and I'm leaning toward painting the woodwork in ivory. That would both lighten everything and call attention to the dark finishes on the furniture. What do you think?"

Viola glanced at the papers. "Looks fine to me, dear, but to my mind a house is just four walls that keeps me from the out-of-doors."

Brodie had warned her that his grandmother would have little interest in the interior of the house, but Chey had hoped, for her own sake, that he'd overstated the old woman's indifference. She saw now that he had not. Laying aside the two papers, she nodded and smiled wanly. Brodie picked up the papers and studied them.

"I like this. It has an airy feel to it."

"I'm glad you approve."

He looked her squarely in the eye and said in a husky tone, "I approve very much, Mary Chey, of almost everything you do."

Her breath caught in her throat. "I, uh, that is, thank you."

He stood there a moment longer, holding her gaze with his. Then he glanced away. "Well, I'd best get this fellow upstairs for a proper nap."

"Oh, I'll do it," Viola said lightly. "You two stick with those color schemes." With that, she turned Seth toward the door.

"Bye-bye, Chey-Chey," the boy called as Viola led him from the room.

"Bye, Seth."

Brodie laid aside the papers he'd studied earlier and brought his hands to his hips, saying, "I'm sorry about that.

Seth's been told not to bother you while you're working, but I'm afraid he conveniently forgets what he doesn't want to remember.''

''He's only three,'' she said.

''Mmm-hmm, not too young, apparently, to appreciate the company of a beautiful woman.''

Chey caught her breath, appalled by the sweet flush of pleasure that his compliment brought. ''Don't do that,'' she ordered softly.

''What?''

''Flatter me.''

''The truth is not flattery.''

''Why won't you just let this go?'' she beseeched him.

''I can't.''

She rolled her eyes.

''All right, I don't want to.''

''Please,'' she whispered.

He leaned close, bringing his mouth next to her ear. ''What's wrong, Mary Chey? Afraid you'll give in?''

She closed her eyes until she could gather the strength to put him in his place. ''No.''

''I don't believe you.''

She stepped away, glaring at him. ''Do you like tormenting me?''

''Yes. But I'd rather make love to you.''

''And I'd rather you fell off the face of the earth!''

He chuckled. ''All that fire,'' he said, ''could be put to better use.''

She turned her back on him then. She didn't hear him leave, but when she finally turned around, he was gone.

Unfortunately, his departure did not signal an end to the interruptions. On the contrary, within the half-hour, Viola opened the door and walked back into the room. To Chey's surprise, the older woman seated herself in the chair at the end of the table serving as Chey's desk.

''Everything okay?'' Chey asked.

''With Seth, you mean?'' Viola said, then she waved a

hand dismissively. "Seth is fine. Sound asleep with the monitor on. Brodie keeps the receiver with him."

"Ah." She couldn't think of anything else to say. Viola, obviously, could.

"You handle my great-grandson very well."

"It comes naturally," Chey commented idly, wondering what this was leading up to. "Actually, it comes with the family, all those nieces and nephews."

Viola nodded and folded her long, slender hands. "I wish you were as adept at handling his father," she stated bluntly.

Chey's mouth dropped open. Anything she might have said, Viola waved away with the flick of her wrist, anyway.

"I'm old, dear," Viola said tartly, "but I'm not dead. I recognized from the first what exists between you and my grandson, and it seems to me that it has only grown stronger over time. My goodness, when the two of you are in close proximity, the small hairs stand up on the backs of my arms. What I don't understand is why you are fighting it so desperately."

Chey gasped for breath, totally overwhelmed. "I don't...it's not..." She broke off, knowing that denial would be useless and insulting. She put a hand to her head. "I never get involved with my clients."

"Well, of course, you wouldn't normally," Viola said. "I can understand that. But he won't be your client forever, will he?" She shook her head and folded her arms. "No, this is not delayed gratification I'm seeing. It's rejection. And forgive me, but I can't help wondering why."

Chey glanced away, very uncomfortable. "I, um, I don't expect you to understand this, but I like my life just as it is."

"And Brodie threatens that somehow?"

Chey was uncertain how to put it. Somehow, she wasn't sure she completely understood it herself anymore. But, no, that was ridiculous. This was a logical decision of long standing. She straightened and looked Viola in the eye. "My career is the most important thing in my life."

"I see," Viola said, meaning that she did not.

"Romantic involvements," Chey pushed on hesitantly, "get in the way."

"Naturally," Viola agreed. "What doesn't? Surely, you aren't telling me then that you've never allowed *anything* to get in the way of your career?"

"Er, no, not exactly."

"Then there is something more, some compelling reason why you are attempting to deny nature its course."

Realizing that she wasn't going to get around this, Chey took a deep breath and laid her cards on the table. "If you must know, I have a policy against dating men with... *encumbrances.*"

Viola stared at her a long moment, then her whole face curved into a smile. Chey had the uncanny feeling that Viola was laughing inside. "Ah. I think I understand. I was, shall we say, unwilling to embrace such encumbrances myself at one time. In truth, I never intended to, but the lack of adequate birth control took that decision out of my hands. Then something I never expected happened. I fell in love."

"With your husband?" Chey asked, curious.

"No, I was already in love with him. I fell in love with 'the encumbrance.'"

Chey literally recoiled. "That's exactly my point. I have no intention of falling in love with any..." She thought of Seth's sweet face and couldn't say it. "With anyone," she finished lamely.

Viola smiled knowingly. "The problem with love," she said, "is that it's not very easily controlled, and after all, it just means making room in one's life for another human being. Or two, in this case."

"One of whom needs a great deal of guidance and care," Chey pointed out.

Viola chuckled. "We all need guidance and care, dear,

even you. That, I am afraid, is the human condition. It doesn't explain, however, why you are unwilling to allow even casual personal involvement with my grandson.''

''I, um, just feel that it's unwise, given all the negatives.''

''Almost any other woman would fail to see beyond the positives,'' Viola stated definitely. ''My grandson is an extremely attractive man, you know. But what does it matter, since you are so dead-set?'' She lifted a sleek eyebrow, then got to her feet. ''It is a shame, though. I've seen the way my grandson looks at you—as if he could just eat you up where you stand. His grandfather used to look at me like that. The memories alone have seen me through more hardship and heartache than I care to recall. I wonder what memories will see you through the hard times to come, for they will come, believe me.'' With that, she sighed and left the room.

Chey stared unseeingly at the color-scheme printouts, wondering if Brodie's grandfather had singed Viola's skin the way Brodie could hers with the simplest of touches. It seemed, suddenly, as if she was missing out on something very potent, and she had to admit, if only to herself, that she was no longer as ''dead-set'' as she had once been, as she ought to be. Why shouldn't she make a few memories of her own, after all? Where would be the harm in merely exploring the possibilities?

Suddenly the fact that she even wondered alarmed her greatly and shook her confidence in her position.

It was time to level the flagstones in the garden room, a sure sign that they were making progress, though for a while it had seemed that they'd actually lost ground. Finally, however, floors were down, walls were moved, doors were closed and others opened. It was cool and comfortable in the house. Paint was going up, bringing color and life to once-dead rooms. Chey felt a certain pride and relief and also an odd sadness, a looming disappointment. She was depressingly aware that when the house was done, she might well never see Brodie Todd again. It was with mixed emotions, then, that she personally oversaw the movement of the exercise equipment to its new home in Brodie's suite. She'd sent a message upstairs to let Brodie know what she was intending and had received one in return that he was busy in his office with an important long-distance telephone call.

While the workmen placed the equipment as ordered, she looked around the room. The cedar-wood floors gleamed so brightly that they reflected the vibrant spring-green walls, which were set off by clean ivory picture-framing. Mellow golds and yellows seemed to draw light from the soft blue ceiling, against which filmy white clouds drifted. It had required scaffolding to get that done, but Chey judged it well worth the effort as it gave the suite an airy, out-of-doors feel. The same color and paint scheme carried over into the sitting room and bedchamber, with variations in accent and primary colors. Keeping with the outdoorsy feel, she'd chosen woody browns and soft grays.

The furnishings were still a problem. While she had every intention of maintaining the neat, uncluttered atmosphere, her inclination was to go with light, simple pieces and ruffled ivy prints to counteract the stark masculinity of the room. But she'd put off making the choices since Brodie was apt to prefer the opposite, and thrashing it out would mean spending a good deal of time alone in his company, something she had avoided assiduously of late, with mixed results.

Brodie was still apt, in any given moment, to appear unexpectedly at her elbow, speaking in intimate half-whispers that never failed to turn her insides to jelly, even when the subject was a mundane business matter. He seemed to approve of what she'd done with his house so far. In fact, he'd cornered her only the day before to tell her how very much he liked how his suite was shaping up. As usual he'd crowded her, made her pulse race erratically with nothing more than the heat from his body and a brush of his fingertips down her arm. She had reacted with her customary nervous detachment, but more from habit than any real desire to resist, a fact he had proven with dismaying ease when he'd suddenly gone away again, leaving her disappointed and craving his touch. She still felt a twist of resentment. It seemed desperately unfair that he could do that to her with so little effort on his part. What would it be like, she wondered, to be "eaten up" by Brodie Todd?

Shivering, she forced the thought away and saw the last weight bench carefully positioned, then paused to take inventory one more time while the workmen all tramped down the stairs. Even then she lingered, until finally she realized what she was waiting for. Brodie. Why couldn't the blasted man show up when she expected? Why must he always surprise her, catch her off-guard? Shaking her head, she moved through the suite and out into the hall, sternly forbidding herself to knock on the door of his office.

Moving toward the landing, she impulsively diverted her steps instead, and turned down the hallway to her left to check on the pair of guest rooms that stood across from what she had come to think of as the hospital suite. In deference to the patient's special needs and the comfort of guests, it had been decided to move the doors of both guest rooms by constructing a narrow, short, hallway between them for access. Both doors now opened off that private little entry. That plan had necessitated the moving of closets and some creative planning for both small baths, however, and they'd encountered unexpected problems along the way. Though she hoped those had now been fixed, Chey had not yet made a physical inspection. Now was as good a time as any.

She was just about to turn into the newly constructed hallway when the bark of a sharp female voice, followed instantly by a shushing sound, drew her up short. Her attention captured, she tilted her head and caught the low murmur of what seemed to be two voices coming from

Janey's suite. Something about those voices struck her as patently odd, almost as if one of them had been raised in anger, but who would be arguing in Janey's suite? Her feet moved of their own accord toward the door. Impulsively, she reached for the knob. Only at the last moment did she think to tap politely on the door and wait to be invited inside.

A wary greeting reached her. "Yes?"

Chey opened the door and stepped partly through, looking across the sitting area toward the bed. Emma Brown sat in a straight-back chair, frowning at her, a book in her hands.

"What can I do for you, Miss Simmons?"

"I, um, I thought I heard voices."

Brown's flat, wary eyes narrowed slightly. "I was reading aloud. The doctors say it's good for her."

Of course. A perfectly reasonable explanation. And yet… Shaking off half-formed suspicions that felt utterly foolish now, Chey debated whether or not to fully enter the room. Her curiosity proved greater than her hesitation, and she stepped inside, moving toward the bed. Was Janey Todd truly as beautiful as she remembered? Or had pity colored her perception?

"How is she?"

"Why do you ask?"

Chey paused, surprised at the response, and fixed her attention on the stout nurse. "From concern, of course. It's very sad, what's happened to her."

"Yes. Sad," Brown echoed.

Disregarding the nurse, Chey walked closer to the bed. The woman who lay there might have been a sleeping princess materialized from a fairytale, her lovely face a study in peaceful repose.

"Beautiful, isn't she?" Brown said, the note of adoration in the normally dull voice as shocking as a shotgun blast in the quiet room. Chey jerked a look over her shoulder.

The woman had come to her feet, and her face fairly glowed as she stared at her charge.

"She's lovely," Chey admitted quietly. "Very."

"It's so unfair," the nurse said with such ferocity that Chey stepped back.

"Accidents happen," she murmured, wondering if the woman was unhinged.

Nurse Brown glanced at her almost in surprise, as if she'd forgotten she was not alone. Then she nodded and folded her hands. "It'll come right, though. You wait and see. She's a fighter. She'll come out of this. Some day."

"I certainly hope so," Chey said doubtfully. It was not likely to happen. Comas of this duration rarely reversed.

"She has to," Brown stated flatly, "for everyone's sake." Her beady eyes narrowed to mere slits. "Especially Mr. Brodie's. Oh, you should have seen how broken up he was when it happened. I've never seen a man so worried or sad. Everyone thought she'd die, but Mr. Brodie wouldn't give up. He wouldn't let her give up."

Chey was unprepared for the impact of those words. They swirled over her like an angry, stinging swarm of bees, each one sharp and burning. She felt suddenly ill with the strength of some emotion so bloated and distorted that she required a moment to identify it. Jealousy. She was jealous of this pathetic, comatose creature! Not because she was beautiful but because for some period of time she had possessed the love and care of Brodie Todd. And perhaps she still did. Shame and shock overwhelmed her as Chey realized how unprepared she was to accept that.

"Why did he divorce her then?" she demanded.

Brown shrugged, averting her gaze. "What does it matter? He hasn't forgotten her. He's taking care of her, isn't he? When she wakes up, they'll get back together."

Staring at the angelic being on the bed, Chey could well believe it; yet something within her rebelled at the notion. The nurse turned away and began briskly straightening the rumpled bedcovers. "How can you be so sure?" Chey whispered.

Brown straightened to gaze down at her patient once more, saying, "She's the mother of his child. That alone binds them forever."

"As it should," Chey muttered.

"It's more than that, though," Brown vowed. "Sometimes even now when he looks at her, you can just see the longing in him."

Chey stared at the delicate woman on the bed. Did Brodie look at his ex-wife with the same longing with which he looked at *her?* Or was Brodie hopelessly in love with his comatose ex-wife and simply trying to get on with his life with the first attractive woman he'd met? The thought hurt. Surely this thing between them was more than that. On the other hand, if he were still in love with his comatose ex-wife, wouldn't he be *safe* for casual involvement? Suddenly it all seemed so clear to her.

This attraction was a godsend for Brodie and perhaps for her, too. Neither of them could support a deep emotional involvement, but they each needed what the other had to offer. Didn't they? How wrong would it be to just explore the possibility of…what? Mutual satisfaction? Fun? What could it do just to get to know him on a personal level, especially if no chance really existed that it might lead to more—and since it was what she wanted to do anyway? Without even questioning her own intention for once, she turned and moved toward the door, a decision made.

"I'm sorry to have interrupted you, Brown. Thank you for your time." She left the room, moving purposefully back down the hall toward Brodie's office, every footstep lighter than the last. It was time to allow herself a few private memories, and surely the relief she felt was an indication that she was doing the right thing.

Chapter Seven

Brodie shifted the telephone receiver to the other ear, covered the mouthpiece with one hand and called, "Come in," before going back to his conversation. "I appreciate that, Ambassador. Why don't we…"

The thought died on his tongue as the door opened and Chey walked in. She looked cool as a cucumber in black jeans and a white, sleeveless sweater, a simple black band holding back her pale hair. He sat up straighter and indicated with his hand that she should take a seat before forcing himself back to his call.

"Uh, why don't we get together and discuss this in person? I'd be delighted to bring you and your family and staff here to Fair Havens in New Orleans."

Chey settled into the chair, even as she whispered, "I can come back."

He held up a staying finger, not about to let her go as easily as that. On the other end of the line, the ambassador was effusively accepting his invitation, detailing who and what would have to be included in his entourage. Brodie had to look away from her in order to concentrate on the conversation.

"Let me check my calendar," he suggested expediently to the ambassador, "and I'll call you tomorrow to set up a definite date."

The ambassador agreed to this, then chatted on while Brodie listened with half an ear, impatient to get the man off the phone. Finally he did so, hanging up quite abruptly and focusing all his attention on the woman sitting patiently in front of his desk. A smile broke across his face as he sensed that weeks spent carefully stoking the flare of attraction between them were about to pay off in some way. At this point he'd welcome even the slightest thaw in his ice princess.

"Sorry to keep you waiting. That was the ambassador of the Sultanate of Legan, a small country in the Middle East."

"I've heard of it," she assured him.

He braced his elbows against the top of his desk and pressed his hands together. "They've uncovered some amazing ruins there, and now that the digging and restoration are done, they're ready to exploit it by allowing a select group of paying customers to tour them. And BMT is going to package and sell the first all-inclusive tours."

She beamed at him. "That's wonderful."

"Yes, it is. In fact, I predict it's going to be one of the hottest vacation spots in the world within the next five years. One small problem." He tapped a finger against the edge of the desk. "I need to bring the ambassador and his party here to finish the deal. How soon do you think we can be ready for them?"

She pursed her lips, one foot swinging back and forth as she thought about it. "Several more weeks, at least."

He was pleasantly surprised. "Really? That quickly?"

"If we work hard, yes."

He lifted his hands in delight. "Excellent!"

"Of course," she said, holding her gaze with his, "you'll have to give me a good deal of your attention from here on out. Details require the most decisions."

His heartbeat quickened. Unless he was mistaken, that was a flame he saw flickering beneath that sheath of protective ice. "That's no problem at all," he told her, allowing the huskiness of his voice to betray his hopes.

"Good." She dipped her head and looked at him from beneath her lashes.

Ruthlessly suppressing the desire to go over the desk after her, he cleared his throat and asked carefully, "Is that what you wanted to see me about?"

She shook her head but said nothing for a moment more. His nerves were stretched paper-thin by the time she finally blurted, "I've been thinking." He forced himself to remain still and silent until she added, "About us."

He sat forward calmly, his heart beating so hard that he feared she could see the movement of his chest. When he thought he could speak in a level tone, he asked simply, "And?"

She twisted her hands together. "A-and maybe we could...well, get to know one another better, spend some time together."

He allowed himself a smile but kept it tight, fearing that if he didn't he'd wind up laughing in sheer glee. "Okay."

"I mean," she went on quickly, "the job will be done in a matter of weeks, so it can't really hurt to, ah, enjoy one another's company, I guess."

He wanted to crow with delight but instead wiggled his foot beneath the desk to release a little of that euphoric energy. "I see."

"I'm not saying we should rush into anything," she went on quickly. "I-in fact, I think we ought to take it slow."

"I can take it as slowly as you can," he told her honestly.

She cleared her throat and looked away. "Excellent. Then we understand each other."

"Just one thing," he said, tapping the edge of his desk lightly with his finger. "What changed your mind?"

Hunching one shoulder, she smoothed a hand across her lap. "Does it matter?"

He thought about that and shook his head. "No. Just curious."

"You didn't wear me down, if that's what you're thinking," she told him tartly. "I've just been working a lot, and I thought it would be nice to get out a little more."

"I see." What he meant was, "In a pig's eye."

"Well, then?" She stared at him until he realized it was his move.

"Are you busy tomorrow?" he asked, holding back his smile.

She skittered a glance around the room. "Tomorrow evening? No, I don't think so."

He beamed, deciding to take it easy on her. "How about a movie?"

The look of eagerness on her face sent a bolt of lust straight to his groin. "I…I can't remember the last time I saw a movie. That would be nice. Thanks."

"My pleasure. Okay, then, why don't you check the listings and pick out something you like."

"I will." She turned and reached for the doorknob, then paused, saying, "Oh, and I'll have a number of fabric swatches ready for you in the morning."

He chuckled. "I look forward to it."

She tossed a smile over one shoulder and left him. He leaned back in his chair, let out a hot breath, and pumped his fist in celebration.

He was nervous. He admitted it to himself as he drove toward her place in the small, extravagant sports car, the tan vinyl top up in deference to the light drizzle that fell to the pavement only to rise again in tendrils of steam. It made no sense, this anxiety. It wasn't as if he hadn't gone on a thousand dinner dates, staged a dozen seductions. He told himself that it was because Chey was not the sophisticate he'd first taken her to be, but the truth was... The truth eluded him, frankly. Perhaps it had to do with prolonged celibacy and the anticipation generated by the past three weeks.

This dating business was trying. They'd been to not one, but three movies, strolled around Jackson Square to watch the painters and performers, been roller-blading in Louis Armstrong Park, listened to a rousing concert at Mahalia Jackson Theater and attended a history lecture at a local university, all without so much as seeing the inside of her apartment or reaching the level of intimacy he so desperately craved. He didn't think he could endure one more hot, groping goodnight kiss or the resulting midnight swim he took later to cool and exhaust himself enough to sleep, so tonight he was pulling out all the stops and taking her for dinner and dancing at BuFord's, one of the city's finest supper clubs.

As he turned the small, dark green car down her narrow street, he patted his pocket once more, assuring himself that it still contained the pair of foil packets he'd slipped inside earlier, then slowed and put on his turn signal. Carefully, he eased the low-slung car onto the sloping drive that cut through the banquette and into the narrow passage beside her shop. As usual, the wrought-iron gate stood open, pushed back against the stone walls. The passage was as deep as the building, perhaps twenty-five or thirty feet, and opened into a small courtyard that was mostly drive. It was a nice place, though. She actually had a garage, a rarity in the French Quarter, and nestled within the heart of the U-shaped property was a small garden with a little fountain, bench and trellises blanketed with honeysuckle and bougainvillea. He killed the engine of the car and got out, a closed, compact umbrella in hand.

"Hey!"

Looking up in the direction of the voice, he saw Chey on the balcony. One look and his blood pressure went straight through the top of his head. She was dressed in form-fitting hot pink that began well below her shoulders and ended well above her knees.

"Come on up!" she called. Tucking the umbrella beneath one arm, he jogged quickly across the courtyard to the stairs that led up to the covered balcony, or gallery. "You look great," she said, her gaze traveling up and down his body, taking in the shiny white T-shirt beneath his black suit coat, his black alligator belt and shoes and pleated, cuffed pants.

He was too enchanted even to thank her for the compliment. The dress was a tube of very elastic fabric that hugged her body like skin. Her long blond hair had been piled in artful chaos atop her head, with long tendrils left free to float about her face and bare shoulders. Beneath the hem of her dress, her long, lean, shapely legs seemed to stretch on and on, ending finally in a pair of glittery silver shoes with straps and tall, thick heels. If she was wearing stockings, they were too sheer to be detected, but he doubted that she was, doubted, in fact, that she wore much of anything under that dress. He didn't realize how long he stood staring at her until she asked timidly, "Too much?"

Too much, he wondered, that little thing? "Lord, no. It's simply…" He dragged his gaze up from her breasts to her face, encountering worried, darkly lashed, bright green eyes and plump lips touched with luscious pink. He was possessed of a sudden, insane urge to peel that dress off her, toss her over his shoulder and find the nearest bed. He looked deeply into those green, green eyes and said suggestively, "You almost look too good to take out in public."

Her sultry smile and the hand she laid lightly against his chest sent a bolt of lust straight to his groin. "Thank you," she whispered. If he'd been foolish enough to hope that she'd just ditch the preliminaries, finally invite him inside and lead him straight to her bed, he would have been bitterly disappointed when she added, "Just let me grab my things."

Thankful for the cut of his trousers, he watched her turn and hurry away on those high heels, that dress hugging her sweet butt with all the fervency of a thoughtful lover. She returned an instant later, having grabbed a small silver purse and tossed a pale, creamy gray Pashmina around her shoulders.

He opened the umbrella and lifted it over their heads as they reached the top of the stairs, keeping it steady as they descended the steps side by side. Unlocking the car with the pocket remote, he walked her to the passenger door, then handed her down inside before hurrying around to take his place behind the steering wheel. After carefully backing out the car, he dashed back through the mist to close the gate and thereby secure the apartment. The look of gratitude she gave him for that kept his blood simmering all the way across downtown to the supper club on the river. They pulled up to the entrance and were met by a white-jacketed valet with an open umbrella who escorted them to the bronze-appointed red door. Chill air and silent, opulent promises of pleasure beckoned them inside. The place was a stylish Art Deco and Old World combination of red vinyl, black marble, mahogany and chrome.

Brodie nodded at the maitre d' and slipped an arm proudly around Chey's slender waist. In short order, they were ushered into the dining room to a red vinyl booth with a gleaming black-topped chrome table. A squat candle glowed within the small, shell-shaped holder on the table's center.

They were given artful descriptions of the night's specials: crawfish wraps or shrimp salad, spicy vegetable soup or fruit compote, prime rib or pompano, potatoes Creole or red-hot rice, asparagus torte or braised broccoli, and for dessert, praline pie with cream or chocolate pecan trifle with flaming cherries. They made their selections, and Brodie ordered a bottle of champagne, knowing that he would have to imbibe sparingly as he was driving. Overhead, a glittery silver ball reflected narrow rays of light on to the empty black marble dance floor, across which a lone, self-absorbed musician played a softly tinkling piano at the edge of the bandstand. The effect was dreamy and intimate.

The moment for conversation arrived. "The house is really coming along. You've done well, Chey."

She inclined her head. "I'm glad you're pleased."

"Besides being very gifted," he went on easily, "you're very fortunate, too, You have great resources right within your own family."

"Yes. They've been very helpful. Of course, if they weren't the best, I wouldn't use them."

"But they are the best," he stated flatly. "Each in his own way." He picked up the water glass that the waiter had just filled and asked casually, "What did they do before you took over?"

She blinked at that. "What do you mean, 'took over'?"

He cocked his head, rather surprised. "Darling, you are effectively the CEO of the Simmons' family enterprise."

"But there is no such enterprise."

He could only gape at that. "Not on paper perhaps, but in reality that's exactly what it is. And you are the organizational genius behind it."

She frowned. "Better not let my brothers hear you say that."

"Oh, they know," he assured her. "Believe me, they know it very well. In fact, they count on it."

She shook her head. "Now that is pure bunk. As far as my brothers are concerned, I'm just the baby sister who hasn't found a husband yet."

"Oh, for pity's sake, Chey! They depend on you to run things. How can you not see that? You may forever be the baby sister, but your brothers definitely respect your business sense and your talents. They never question your orders, Chey. They always do exactly what you ask of them. In point of fact, they follow your orders explicitly because they know that you know what you're doing. I've seen it time and again."

She studied his face a moment, then said softly, "I wish I could see it."

"I think maybe if you'd get that chip off your shoulder you'd be able to," he told her bluntly.

"I don't—" she began heatedly, then quickly subsided. "Okay, maybe I do. I just get so tired of being told that I should get married and make babies! Why do they keep harping on that if they really think I can do other things well?"

"They just want you to be happy," he said. "To them, that's how it's done."

"Which is why I don't fit in very well," she mumbled. "They all...think alike, fit together."

He sat back and regarded her steadily. "It's hard to be the different one, isn't it? The Simmonses are an extraordinary clan. Why don't you see that while you may be different, you're also the very top of the heap? They see it, and they're proud of you. At least your brothers are. I mean, every one of them just bursts his seams when he talks about you."

Her eyes had grown round. "Really?"

"Absolutely."

"All they ever say to me," she grumbled, "is that I'm breaking my mother's heart because I'm not pregnant and hanging on some man's arm."

He chuckled. "Brothers are like that. They think it's their job to make you do what they think you should. I know it's irritating, but it just means they love you."

She propped her elbows on the edge of the table, bowed her head and shaded her face with her hands, thumbs hooked beneath her chin, fingers cupped like blinkers. After a moment she sighed and looked up again, her eyes narrowing. "How did you get so smart, Mr. Todd?"

He shrugged. "A little experience. A lot of observation, one of my few talents, by the way."

A smile quirked the corner of her mouth. She folded her arms against the table edge. "Oh, right. BMT materialized right out of thin air and dropped into your lap. You didn't have a thing to do with it.''

He waved a hand. "Pure play, I assure you. I was merely *observant* enough to realize that I could actually make a living at it.''

She put her head back and laughed heartily. When she looked at him again, her eyes sparkled with warmth. "You're a dangerous man, Brodie Todd," she told him. "I like you a lot.''

He leaned close, reached out and clamped a hand around the nape of her neck, pulling her face into a nose-to-nose juxtaposition with his. "It's a start," he said softly. "Maybe your feelings will even catch up with mine before long.''

She lifted a brow at that, and he could see the question— and something else he couldn't quite pinpoint—in her eyes. Another moment and she would ask him what his feelings were exactly. He realized suddenly that he didn't really know. They certainly went beyond mere lust, but just how far beyond, he couldn't have said. So he kissed her. The wine arrived an instant later, interrupting the brief but heady intimacy, and soon after a friend dropped by unexpectedly with his wife. Brodie slid out of the booth and onto his feet, delighting in rescue.

"Livvie!" Chey exclaimed, before he could even speak. Obviously, Chey knew them, too. She hastened to make introductions. "Allow me to present Mr. Brodie Todd. Brodie, this is—''

"Marcus and Olivia Childs," he interrupted smoothly, shaking Marc's hand and leaning forward to kiss his wife's cheek. "We're old friends, actually. Marc has leveraged more than one expansion of my business.''

"And very profitably," Marcus confirmed. Decades older and inches shorter than his beauty-queen wife—his third—Marc was by day a shrewd investment banker and by night a mature, upper-crust version of the ubiquitous party animal. A purely social person, he loved nothing more than seeing and being seen. He clapped Brodie on the shoulder and said to Chey, "You are looking particularly ravishing tonight, my dear." To Brodie he explained, "Chey redid the old house, you know," meaning the thirty-room mansion in the heart of the Garden District that had been in his family for generations. He smiled at Livvie indulgently. "Wives like to redo." He would know.

"Chey is refurbishing my old den, too," Brodie said blandly.

"So I heard," Livvie cooed, batting her big black eyes at Chey. "I'd love to see what you've done, sugar."

"Well, I'm sure Brodie will invite you over once everything's done."

"Absolutely," Brodie promised.

"Speaking of invitations," Marcus said, tightening his grip on Brodie's shoulder, "I have one for you. How would you like to join my krewe?"

Brodie looked to Chey, astonished. She lifted both eyebrows at him. Brodie lifted his at Marcus. An invitation to join one of the city's unique social clubs was a rare and coveted distinction. The krewes were responsible for the famous parades and balls that marked Mardi Gras and much of the commerce of New Orleans. "I'd be honored."

Marcus pounded Brodie on the back. "In that case, *mon ami*, a toast is in order." Brodie waved over the waiter, who brought two more glasses. Chey stood as the champagne was poured. Marcus gave the classic New Orleans salute. *"Laissez les bon temps rouler!"*

"Let the good times roll!" Brodie echoed heartily. Some polite hugging and kissing ensued before the Childses departed to join a large party waiting at another table.

"Talk about your social coup," Chey said as he seated her once more.

"I really didn't expect it," he replied truthfully, "at least not for a long while." He quickly changed the subject, lest she think him preening. "I wonder what other mutual acquaintances we have."

They chatted about that until the first course arrived. The conversation moved on to music, movies and books, until the pianist departed and the band members began gathering on the small elliptical stage. Brodie looked around and noted that the place was filling up. Checking his watch, he was surprised to find that they'd spent nearly two hours over the meal. When the waiter approached to ask if they were ready for dessert, they decided to put it off for a time. Brodie asked for more water, then refilled Chey's glass with champagne. The band played the first number, a peppy zydeco tune, and segued right into the next. Chey smiled and swayed her head to the jolly beat, her toes tapping beneath the table. The third tune was a swingy, nostalgic number that purely infected Brodie. He slid out of his seat, walked around the table and held out his hand. Without the slightest hesitation, she placed her own in it, and he pulled her to her feet.

They took it easy at first. He saw quickly that she wasn't trained, but she made up for it with a smooth, natural grace and a great deal of faith, so he stepped up the program. Pulling her close with an arm wrapped snugly around her waist, he thrust his knee between hers and twirled her around the edge of the crowded floor. It felt as natural as breathing, the fit of their bodies so perfect they might have been made for one another. He tried a few of his favorite maneuvers. She stumbled through some of the more complicated steps, but they laughed about it and kept going. Brodie peeled off his coat before the next number and got serious. She caught on fast, an eager pupil. People started giving them room. By the end of the third dance, they were applauded.

Laughing and thirsty, they moved to the table for drinks. "I predict you'll be taking flings before the night's out," he said, handing her down into her seat.

She looked up at him uncertainly. "What are flings?"

"Tosses, uh, overhead steps. I fling or toss you up and into maneuvers then catch you again."

"In your dreams," she told him firmly, reaching for her glass.

He moved around the table and slid into his side of the L-shaped booth. "No, really, you could do it."

"*Could* and *would* are two different verbs," she said meaningfully. "Besides, I'm not dressed for something like that."

He grinned and confessed, "I wondered if you were wearing anything under that dress."

She blushed a fiery red. "Of course I am."

Running a fingertip around the rim of his glass, he considered a moment and finally concluded, "A thong. Anything else would show."

She leaned forward, shushing him urgently, and laid her hand over his mouth. He smiled against her palm, then nipped it with his teeth. She yanked it away. He caught it and brought it back to his mouth, breathing heat into the heart of her palm then leisurely licking it. Her mouth dropped open, but she didn't pull away. He carried the hand beneath the table and placed it on his thigh, then refilled her glass with champagne. She tossed back half of it in one gulp before slowly pulling her hand away from his leg.

"You, um, you aren't drinking," she observed, cradling her champagne flute with both hands and studying it. "You've only had one glass so far."

"I'll have one more before we go."

"Only one?"

"I'm driving," he reminded her.

"I'm not," she muttered, tilting back her head and draining the glass. He immediately pulled the bottle from the ice bucket and emptied it into her glass, then signaled the waiter for another, not that he wanted her intoxicated, but he did want her to have a good time.

When the second bottle came, they ordered dessert, choosing the praline pie. She had hers without the thick, warm, brandied cream. He had another glass of the champagne, then pulled her out onto the dance floor once more.

No longer caring about the steps, he just wanted to get next to her, and she seemed of the same mind, winding both arms about his neck and pressing herself against him. The floor was crowded, so they didn't have room for much more than undulating with and against one another. It was enough to drive him wild. When the music ended, he kept her close, making sure she felt just what it was he wanted now. Her movements were restless and infinitely arousing.

"Ready to go?" he asked pointedly.

Her answer was a simple, knowing "Yes."

He grabbed her hand and hauled her back to the table, where he spent precious seconds throwing down bills and gathering their things. They walked swiftly through the dining room and foyer, so close that their bodies bumped against each other. The valet took off for the car at a run when they emerged onto the banquette. The drizzle had stopped, and the cooling night had caused a fog to rise and swirl around them. Brodie shuffled his feet impatiently, then just gave in, tossing his jacket over his shoulder and reaching for her. She slid her arms around him, the Pashmina cloaking them both softly, and kissed him with the same hunger that was battering him so mercilessly. They broke apart only when the car arrived.

He put her inside, tossed his coat behind the seat and slid beneath the wheel, asking, "Mind if I put the top down now?" She shook her head, fastening her safety belt. He hit the button. "Good. I need cooling off, frankly."

She put her head back against the seat and said, "I think I'm drunk."

"You didn't have that much alcohol."

"I didn't mean the champagne."

He gunned the engine. Only the fog kept him from racing through the streets. It swirled around them, enveloping them in a cocoon of defused intimacy as they drove back to her place. Finally they pulled into her courtyard. He put up the top, killed the engine and hopped out, hurrying around to open her door. Releasing her belt, she swung both legs out and stood.

"You're staying, aren't you?" she asked breathlessly.

It was the invitation he'd been hoping for. "Absolutely."

She slid her arm through his, and together they turned toward the stairs. When they reached the top, she opened her tiny pocketbook and plucked out her keys before unlocking the first door they came to and leading him inside.

She neither turned on the lamp nor closed the door, and the fog muted the light from the balcony. He stood just inside the doorway of the small room, noting with half a mind the sparse elegance of painted wood and neat antique pieces. She tossed the shawl over the back of an armless rocking chair, dropped her purse onto the seat and lifted first one foot and then the other to remove her shoes. Then she glided across the room to a large armoire, opened it and flipped a switch on the stereo. Dreamy music filled the room.

Brodie closed the door behind him, walked across the floor and slipped his arms around her waist from the back. She laid her head against his shoulder, inviting him to taste the graceful curve of her neck. Lowering his head, he put his mouth to her skin, tasting her. She sighed, and lifted a hand to free her hair, plucking and dropping the pins and clips. He moved his hungry mouth to her ear, nipping and probing. When he lifted his hand to her breast, she moaned and arched her back. With one hand he cupped the firm mound of her breast through the springy elastic. With the other, he reached around and tilted her chin, pushing her head back until he could cover her mouth with his. Need slammed through him. He moved both hands to the top of edge of her dress and folded it down.

When he cupped her bare breasts, she shuddered and made a sound that filled his mouth and reverberated throughout his body. Absolutely desperate to get her skin next to his, he broke away long enough to reach back behind his own head, grip a handful of shirt and tug it up, over and away. He shook free of it and reached out to turn her to face him. The sight of her took his breath away. Her breasts were round and full and tipped with small, pink nipples that stood erect for his touch. He filled both hands and felt the jolt of connection in his groin. She swayed toward him, lifting both arms around his neck, and he hissed in a breath of supreme satisfaction when her cool, bare skin met his. Bowing his head, he closed his eyes and held her against him, swamped with need.

She moved, and he moved with her, matching his pelvis to hers, swaying gently to the music. Then he picked up his feet, and they were dancing, chest to chest, her warm, moist breath heating his collar bone, her belly rubbing against his fierce arousal. A few minutes later, he hooked his thumbs in the folded-down top of her dress and pushed. Twisting against him, she helped him work it past her hips and thighs, until it dropped to her feet and she stepped out of it, pressing her body and mouth to his in a silent plea.

Desire pounded in his temples, insistent, stronger than any urge to savor the moment. Obeying it, he dipped slightly, scooped her into his arms and pulled his mouth from hers to gasp, "Are you sure?"

"Yes. No! I don't... Do you have protection?"

He laid his forehead against hers in relief. "Of course. Which way?"

She pointed toward a door tucked into a corner beside the bookcase. He carried her through it and into a large, airy bedroom where moonlight spilled across the floor from an unshuttered window. A high, delicate spindle bed swathed in bunches of white mosquito netting stood against one corner. He carried her toward it, vaguely taking in cool, blue-gray walls, white woodwork and a ceiling fan that circled lazily overhead.

Sitting on the edge of her bed, he shifted her onto her feet, standing her between his legs. She braced her hands on his shoulders while he stripped away his shoes and socks, unbuckled his belt and opened his pants. Then he clasped his hands around her waist and brought her closer, finding a luscious nipple with his mouth. Moaning, she leaned into him, her hands cupping the back of his head. Quickly, he found the narrow straps of her thong panties and tugged them over her hips and down her legs before moving his attention to her other breast. She was breathing through her mouth in great huffs by the time he slipped his hand between her legs and found her wet and hot. She cried out, hands fisting in his hair, when he pushed his finger into her. Pressing his face between her breasts, he explored inside her shuddering body.

In no mood to go slowly, he reluctantly left that sweet place between her legs, stood, pulled the foil packets from his pocket and shoved down his slacks and briefs, kicking them away and reaching for her. She slid a hand down his chest and over his belly to skim the hard length of him, but he grabbed her wrist before she could do more, gasping, "Oh no! I'm hanging by a thread as it is."

"Then do it now," she moaned, undulating against him.

He was tempted. Oh, was he tempted. But he was dangerously close to explosion, and even more than he wanted to be inside her, he wanted to hear her sweet cries of completion, to make his mark on her heart and soul as well as her body. Sweeping her up into his arms again, he turned back to the bed, yanked the covers away with one hand and lay her down, her head against the pillow. Then he put on the condom, sat on the edge of the bed beside her and began to drive her crazy with his hands and mouth. She was mindless by the time he spread her legs wide and settled between them, his upper body weight braced against his locked arms. Slowly, he put himself where he most wanted to be. His head spun. His lungs seized. His heart stopped completely then began to wham madly against the walls of his chest, driving him convulsively deeper into her liquid, silky core.

"Brodie," she whispered urgently, lifting her mouth to his.

He tried to pay close attention to the signals her body sent him while driving himself closer and closer to her heart, but it was difficult. Eventually, however, he realized that the deeper he went, the more she held back, fighting him emotionally. She was running from him again, not physically but emotionally, pulling back in panic as he pushed and shoved and rocked her closer to a place she feared, a place, perhaps, where she had never before been. She began shaking her head, tears leaking from beneath her closed eyelids. In pure desperation, knowing that he dare not let her distance herself from him now, he began to coax her.

"Chey. Honey, please. Come with me. I need you there, Chey. Please."

She let go. He felt it as something that expanded inside his chest, growing lighter and lighter until it exploded in the sound of her cry and a cataclysmic quaking inside her body, and then he was there with her, blind and euphoric and strangely whole. He blinked and unexpectedly found himself in a place where he had never been before either, and with a sense of exhausted wonder, he finally put a name to those confusing feelings of his. Love.

Chapter Eight

She couldn't believe what she'd just done. What a fool she was to have thought, even for a moment, that she could indulge in casual sex with this man. And that was what she'd thought, deep down—that she could yield to the first real attraction she'd truly felt for a man and then just neatly file it away in its own narrow compartment and get on with her life. She'd thought she was being so sensible, taking her time, getting to know him first. She hadn't realized how devastating making love with him would be. She hadn't even realized that such depth of feeling, both sensual and emotional, could be evoked!

Had she understood what making love with Brodie would be like, she could never have convinced herself that it would be safe. The man was not only a client; he was a father, for pity's sake, and emotionally married to a comatose woman who was ensconced in his very house! Those were reasons *not* to get involved, and yet she had convinced herself of the opposite. No doubt about it, she had made a terrible mistake. She didn't realize that she had spoken the thought aloud until Brodie rose up in bed next to her, twisting at the waist as he confronted her.

"A mistake? *This* was a mistake?"

She was shocked and shamed by the pain in his voice. Reaching for the bedsheet, she tucked it around her and pushed up on one elbow. "I didn't mean to say that."

"But you do mean it," he accused, swinging off the bed.

Chey sighed, feeling drained and weak, her muscles like jelly. "This was my mistake, not yours. I should never have allowed this to happen."

"Don't try to tell me that you didn't enjoy making love with me!" he exclaimed, yanking on his pants.

"It's not that," she said weakly. The truth was that she'd enjoyed it too much. "I only meant that it shouldn't have gotten this far."

"It's really only started! Everything that came before was just spinning wheels! This, Chey, is where *we* really begin."

She sat up, tucking the sheet beneath her arms and folding them atop her knees. "What I'm trying to say is, there can't be anything more. It's simply—"

"Nothing is simple with you!" he interrupted hotly. Chey blanched, stung. "At least with Janey I knew what I was getting!" He jammed his feet into his shoes, muttering, "I don't know what the hell your problem is, but I know that if you don't overcome it you'll spend the rest of your shallow life alone!"

"My life isn't shallow!" she refuted, angry now.

"Oh, yes, it is," he told her, heading for the door, "and only God knows why I even care! It must be a personal character defect, this getting involved with shallow women!" With that he strode from the room. A moment later, the parlor door slammed, and she was alone, more alone, somehow, than ever before.

He was not at all certain until she actually walked into the newly refurbished breakfast room that she would even show up again. Relief mingled with dismay as one of his many fears was confirmed in that first glance. It was the old, uptight Chey who was back, not the charmingly shy, seductively soft woman he had gradually coaxed into the light these past weeks. He stood, hoping that she wouldn't bolt when she saw that he was alone in the room. Instead, she crossed coolly to the buffet and helped herself to a cup of coffee before turning to face him. They both spoke at the same time.

"I owe you an apology."

"I'm sorry for—"

They both broke off. She smiled wanly. "You go first."

"Okay, for starters, I'm sorry I called you shallow."

She looked down at the cup in her hand. Then her shoulders squared and she lifted her chin. "Apology accepted." She took a deep breath and got right down to it. "This is all my fault. I knew right from the beginning that nothing could come of this relationship."

"Nothing permanent you mean," he interrupted, gritting his teeth. "Because what happened last night was definitely something, something amazing."

She blushed a painful scarlet. "Be that as it may, it can't happen again."

"Why not?"

She bit her lip and launched into an obviously rehearsed explanation. "You deserve to know that I broke not one personal taboo by getting involved with you but two. The fact that you're a client is bad enough, but you're also…a father."

He was truly taken aback. "It's Seth?"

"No, not Seth," she answered quickly, "not Seth personally. It's any child. Actually, it's me. I don't want to be…I'm not cut out to be a mother."

For a moment, he could do no more than gape at her. Then suddenly he felt two emotions at once, a crushing sense of disappointment and utter disbelief; disappointment because he was in love with this woman, disbelief because he'd seen her with Seth and knew her to be a natural mother. Good grief, she was the great mother of her whole family. Didn't she realize that? No, of course, she didn't. Well, he knew something about parenthood that he hadn't known before Seth—and he suspected that it was something Chey had yet to learn as well. He tried to choose his words carefully.

"You know, I didn't put much premium on being a parent, either, until Seth came along. I mean, my business and one of my greatest pleasures is travel, and kids aren't exactly conducive to that, at least not the sort of travel in which I specialize. But we work it out. If I don't fly off as often as I used to, well, somehow it just doesn't matter."

"That's just it," she said, gesturing towards him, "that selflessness. Parenthood requires a dedication I've never felt for anything but my work."

"You've misconstrued what I'm trying to say," he told her a little impatiently.

"I know what I'm talking about. My father died when I was eight, and even then I marveled at the depth of my mother's selflessness. She had, has, room in her life for nothing else but her children. I don't want to be like that."

"Well, ten children could be rather consuming," he pointed out.

"Ten or one, it makes no difference," she insisted stubbornly. "I see it every day with my brothers and sisters. A good parent *always* puts the child first, and I don't think I can do that. I don't *want* to do it."

"I didn't want to do it, either," he blurted, exasperated, "but when Seth came along, I had no choice in the matter!"

"But I *do* have a choice," she stated firmly, "and I've made it. I don't want children."

"So you're saying you could never love a child?" he asked, truly needing to understand the situation.

"No, of course not. I love my nieces and nephews, but

thankfully, it's not likely I'll ever be called on to parent any of them."

"But you would if you had to."

"It's not likely I'll ever have to."

"Chey, I've seen how you interact with your family. It's much the same as a mother with her child. You guide and direct, want what's best for them, stress the finer elements, praise their success. In essence, you mother them."

"Even if that were true," she retorted doubtfully, "it means my plate is full."

"So, you're saying that you won't sleep with me again because I might expect you to someday be a stepmother to my son?"

"It's not that I think you want to marry me," she answered smoothly.

"Why not?"

She blinked at him. "I... Well, that was the whole point!"

"The point of what?"

"Of being with you."

He stared at her, slowly tilting his head to one side. "You thought I would never want a permanent relationship?"

"Yes, of course, but I didn't realize then that sex isn't as simple as it seems to be."

"I see." He stroked his chin, fingering the short hairs there and thinking that he might see more than she wanted him to. She was as shaken by what they'd shared as he was. More so, in fact. "All right. If that's how you really feel."

Her relief was palpable. "Thank you. I...perhaps we should just pretend that last night didn't happen."

"Sorry, darling," he replied honestly, "I'm not that good an actor."

She worried her bottom lip with her teeth, and he thought he might like to do that himself sometime. He sucked in a calming breath and determinedly cleared his head.

"But we do have a job to finish here," he said, "and it'll be a lot easier for both of us if we can do it as friends."

She heaved a sigh. "Friends. Thank you. That's more than I dared hope for, frankly."

"I always like to give a lady more than she expects," he said with a smile, knowing perfectly well that she did not expect how much more than friendship he intended to give her.

"A picnic," she said stupidly, the evidence laid out before her on the ground in the form of a blue blanket and a basket of food. It was a very intimate setting here at the back corner of the property. Spanish moss hung from the overarching branches of a centuries-old oak, beneath which a number of large terra cotta pots had been arranged, exotic blooms spilling over their rims.

"I thought this would be better than lunch at the same table as Grandmama and Seth," Brodie told her, his mouth close enough to her ear to send shivers up her spine. "Besides, it's too nice a day to be cooped up inside. Sit."

She debated for a moment while he went down on one knee to set out and uncover plates of thick quiche and asparagus and pineapple salad. Was this an attempt to be thoughtful or something else? No matter, her options were few in this situation. If she refused to join him, he'd know how much his company unsettled her. Her only recourse seemed to be to stay and soldier through. Shouldn't be too difficult. They were here to discuss business, after all. She sat. He handed her a plate, linen napkin and flatware, before stretching out on his side next to her.

She put a fork into Marcel's shrimp quiche and said crisply, "You have to make a decision *today* on the chair in the Western American room."

"Mmm," he answered, savoring the bite of quiche in his mouth before answering, "I have made a decision. I've decided that you ought to decide."

She dropped her fork to her plate. "Then what are we here for?"

"Lunch. Oh, and hockey."

"Hockey?"

"I love hockey," he said complacently. "Became addicted to it while I was in Dallas, but no one around here will let me talk about it. I need the ear of a friend too polite to ignore me."

A friend. It suddenly didn't sound so innocuous. "But I don't know anything about hockey."

"Then let me educate you," he said enthusiastically, waving his fork at her. "Now then, a face-off is…"

They talked hockey for an hour that seemed like ten minutes. She asked stupid questions, and he replied with the seriousness and solemnity of a college professor. The crazy thing was that she actually learned something, even when the conversation deteriorated into inanities and silliness. Then, without her even knowing how it happened, he had one hand hooked around the back of her neck and was drawing her close for a kiss. Even as she allowed her eyes to drift shut, she knew it shouldn't be happening. And then it wasn't. Dropping his hand, he sat back on his heels. "Sorry. Forgot myself for a minute there. You're just so easy to be with sometimes that it feels natural to…well, never mind."

She was reeling, her body purely humming with desire and remembered fulfillment, her mind trying to grasp the fact that *he* had called the halt, which basically meant that all her best intentions were as substantial as mush. Suddenly a little redheaded blur threw itself at Brodie, who caught it in his arms, fell onto his back and began laughing. "What are you doing here?"

"I fin' woo!"

Brodie pushed him into the air, holding him off at the ends of his long, strong arms. "You sure did find us. Where is Grandmama?"

"Right here." Brodie sat up, swinging Seth onto his lap.

Viola stood to one side, trying to catch her breath. "He's just too fast for me. I thought you might watch him for a little while. I feel in some need of a nap."

"Of course," Brodie said. "We're finished here. Chey will help me get him and the picnic basket back to the house. That is, if she doesn't mind."

Chey looked at Seth. Whenever he was around, she felt this terrible pull as if she were being sucked into a whirlpool from which there was no escape, but she couldn't refuse to help out. That would be selfish in the extreme, and in truth she welcomed the distraction. "Not at all," she said smoothly.

"If you need me," Viola said with visible relief, "you know where I'll be."

"Have a good rest, Grandmama," Brodie said as she headed back toward the house. Then he smiled at Chey, set Seth aside and began packing away the debris of their lunch, saying, "This won't take a moment."

"Here, let me help," she said, gathering up her own things.

"I hep!" Seth exclaimed, rushing to pick up a fork and stepping on a china plate in the process.

Brodie quickly rescued the plate and gathered in the fork, saying, "No, thanks. I'm cleaning up after myself. That's what we're supposed to do, remember?" Seth nodded, then toddled over and plopped down in Chey's lap. Brodie sent her an apologetic but beseeching look that she simply could not refuse. She wrapped her arms around Seth and engaged him in conversation, asking what he'd been doing that morning. He gave her a disjointed recital of his morning's activities while Brodie repacked the basket.

"Okay, that's everything."

Chey set Seth on his feet and allowed Brodie to give her a hand up. He quickly folded the blanket and tucked it under one arm, hoisting the basket with the other. He reached for Seth's hand, but the blanket limited his reach and Seth was able to dance out of the way, attaching himself to Chey instead. "I go wif Chey-Chey," he said petulantly.

Brodie brought his hand to his hip, preparing to be stern, but Chey simply took the boy's hand in hers and turned toward the house. It was a minor thing, holding a child's hand. It was better not to make a big deal of it. That great sucking sound that she heard was all in her mind. Brodie fell in beside them, and before long Seth reached up for his hand, too, and there they walked, Seth between them, one little hand in hers, the other in his father's, as if they were a family.

Then Seth picked his feet up off the ground, swinging at the ends of their arms, and cried gleefully, "Wheee!"

He put his head back, face beaming up at them. Such a simple thing, and yet it brought him such joy. Chey laughed, even as she felt the waters closing over her head. The current was pulling her down, after all, and she could not seem to prevent it no matter how hard she tried.

"Calling it a day?" Brodie asked, arms folded across his chest as he leaned there in the doorway of the smoking room, which Chey had started to call the study. Chey nodded, keys in hand.

"It's time. I'm not getting much done for some reason, anyway."

"Hard to concentrate when it's this hot, isn't it?"

"Don't know why," she said by way of tacit agreement. "The house is cool."

"It's the heaviness in the air," he theorized. "Humidity, I guess. Tell you what, let's go for a swim. The water ought to be about perfect now."

It sounded very tempting, but she shook her head. "I don't have a suit."

"Grandmama might have something that will work for you," he suggested.

She shook her head again but reluctantly. "Another time."

"Aw, come on. Marcel's made up a big pitcher of lemonade. We'll take a dip, have a cold drink. By dinner time you'll be thinking it's March."

She laughed, temptation bursting over her. "I could go get my suit."

"I'll take you," he said. "We can race across town with the top down. Come on," he coaxed. "I've been a good boy, haven't I? Where's the harm?"

She didn't really want to refuse, and he had been the very soul of a thoughtful, caring friend. She nodded, and they went out together.

It was viciously hot out, the sun seeming to boil the humid air around them, but somehow the discomfort floated away on a steamy breeze as they drove through town. He waited in the courtyard next to the car while she ran up and changed into a shiny blue one-piece suit and a yellow cover-up. She hurried back down the stairs with a tube of sun block and a beach towel under one arm, rubber flip-flops on her feet. He grinned appreciatively as she drew near, so she skirted wide around the car and let herself inside.

Shaking his head, he dropped down behind the wheel and started the engine. Soon they were back at the mansion, the car parked in its assigned bay in the redesigned carriage house. Avoiding the covered passage to the house, they walked, instead, into the garden. The inside of the pool had been painted a deep cerulean blue, and the water sparkled invitingly. A large carafe of lemonade sat inside a big glass bowl of ice on a low, iron lace table between two chaise lounges. Chey had rubbed waterproof sunscreen onto her arms, neck and face while they drove across the city, but she knew that wasn't enough to protect her fair skin, so she laid aside her towel, shed the cover-up and uncapped the tube. She was just about to squirt white cream into her hand when the tube was plucked from her grasp.

"I can get the places you can't," he said, turning her away from him.

She couldn't argue with that. Her hair was already pinned up, and she left it that way while he rubbed cream over her back and shoulders, slipping his fingers beneath the straps and low back edge of her suit to be sure she was completely covered. He went down on his haunches and began to slather the backs of her legs. Chey had to close her eyes and concentrate on blocking the shivers brought on by his touch. When he reached round her to get at the fronts of her legs, she stepped away, saying, "I can do that."

He rose to his feet and handed her the tube before walking into the bathhouse. She quickly finished with the sunscreen and unpinned her hair, combing it out with her fingers, then kicked off her shoes and moved to the shallow end of the pool. The cool, silky water lapped around her as she descended the broad steps. Sighing with pleasure, she pushed into the deep end with long, smooth strokes before arching her back and slipping beneath the water. She rose back to the surface, her face turned up to the sun, cool water sluicing off her head and shoulders, to find Brodie standing at the edge of the pool in black, boxer-type trunks. Lifting his hands over his head, he bent his knees and dove cleanly into the deep end. She waved her arms and kicked her legs to stay in place until he reached her, cleaving the water with his head and shoulders.

He was a gorgeous hunk of man, and she flashed on that night in her bed with him, those broad shoulders above her, that sleek, muscled chest with the line of dark hair down its center, his lean, handsome face, pale eyes staring down at her so intently. For an instant she was there again, lost in a fog of exquisite sensation, the hard length of him filling her to perfection. The sense of connection in that moment before he had begun to move had been staggering, and it had grown as he'd continued kissing her and driving her with him to the edge of something she could barely acknowledge even now. What he had made her feel that night had seemed almost unnatural in its intensity and richness, and yet, her body had yearned toward it with a desperation that still frightened her.

"You swim well," he said, wiping the water from his face with one hand.

"All the Simmonses swim well," she said, beginning to stroke back toward the shallow end of the pool.

"Oh? Why's that?" he asked, easily keeping up with her with a strong kick and lazy sidestroke.

"We have an aunt and several uncles who live down the bayou," she explained after finding her feet in the shallow end. "For a poor kid, a trip down the bayou was as good as it got for summer vacation."

"Bayou waters can be deep," he said, standing beside her. "My brother and I spent lots of time boating out in the bayous. He always loved it." He looked away. "That's how he died, a boating accident during a fishing trip to the bayou."

"Oh, I'm sorry," she said. "I didn't know."

"No reason you should've."

"You must miss him a great deal."

He nodded, a faraway look in his eyes, and said softly, "Imagine losing one of your brothers. Then imagine that he was your only brother."

Everything in her rebelled at such a thing. "How long has it been?"

The look he dropped on her face was decidedly odd and a little unsettling. "It'll be four years in September."

"That's next month." Something clicked into place. "He never saw Seth."

"No. He never saw his own namesake."

When Brodie turned and started wading toward the steps, she hurried to catch up, worried that she had somehow offended him. "Is something wrong?"

"Not at all. Ready for some lemonade?" he asked. The subject of his brother's death was clearly closed.

She blinked. "Sure."

"Don't get out. I'll bring it down to the steps."

She sat on the third step, wondering why he couldn't talk about his loss even after all this time. He came back with two plastic tumblers full of ice and pale yellow liquid, one of which he handed down to her before sitting next to her on the step, the water flowing and shifting around them. She took a long drink of the cold, sweet lemonade and felt the temperature sliding lower.

"Now what do you think of Grandmama's pool?" he asked after a moment.

"It's beautiful. Everything about this place is beautiful."

"Maybe that's why you seem to belong here," he said softly.

She looked down at her glass, both thrilled and dismayed, but before she could say anything, a familiar little voice cried out, "Daddy!" Brodie sighed and sent her an apologetic look, but the smile he turned up to his son was genuine.

"What is it, son?"

"Wook," Seth instructed. Chey looked, too, and saw Viola coming toward them through the open gate in the pool fence, a grim expression on her face, two men in baggy jeans and sweat-stained shirts following along behind her. Brodie muttered a curse beneath his breath, set his tumbler on the edge of the pool and got up off the step, standing in the water with his hands on his hips.

"What the hell are you doing here?" he demanded the instant the group was within hearing.

The man who answered him was older, perhaps fifty, with short, silver-streaked blond hair. A small man with abnormally long arms and body, he looked stunted, his gray eyes cold and calculating. "Well, now," he said, "where else would I be when this is where you've taken my girl and my grandson?"

A muscle flexed in the hollow of Brodie's jaw. "You could have called first, made sure the visit was convenient before coming all this way."

"Not so far," said the other man. He was a younger,

somewhat blunter version of the elder, except for the bright, strawberry blond of his hair. Chey realized with a shock who these men must be. She saw a hint of it in Seth's face, but it was the hair, confirmed by the old man's words, that brought it home to her. These two men were father and brother to Janey Todd, grandfather and uncle to Seth.

"What's that supposed to mean?" Brodie asked, folding his arms.

The older man smiled, and something about it chilled Chey. "No reason for us to stay on in Dallas when the girl and the boy are here, is there?" he asked.

Brodie's face darkened even as the younger man brayed, "That's right. We're living here now."

"Not so high as you, o' course," the older man said, his gaze drifting around the place and coming to rest on Chey. "Don't waste no time, neither, do you? But then women always have flocked to you. Must be all that money."

Chey could see that Brodie's hands were fisted. "You call before you come into my home again," he ordered flatly, ignoring the insult.

"Oh, sure," the older man conceded easily. Then suddenly he went down on one knee at the edge of the pool and stuck out a hand to Chey. "How do, ma'am? Name's Harp, Harp Shelly, and this here's my boy, Dude." He jerked his head toward Brodie, adding, "I'm his father-in-law, don't you know."

"Ex-father-in-law," Brodie corrected smartly.

Chey didn't look at Brodie before she slipped her hand in and out of Harp Shelly's, blunt, thick one and gave him her name. "Chey Simmons."

"You know about my girl?"

"Yes. I'm sorry for the tragedy that has befallen your family."

Harp nodded, studying her. Then he abruptly rose and said to Brodie. "I'm thinking Dude and me'll take the boy for the day tomorrow."

"No," Brodie said, and the older man instantly bristled.

Viola jumped in. "We, um, have plans tomorrow." She
threw a desperate look at Chey, her hands twisting together.

Chey took the hint and surprised herself by quickly lying.
"Yes, we're taking Seth to the zoo." It was the first place
she'd thought of. That she had included herself in the out-
ing didn't even occur to her.

Seth jumped up in the air and clapped his hands together,
crying, "Yeah! Zoo!" At the same time, Brodie flashed a
surprised look in her direction.

"We have a wonderful zoo in New Orleans," she went
on brightly, careful to keep her gaze locked on Harp Shelly.
"We plan to spend the whole day."

"In any event," Brodie put in firmly, neither confirming
nor denying the plans, "Seth is too young to spend the day
away from the house with strangers."

For a second, Harp Shelly's face registered intense anger,
but then he seemed to push the emotion away as he bent
and addressed his grandson. "We're not strangers, are we,
boy? You remember your old granddad?"

Seth looked uncertain and moved closer to his great-
grandmother.

"You remember Uncle Dude!" the younger man insisted
and made a funny face, sticking out his tongue and crossing
his eyes. Seth giggled but stayed glued to Viola.

"You can come and see him here," Brodie said, "but
be sure to call first."

Harp Shelly just looked at him and announced, "I'll see
my girl now."

Chey began to wonder if Brodie would deny him this,
too, but then Brodie turned to Viola and instructed, "Ask
Kate to take them up. Keep Seth with you." To Harp he
said, "Too much company at one time isn't good for Janey."

"Glad to see you're taking good care of her," Harp
sneered before abruptly turning away and starting back to
the house.

Viola gave Brodie a sympathetic, worried look, then took

Seth by the hand and followed Harp. Dude stood staring at Chey, as he'd been doing for some time, then turned at the last minute and went after them.

"Lousy son of a bitch," Brodie said, watching the men go. He glanced at Chey unapologetically and added bluntly, "I despise that man."

Chey smiled sympathetically. "I take it you don't trust him with Seth."

"Harp Shelly is an ex-con who lives one step away from jail. I wouldn't trust him with a dog. Frankly, I'd ban him entirely from Seth's life, if I could."

"Why can't you?" she asked, but his gaze slid away from hers.

"He is Janey's father, whether I like it or not, but I don't want Seth in that man's care, so I have to thank you for jumping in when you did. The zoo, though? You know you're stuck with it, don't you? Seth's already counting the minutes, and he's too young to fob off even with the most carefully reasoned excuses."

She hadn't even considered that. "I don't really have a choice, do I?"

"None," he confirmed, grinning apologetically.

She sighed. "Well, it's been quite a while since I last visited the zoo, and I don't suppose a day off will hurt."

"I'll see to it that you don't regret it," he promised, and she very much feared that he would do just that.

Chapter Nine

She was walking on dangerous ground. She knew it for certain that next day at the zoo, where a plump, grandmotherly woman looked at her and Brodie with Seth and said wistfully, "What a lovely family." She knew it again a few days later as she and Brodie hurried along the street in the rain, shopping for decorative accessories. They huddled beneath the same umbrella, gazing into shops packed with damp tourists and surreptitiously enjoying the proximity, their warm bodies bumping and sliding together. She knew it once more soon after, when, to mark the day of his brother's death, Brodie coaxed her onto a rented boat for a leisurely tour of the bayou where the accident had occurred and he shared with her his pain over the loss.

No doubt about it, she was playing with fire, but she couldn't seem to stop. She should never have toured the art museum with him, looking for "ideas," should never have let him talk her into those lunches out, "for perspective's sake." It was beyond foolish, those trips to the library where they sat whispering with their heads together over reference books that she knew by heart. She had become greedy for every moment of his company that she could justify, and it had come to the point where she could no longer hide from herself the fact that she was falling in love with him. But that was not the worst of it. The worst of it was Seth.

No matter how hard she tried, she could not hold herself aloof from that little boy. He simply wouldn't allow it. Adoration was his birthright, and he claimed it with all the confidence of those truly loved. What does one do with a child who climbs into one's lap uninvited to bestow smiles and hugs? How does one immure oneself from sweet giggles and infectious belly laughs? How does one refuse to become a favorite when it is impossible to turn away from effusive welcomes and reluctant farewells, when firm corrections are accepted with regretful sincerity and coolness is instantly forgiven with the slightest thaw?

Somehow, the determination, the conviction, the principle that she could not, should not, would not even wish to become his mother became too slippery to hold. She truly did not wish to bear a child, and she could still dispassionately and honestly conclude that she did not wish to be *a* mother, but somehow she could be *Seth's* mother. Not that she expected it to happen or even felt that it should.

For one thing, she could never give up her career. That much she knew without question, and despite the assertions of the popular culture, she was not certain that this motherhood business could be conducted properly in combination with any other. Just as troubling, however, was a certain brick wall into which she kept stumbling as she wandered through the life and mind of Brodie Todd. Quite without meaning to, she found herself attempting to breach it one afternoon.

"Why don't you talk about Janey?"

He immediately went stiff but did not put down the product material he had come into her office to read. "Do you talk about the most unpleasant things in your life?'' he asked, an edge of defensiveness in his tone.

''Not often, but I've done more of that with you than anyone.''

Finally, he put down the papers and carefully poured himself a glass of ice-water. ''What do you want to know?''

She decided it was best to start at the beginning. ''How did you meet?''

''She was my secretary, in an office I didn't go to very often.''

He no longer had a secretary. Why? Because he couldn't bear to see some other woman in that capacity? ''What made you want to marry her?'' she asked cautiously, pleased that it came out in such a casual manner.

''She was pregnant,'' he said bluntly.

That was a shock, and she wasn't certain how she felt about it. So he had married Janey because he'd had to; yet, he was taking care of her when no obligation to do so existed. ''Why did you divorce her?''

''The marriage was over.'' It was obvious he was saying no more on that subject.

''Are you still in love with her?''

He looked down at his glass. His jaw flexed, and he answered flatly, ''No.''

It was what she'd wanted to hear, but something about his voice bothered her so much that she dared not continue. After a moment, he picked up the papers again, leaving her with a sinking feeling in the pit of her stomach. The brick wall stood as firm as ever, despite the peek she'd managed over its top.

Brodie watched the small coupe disappear as Chey turned the car onto the street. He wondered if he should tell her the truth, then immediately dismissed the idea. No reason she should know. Perhaps someday, if she actually came to love him—and Seth. She was not immune to either.

He had hope, but it was too soon to trust her with the most significant secret of his life. He yearned to share it with her, yearned to share everything with her. How ironic was it that he should fall in love with the one woman who did not want all that he had to offer?

He went back into the house and started up the stairs. It had been days since he'd visited Janey's rooms, and Chey's questions had started him thinking again about their odd relationship. Whatever their personal dealings had been, Brodie was well aware that he owed her greatly for Seth, and for that reason he had promised himself that he would never allow her to become a burdensome responsibility. She was a person, and he would treat her as such.

Surprisingly, as he drew near her door, he heard voices. Words were indistinct, but the sounds had the cadence of casual conversation, when voices overlap as one person talks over another. Startled, he opened the door rather abruptly and went straight in. Brown was standing over the bed, and she jumped when the door opened at her back, whirling, one hand pressed to her chest.

"Oh, Mr. Brodie! You scared me half to death."

"I'm sorry, Brown. I thought I heard voices."

She glanced at Janey and said, "It was just the radio. I play it for her 'cause the doctors say stimulation's good for her, but sometimes they talk more'n they play music. Why they think a body wants to hear all that jabbering I don't know, and I wonder if it doesn't confuse her sometimes, hearing strange voices, so I turn it off when they get to gabbing."

It was a reasonable explanation, and yet it felt strange in some way. Perhaps it was that Brown usually spoke no more than necessary, and now she seemed positively chatty. He dismissed it. "I just want to sit with her a minute."

Brown nodded uncertainly, but then she turned and trudged around the end of the bed. Why did he have the feeling that something was off-kilter?

"Have you seen any changes in her lately?" he asked,

halting the usually taciturn nurse. She turned slowly, hands folded tightly over her rounded middle.

"Well," she said thoughtfully, "I think she might have known when her pa and brother come. She didn't make no noise or nothing, but it was like she wanted to, you know? It's like she's in there trying to get out."

"But no eye contact?" he clarified. "No overt movements, and no words?"

"That's right. Not while I'm here. But I ain't with her ever' minute, 'course."

"She's not likely to make responses without stimulus," he said dismissively.

"I'm sure you're right," Brown murmured with a last look at the bed before lumbering off toward her own room.

Brodie moved to the bed and lowered himself to sit on the side, looking at that pretty face. He felt a great rush of sadness, not just because of the accident but for everything. What a wasted life! Seeking to make some kind of meaningful contact, he picked up her delicate hand, cradling it in his.

"I'm sorry I haven't been in to see you lately," he began. "Seth and the house and the business…" He felt a twinge of guilt at the lie and a deeper, more poignant emotion beneath it. "Actually, it's more than that," he admitted softly. "I doubt you'd be happy to hear it, but somehow I need to say it and you seem to be the only one I can say it to just now. How odd is that?" He shook his head wryly. "The point is, I've met someone, and I've fallen in love with her." He couldn't be certain, but for an instant he thought he felt movement in Janey's hand. He gripped it more tightly, studying her face. "Janey? Can you hear me? Can you speak to me, open your eyes?"

Her eyes rolled beneath her eyelids, but he'd seen that many times. The doctors insisted that these little jerks and eye flutters were involuntary; yet, it sometimes seemed to him that it was just as Brown claimed, that Janey was in there somewhere and responding as well as she could to what was being said and done around her. He tilted his head, thinking that if the old Janey still existed, this sort of talk was exactly what it might take to reach her.

"Perhaps you'd like to hear about her," he said conversationally. "You've met her, sort of. Her name is Chey Simmons, and she's a delectable little blonde with six brothers and three sisters. The fact is, I love her, and I intend to marry her." Someday. Maybe.

This time, he could not mistake the way Janey's fingers curled against his. The pressure, though brief, sent a bolt of shock through him. He leaned close, took her face in his hands.

"Janey? If you can hear me, if you understand, open your eyes. You can come back, Janey. It's not too late. You're a beautiful, charming woman. You can have such a good life."

Nothing, nothing at all. He tried one more time.

"The money is still there, Janey, every cent, just waiting for you. That's reason enough to wake up, isn't it, all that lovely money?" But apparently it wasn't, for the woman on the bed slept on, oblivious. Comatose.

He stared down at her for a long time, then he tenderly smoothed her hair around her face and gave up. Shaking his head, he sat for a moment longer, the hope draining out of him. The relief he held resolutely at bay. He wouldn't let himself be glad that all the old problems slept on with her. Nothing was worth the living death that held her in its grip. Nothing. He stood, bent and pressed a kiss to her forehead.

"Rest now," he said with a sad smile, "then wake up, if you please, and get on with your life, because I'm certainly getting on with mine."

He walked smoothly across the room, thinking that he had accomplished one thing, at least. He had crystallized for once and all what he wanted from Chey Simmons. Nothing short of always, and he meant to do everything in his power to have it.

* * *

It was the christening, the first dinner party, however informal, in the newly renovated dining room, and Chey was pleased to be included, if a little apprehensive. Something in Brodie's manner of late told her that the easy days were behind her. It was as if he had abandoned the facade of friendship and was actively courting her again, employing a deadly charm underlaid with steely determination. And to her dismay it was working. She saw herself being coaxed closer and closer to a place she'd sworn she'd never go and wondering if the destination could be as sweet as the journey.

Brodie had invited Georges to dinner, as well. It was their moment of glory, though the house was not finished yet. Much, in fact, remained to be done, especially with the family rooms, which had been assigned a lower priority after the situation with the Legantine representatives had heated up. Nevertheless, Brodie seemed eager to begin enjoying the benefits of their labors and to express his appreciation.

Chey dressed with care in a simple black, sleeveless sheath and flat sandals. Shiny black clips held up the sides of her hair in two simple twists, leaving the back to flow freely over her shoulders and down her back. Georges had chosen a grass-green sport coat to offset his monochromatic ensemble of navy blue slacks, shirt and tie. Brodie answered the door in dark gray slacks and a light gray, collarless shirt with the sleeves rolled up. His wide smile did nothing to disguise his amusement at Georges or the heat in his eyes for her. A slow burn ignited in her blood stream at the sight of him.

"Drinks in the garden room," he told them, snagging her hand. "It's warm, but Grandmama insisted. Anyway, Marcel says dinner is only a quarter-hour off. I hope you like mint juleps."

"Mint juleps! Fabulous!" Georges said, rubbing his hands together and starting off down the hall.

Chey shared a smile with Brodie as they followed, her hand firmly clasped in his. "Speaking of fabulous," he said silkily, "I'm glad you left your hair down."

She smiled, the heat in her blood spiking several degrees. "Thank you."

As soon as they entered the room, Georges went straight to one of four wide, rolled-arm, antique rattan chairs, which Chey had discovered in South Carolina via an Internet search, and made an elaborate display of kissing Viola's hand. Seth, who occupied Viola's lap, giggled while Brodie placed Chey in the chair next to Viola, then sat down, leaving the last chair for Georges. Viola sent Seth to his father, then sat up and pulled around a wheeled drinks table containing the ingredients for her brew.

She began by pouring a little ice water into a silver cup, then added a portion of confectioners sugar and a large sprig of mint, which she mashed together with a small wooden spoon. Next she filled the cup with crushed ice, stuck in another sprig of mint and poured good Kentucky bourbon to the rim. A small straw jammed straight to the bottom was the final touch. Viola passed the cup to Chey and began filling the next while Chey sipped the burning sweet mixture judiciously. Both cold and hot, the sweetened bourbon took her breath away while the mint seemed to fill her nasal cavities. Within minutes the room was uncomfortably warm and Chey was very relaxed. She was feeling lovely by the time Marcel announced that dinner was on the table.

The rare Thomas Sheraton mechanical expanding mahogany table that she'd had shipped all the way from England had been expanded to its full twelve feet beneath a pair of exquisite brass chandeliers, but they were eating family-style, so places for only seven had been set near one end. Viola had fashioned a beautiful centerpiece with ivies and flowers from her garden in an enormous silver-and-china epergne from Chey's shop. A perfectly gorgeous salad in a shell-shaped crystal bowl the size of a small fish pond immediately caught Chey's eye, but the mingled aromas rising from a silver basket of freshly baked Italian bread and a china platter of spaghetti covered with Portobello mushroom caps and a mound of chopped vegetables in a delicate sauce literally made her mouth water.

Dinner was a leisurely, relaxed ninety minutes of fabulous food, conversation and laughter. Marcel and Kate joined them at the table, but Brown had declined her invitation. No one missed her, as Brodie, Marcel and Georges set about entertaining the ladies. Seth laughed, kicked the chair in which his booster seat had been placed, and managed to smear food on his clothes, hands and face, but he sat as still as a child could be expected to and eventually got as much food in him as he wanted. He did not seem to mind being the only child in a room full of adults, nor did he appear bored, but he did begin to droop sleepily before the end of the meal and even refused the airy, chocolate-filled cream puffs that Marcel had made for dessert. Just as soon as Viola had done justice to her own confection, she got up and prepared to take the child up to bed.

Georges volunteered to carry him up the stairs. She cleaned the boy's face without the least protest from him, then had Georges carry him to his father, for a sleepy good-night kiss and hug. Marcel and Kate got air kisses, but Chey received an exuberant hug. As Georges carried the boy away, Viola right behind them, Marcel and Kate got up to clear the table.

Brodie reached for Chey's hand, saying, "Let's take a walk outside."

"After that meal, I could use a little exercise," she said, rising to her feet and allowing him to lead her from the room. "Marcel continues to outdo himself," she commented as they left the house.

"I have to work hard to keep off evidence of his expertise," Brodie said, as he opened the gate so they could walk around the pool, protected from mosquitoes by the flickering citronella torches.

"You don't work hard at anything," she told him archly as they skirted the narrow end of the pool.

"Not true," he disagreed good-naturedly, turning the corner with her to stroll the length of the pool gate. "I work very hard at enjoying life. And lately I've been working very hard at something else." Suddenly the sensual tension earlier dispelled by mint juleps, good company and delicious food erupted anew. Glancing up and away, Chey caught a flicker of movement on the upper gallery. Her immediate impression was that it was Brown, but she didn't give it another thought. She was more concerned about the man who now drew her to a halt beside him. "I can't be just your friend, Chey. It's gone far beyond that for me."

She had to swallow down her drumming heart in order to whisper, "I know."

"You aren't running," he said softly, drawing her toward him.

"I'm not running," she confirmed, catching her breath as his mouth covered hers.

One part of her was enthralled while another was horrified. Then all of her was afire. Her arms lifted and wound about his neck, her body bending into his as he crushed her against him. She wondered dimly how she could fight this and then why it was that she should. With his mouth and hands and his own need, he created a maelstrom of sensation and desire that so captured her she did not hear the shouts until he lifted his head and half-turned toward the house.

"Mr. Brodie! Come quick!" It was Brown, pounding toward them in ungainly haste.

Brodie frowned, muttering, "What the hell?"

Brown drew up at the pool fence, her hands gripping the pointed ends of the wrought iron pickets. "It's happened!" she gasped. "You've got to come and see for yourself!"

"See what?"

"Janey, she's awake!" With that stunning news, she

whirled and began running back toward the house, crying,
"Come on! Hurry!"

For an instant, Brodie seemed as stunned as Chey. Then
suddenly he grabbed her hand and lurched toward the
house, exclaiming, "Sweet God!" He literally dragged her
along in his wake, sprinting across the grass. She finally
jerked her hand free, unable to keep up, and attempted to
catch her breath. He paused halfway across the garden
room and looked back at her.

"Go on. I'm right behind you." He twisted back and
forth in obvious turmoil, so she pushed off again, insisting,
"Go on!"

He turned and ran for the hall and the stairs, catching
Brown as she pounded on. Chey was mere yards behind
them. Over and over the thought echoed inside her head,
She's awake, she's awake, she's awake. His ex-wife, the
mother of his son, was suddenly, inexplicably awake from
her long coma. She made the top of the stairs just in time
to watch Brodie sprint down the hallway, Brown huffing
painfully behind him. When she swung through Janey's
open doorway, only a step behind Brown, he was standing
frozen.

Janey sat on the edge of the bed dressed in a pink silk
nightgown, the brush she had been pulling through her
long, pale red, fluffy hair paused in midair. "It's true!"
Chey heard Brodie gasp over Brown's wheezing beside her.
Then, he laughed and exclaimed, "You're awake!" At his
exclamation, Janey's angelic face lit with a smile and she
dropped the brush, holding out her hands to him.

"Brodie!"

Chey knew her mouth was hanging open, but she
couldn't seem to close it. She became aware, only as Brodie
slowly crossed the floor, that the room was crowded with
people. Indeed, Brown and everyone who'd been at the
dinner table, with the exception of Seth, were standing there
gaping at the awakened beauty, who, in turn, had eyes only
for Brodie.

"You've grown a beard," Janey chortled. "I love it."

Brodie was shaking his head. "When...how...?"

Suddenly she hopped off the bed, stumbled slightly, and then literally threw herself at him, crying, "I'm back, darling! And, oh, I love you!"

Chey watched with cold, stinging detachment as Janey wrapped her arms around Brodie's neck and shoved her body up against his, going up on tiptoe to kiss him. Brodie's hands went to her waist, but he seemed too stunned to actually kiss her back. Janey sank down, collapsing against him weakly.

"I'd better go back to bed," she declared apologetically. "Brown says I've been asleep a long time and I'm weak because of it, but when I saw my handsome husband standing here, I felt positively supercharged."

Husband. The word seemed to reverberate around the room. It was whispered by several lips, even, Chey very much feared, her own. Brodie finally seemed to get himself in hand. He partly pushed, partly carried Janey back to the bed and eased her up onto it. When she was settled back against the pillows, he stepped away and brought his hands to his hips, asking, "What happened?"

"That's what I'd like to know," she said, huffing a little. "The last thing I remember is our baby's first birthday, and then I wake up here in this strange place and Brown says it's a miracle of some sort." She smiled and lifted a hand toward him. "I was upset, but it's all right now that you're here. You always make everything all right." She waved a hand, beckoning him closer, then whispered, loudly enough for everyone to hear, "Should all these strangers be in here?"

Brodie stepped back from Janey and glanced around the room. "There aren't any strangers here," he said. "They've all been concerned about you in one way or another."

When his gaze came to rest on Chey's, she saw the question there—and the doubt. She knew suddenly that she was the one person who truly did not belong here, and that it was best if she left immediately, for everyone's sake. What a fool she had been to think, even for a moment, that it might be otherwise! She turned blindly toward the door, but before she could step through it, she felt a hand close around her wrist.

"Chey! I haven't introduced you." He pulled her closer to the bed. Even though she shook her head imploringly, she found herself standing next to Viola, who slid a supportive arm about her waist. Brodie glanced around once more, his gaze coming back to Chey. Then he switched his attention to Janey.

"Let's start with the occupants of the house," he said, and laid a hand on his grandmother's shoulder. "This is Grandmama, otherwise known as Viola. I'm sure I spoke of her many, many times, and she, of course, is why we're all here." He looked at Janey and explained, "Grandpapa died some months ago, and I decided it was time to gather what was left of the family in one place. Since removing Grandmama from New Orleans was unthinkable, we came here. She's been an invaluable help with Seth."

"Oh," Janey said. "Well, yes, that makes perfect sense." She smiled at Viola and said, "I did wonder." Not one word about her son, Chey noticed.

Viola looked at Brodie meaningfully. He just patted her shoulder and moved on to the couple standing together at the foot of the bed. "Kate looks after the house, somehow managing to keep it spotless despite all the remodeling that's gone on, and Marcel feeds us all sublimely. Finding the two of them alone was worth the move to New Orleans."

"You mean we have servants?" Janey asked, delight naked in her voice.

"No," he answered flatly. "We're all family here. I actually think of Kate and Marcel as the indispensable ones. I need them around here so badly that I'm actually willing to pay, and pay well, to keep them here. They are *not* servants.''

"Just like Brown,'' Janey said, flashing a glance at her nurse.

He stared at Janey, then said carefully, "I suppose that's a good analogy.'' With that he moved back to Chey. Taking her hand in his, he said, warmly, "Chey Simmons is the genius who has transformed this big old house into a home of which we're very proud. And Georges is her assistant.''

Janey's bright blue gaze sharpened. "I guess that means you're the decorator,'' she said innocently. Then she glanced around the room, flapping an arm in helpless frankness. "I hope this isn't what the rest of my house looks like. It might as well be a hospital!''

My house. Everyone in the room, with the exception of Janey and Brown, stiffened at the impact of those words, but it was left to Brodie to set her straight, which he did, though not in the way Chey might have chosen had she possessed any right to have made the choice.

"Chey had nothing to do with this part of the house,'' he said firmly. "And it looks like a hospital room because it is. You've been very ill.''

"We're all glad you're better, Ms. Shelly,'' Kate said then.

"Ms. Shelly?'' Janey echoed. "What on earth do you mean by that? A married woman is known by her husband's name. It's Mrs. Todd and proudly so.''

Mrs. Todd. Chey's heart plummeted straight to her toes. Obviously the woman couldn't know that her husband had divorced her while she was ill. All the more reason, one Chey had allowed herself to forget, why she should not have allowed herself to become involved with this man. Brodie looked at Chey in helpless shock while Viola calmly said, "I think someone should call the doctor.''

Brodie pinched his nose with thumb and forefinger and nodded. "You're right. I should speak with him immediately and proceed from there." Heaving a great sigh, he rubbed his hands over his face.

"I should go," Chey said softly.

"We should all go," Marcel said in his deep, quiet voice.

Brodie didn't argue, just dropped his hands and said resignedly to Chey, "I'll walk you out."

"No," she refused, holding up a hand. "You're needed here."

"We'll walk down together," Georges said, taking her arm and turning her toward the door.

Chey looked back over her shoulder just as Janey leaned forward and snaked a possessive arm through Brodie's, as loving a wife as Chey had ever seen. *She's the mother of his child,* Chey thought, *and soon she'll be his wife again.* The pain that thought caused was as deep as it was amazing, and telling herself that it was all for the best did nothing whatever to lessen it.

Chapter Ten

Chey was avoiding him again, and he didn't doubt why. Before Brown had interrupted them with the astounding news of Janey's reawakening, he'd felt certain that he was making important headway, and Janey's inconveniently timed recovery could not be allowed to interfere with that, no matter what Chey was thinking. But first he had to find Chey and tell her the truth.

He'd have done it that very same night if Harp and Dude hadn't shown up on his doorstep within the hour of Janey's awakening. Brown's doing, no doubt. Every time he turned around now, he was falling over Shellys, damn them. Not that he begrudged Janey her recovery.

God knew that the moment he had seen the woman sitting up there on the side of the bed, awake and brushing her hair, had been one of the happiest of his life. He just hadn't realized in that moment that she was going to complicate things so badly. But he should have. Oh, yes, indeed, he should have. Experience, after all, was a hell of a teacher, and experience had taught him that things were never as simple as they seemed when a Shelly was involved.

The timing of Janey's recovery was just entirely too coincidental for his satisfaction. More suspicious still was Janey's supposed amnesia. It was one thing to forget a divorce had taken place, it was another entirely to remember a marriage which had never existed.

Janey seemed determined to convince even him that a happy, loving marriage had been their norm, when no such thing could be further from the truth. He should have told Chey how it had been. He should have explained it all, but he'd stubbornly clung to his own fiction, and if he allowed it, Chey would embellish that with understandable but erroneous assumptions, and he would lose the only woman with whom he'd ever found a snowball's chance in hell of making a happy life.

The first forty-eight hours following Janey's recovery had been filled with trips back and forth to the doctors for tests and consultations, all necessary, he knew. He was about out of patience, however, with Janey, who seemed as determined as ever to crawl into his bed, with Chey who seemed determined to avoid him, with Janey's irritating family and with Brown, who was suddenly present in his household in a way she never had been before. His impatience extended to the doctors, as well. They simply wouldn't give him a straight answer about Janey's condition and the advisability of just enforcing the truth. The one situation he was determined not to allow to continue much longer, though, was Chey's avoidance. And yet it did continue for nearly a week.

He called. He called the shop at least twice a day and her apartment repeatedly at night, but she neither returned his calls nor acknowledged his messages. Georges at least sounded sympathetic and apologetic these days, rather than merely unctuous and prissy, but Chey remained elusive.

Finally, Brodie reached his limit. He held a trump card,

and he was not above playing it; so, when she failed to respond to a strict summons on Monday morning, on Monday afternoon he simply closed the bank account he'd set up for her. He was frankly surprised by how much cash remained at her disposal. A good portion of it rightly belonged to her, though several bills were outstanding and the house was not truly finished. Nevertheless, he withdrew every cent and dared her to ignore him again.

Because his office was situated on the front of the house, he saw her small coupe turn onto his drive that next day, a Tuesday, just after lunch, but he was so frustrated that he didn't even go down to let her in himself, choosing instead to take a little extra time to tamp down his nerves. Kate had standing instructions to bring Chey straight to him whenever she arrived. So he watched, his pulse pounding in his temples, as she got out of the car and walked to the porch, buttoned up in a designer suit, her glorious hair wrapped tight against her head. Then he waited.

He was sitting at his desk, his fingers templed over the blotter when she finally tapped on the door, opened it and slipped inside. His first impulse was to jump up from his chair, grab her and drag her off to his bedroom in order to convince her, in the surest way he knew how, that she must absolutely never evade him again, but he'd seen cheerier expressions on political prisoners, so he restrained the impulse. Consequently, the first words that came out of his mouth, a pure product of rejection and frustration, surprised even him.

"Well, thank you for this effusive show of support."

Her mouth dropped open, indignation sparked in her eyes, and the fight was on. "Now I like that, coming from the man who has just robbed me blind after weeks and weeks of work!"

"Nobody's robbed you of anything," he snapped, already regretting the tack he'd taken. "But what did you expect? One minute I'm pouring my heart out to you, and the next thing I know you won't take my damned phone calls!''

She compressed her mouth into a straight line and dropped down into the chair in front of his desk, arms folding protectively. "You're leaving out one very important fact," she said tartly. "Your wife is no longer in a coma."

"She's my *ex*-wife!" he all but roared, shoving a hand through his hair. "And that's exactly how she's going to stay."

Chey looked down at her lap. "It's obvious that Janey still loves you." The tiny quaver in her voice gave him immense hope.

"Janey has never loved me," he retorted. "She doesn't know how."

"Maybe so," Chey replied doubtfully, "but it's clear that she wants to be married to you."

"Nothing's clear with Janey," he scoffed, "and it doesn't make a tinker's damn, anyway." He lowered his voice. "I wasn't playing around out there, Chey. I'm in love with you. *You*. Not Janey."

A soft, wistful look came over her, but she shook her head stubbornly. "Brodie, you need time to explore your emotions more fully. She's the mother of your son, and you owe it to Seth and yourself to take the time to get to know her again."

"I need time to make sure she's healthy," he said firmly, "and that's all I need time for. Believe me, mine and Janey's marriage was never what she's making it out to be now. Never. And it never could be."

The door opened, ratcheting his gaze upward from her face to the grizzled, sly and unwelcome countenance of Harp Shelly.

"Oops. Sorry," Harp said, entirely too smoothly and not at all repentantly, to Brodie's mind. "Didn't know you had company."

Brodie clamped down on his jaw, barely restraining the urge to hurl a paperweight at the skunk's head. "I'm busy here,'' he said bluntly, but Chey was already getting to her feet.

"We can finish our discussion later."

"We haven't settled anything," he insisted.

"It can wait, especially if you take care of that banking problem."

"I don't want to wait," he said, knowing he sounded like a spoiled child. "Let's discuss this over dinner."

"I'm not sure that's a good idea," she demurred.

"Ya'll can settle this later," Harp interjected petulantly. "I think my girl's problems are a little more important than your decorating scheme." He narrowed his eyes at Brodie and added, "I'm bettin' my grandson would feel the same way if he was old enough to hear some true things."

Brodie almost came out of his chair at that unsubtle threat. Seth would know everything there was to know, but he, Brodie, would be the one to do the telling.

"You want to tell some truth, Harp?" Brodie asked angrily. "Tell yourself that you're wearing out your welcome fast and ought to be on your best behavior from here on out."

"I'll let you two talk," Chey said quickly, slipping past Harp toward the door.

"Chey, we haven't settled anything," he said as she went out the door.

"Later," was the only reply. Brodie murdered Harp Shelly with his eyes, but that demon just grinned and sat down.

"Now then," he said. "I found me the right doctor for my girl, and he's going to be the one to tell us what's what."

She was oddly unsurprised when the intercom buzzed, though the hour was late, almost eleven, and she was not, technically, expecting anyone. She didn't have to think about who might be standing down on the sidewalk next to her gate buzzing for admittance, however. The only question was whether or not to answer him. In the end, he gave her no choice, his voice coming through the speaker, strong and implacable. "I know you're there, Chey. I'm coming up."

Thinking to stall him, she hit the button on the wall speaker and said quickly, "It's late, Brodie. I'm getting ready for bed."

He didn't answer, but not two minutes later, he knocked on her door. She yanked it open, irritated now.

"How did you get back here? The gate is locked for the night."

"Your gate is not tall enough," he told her impatiently. "A determined man can get over the top, and I'm very determined, so you might as well let me in."

His face, though set in rigid lines, showed signs of exhaustion. She didn't have the heart to turn him away, despite deep misgivings. With a sigh, she stepped back. He swept inside, movements agitated. She closed the door behind him, saying, "Brodie, we don't really have anything to talk about. It's not just Janey, you know."

"Will you be quiet and listen to me?" he snapped. But then he dropped down onto the divan and put his head into his hands. "I'm sorry. It's just that I don't quite know what to do." He looked up at her then, pleading in his eyes. "I should have told you this before," he said. "It doesn't matter now why I didn't, but you have to hear me out. Please."

She couldn't imagine what he might say that could make a difference in their situation. He should be with Janey, the mother of his child, and she should be concentrating on her work. And yet, he seemed so desperate that she couldn't refuse. "All right."

He closed his eyes and began. "Janey was my secretary. I didn't have much use for one, really, but since I don't get into my headquarters office very regularly, I needed someone to answer the phone and relay the occasional message. My chief of operations back in Dallas hired her. The first time I saw her, I was struck by her appearance, that sexy innocence. But she made a big play for me right away, and it turned me off. It smacked of calculation, frankly. When she saw that she wasn't getting anywhere with me, she turned her attention to my brother.''

Brodie sat back and pressed a hand to his temple. "Seth was nobody's fool," he said consideringly. "He knew what she was almost as soon as I did. Only he figured that he had nothing to lose. We both assumed that it was money she wanted, and Seth didn't have any. He went for the romp, the play time, and he was quite sure that was all it was to her, too.'' Brodie sat forward again, elbows against his knees, hands clasped together, and she could tell that the next part was difficult for him. He cleared his throat. "The very day he left on that last fishing trip, he told me that he was going to marry her.''

"*He* was going to marry her?'' Chey echoed in surprise.

Brodie nodded. "I was helping him get his boat ready, when he popped us each a beer and said abruptly, 'I'm going to be a father.' I almost choked.''

Brodie just looked at her, waiting for her to understand. When she did, it took her breath away. "You're not little Seth's father!''

"Yes, I am,'' he said, "now. Now I am.''

She slumped back against the cushions, stunned. "Oh, my God.''

"You have to understand how it was with my brother and me,'' he told her. "I fell into the travel business by just following my passion and planning my own trips. People began asking for my help and before I knew it I was in business. Seth didn't have anything like that—until he found out that he was going to be a father. I've often thought since that he fell into his passion the same way I fell into mine, completely by accident. He didn't love Janey. He never loved Janey, but he loved the very idea of being someone's dad, and he absolutely would not, could not, leave his child to be raised by Janey and the Shellys.''

"But to marry without love,'' Chey exclaimed.

"He had no choice," Brodie told her. "He knew them by then, you see. He knew all about Harp's prison record, about Dude's propensity for petty crime. He said Dude wasn't smart enough to be a real criminal like his father and that Janey wasn't strong enough to stand up to the old man's manipulative bullying. Seth was dead-set on marrying her for the sake of his child, and he would've been the best dad who ever lived. Only he didn't live. He went on that fishing trip, and he died, leaving the child he loved and wanted so much unprotected."

"So you stepped in," she said, knowing it was true.

Brodie shrugged his shoulders. "What else could I do? I didn't doubt that they'd sell me the child, and believe me, I was willing to pay, but the attorneys said the best way was not even to adopt the child but to get my name on the birth certificate. In most states, the father of record is the father, period, unless he himself decides to contest the parentage of the child or give up his rights."

"So you married her to get your name on the birth certificate," Chey said, amazed. "It never even occurred to you to let her raise Seth on her own, did it?"

He scoffed at the very notion. "If he even exists for her, I haven't seen it. Turning him over to her would be the same as turning him over to the Shellys and Brown. Would you have given him over to the likes of Harp Shelly?"

Even she, who had determined long ago that she wasn't cut out for parenthood, couldn't have done that. "No, not if Harp's all that you say he is, and I don't doubt that he is. But you must have felt something for Janey, over time."

He shook his head. "I made a deal with Janey. We signed a prenuptial agreement. In the event of divorce, she got a cool million, and the divorce was a done deal from the beginning, Chey. We didn't put it on paper, of course, but that was the deal. I married her. I was listed as the baby's father on the birth certificate. After one year, we split, she took the money, I kept the child. She agreed to it happily and even told me that if I hadn't offered her a deal, she'd have aborted the baby. The pregnancy was her toehold on BMT, you see. That's all Seth's ever been to her, a finger in my pocket.''

Chey was speechless for a long moment. She did not quite understand the need of some women, perhaps most women, to bear a child, but neither could she understand how a woman could use a child as Janey evidently had. All was not yet clear, however. "I don't understand what's happening now, then.''

"I think I do," he said. "I made a mistake with Janey. Even after she cold-bloodedly agreed essentially to sell me her child via marriage and divorce, I felt sorry for her. I was sure that she was being manipulated by Harp, and I still think she was. I just didn't realize how greedy she is. About six months into the marriage, I allowed her to buy a house in an exclusive part of Dallas and spend a bloody fortune decorating it. She spent a half-million dollars, Chey, and I was ashamed of the place. It was hideous—hot-pink stucco and fire-red tile, tacky plaster statues, gold leaf. The woman has no taste, except for spending money. She has a taste for that, and she quickly realized that the million bucks she had coming wasn't going to last her as long as she'd thought. That's when she decided that she wanted to stay married.''

"But you didn't?" Chey mused.

"I definitely did not," he told her, looking straight into her eyes. "She tried to make me believe that she was in love with me, but once she realized that it simply made no difference because I wasn't in love with her, it got ugly. Some of the scenes I endured were unrepeatable. She fought the divorce and tried to renegotiate the prenup. When that didn't work, she threatened to sue me for custody of Seth. I was preparing to offer her another million despite my attorney's advice against it. Then, the night of Seth's first birthday, she showed up drunk, and I had to drive her home. She made such a scene that all the neighbors came out to see what was happening. I left her screaming in the front yard. A couple hours later, Harp found her in the back at the bottom of the pool. It was being drained for resurfacing. She had apparently pitched a fit, tossing around a bunch of pot plants and some patio chairs. Somehow she fell and literally cracked open her skull.''

''And after all that, you took care of her,'' Chey said with pure wonder.

''Someone had to,'' he remarked. ''Harp and Dude couldn't even if they would have, which they wouldn't. Harp kept saying, 'She's no use to anyone now, no use to anyone.' Made me wonder if maybe he hadn't been masterminding the whole setup. No matter what he says now, he had no interest in her once it became obvious that the coma might be permanent. Only Brown seemed to want to help her. So I saw to it that she could. It was the least I could do,'' he said, ''for the woman who gave me Seth. I named him that because in some ways it was as if she had given me back my brother. I don't wish her ill, but I will not let her come between me and those I love.'' He reached for her hand, ran his thumb across the backs of her knuckles and added softly, ''In case you somehow don't know, I'm talking about you and my son.''

She lifted her free hand to cup his cheek. She didn't know what to say. He was perhaps the finest man she'd ever known, and that was saying something, all things considered, and she knew that she loved him. How could she not? But being his wife came with being a mother to his son, even with Janey in the picture, and she just didn't know if that would be fair to any of them. No matter how desperately she wanted it, she wasn't sure that she could be what Seth needed or even what Brodie needed. And yet, she couldn't seem to walk away from him, either, especially not after what he had just told her.

''You said you thought you knew what was going on with Janey now. Is she pretending, do you think, trying to hold on to you via some quirky spin on amnesia?''

He nodded. ''Yes, I think so. I don't have any proof, of

course, and until I get it, I can't really afford to do anything about the situation."

"You know," she said, thinking back, "one day I was upstairs, and I was so certain that I heard someone talking, someone having a conversation, in Janey's room, that I went in. Brown was there, and she said…I can't remember what she said now, but I felt terribly foolish at the time. Now, I have to wonder."

"So do I," Brodie said, getting to his feet. "In fact, I did the very same thing. Brown said it was the radio, but I wondered. I really did." He began to pace back and forth between the hearth and the couch. "Now that I think about it, that was the night I as much as told Janey that I was going to ask you to marry me. I thought for a moment that I'd gotten some response, then I decided I was mistaken."

Marry him. For a moment, Chey couldn't seem to catch her breath, but then she shook free of it and forced her mind to work. "Her awakening was pretty convenient, especially if Brown was there on the gallery, watching us kiss."

"What do you mean?"

"I didn't think much about it at the time," she told him, "but I distinctly recall glimpsing Brown watching from the upstairs gallery on the back of the house."

"Makes perfect sense," he said, sitting down again. "Janey had to be pretending to be in a coma, at least for a time, and then 'woke up' as soon as it became obvious I was getting serious about you."

"But why would she do that?" Chey asked. "Why pretend to be in a coma?"

"Because she knew that as soon as she was on her feet again, I'd move her out of the house. The only question is, when did she really wake up?"

"Brown must be very devoted to Janey to go along with something like this," Chey surmised.

"Absolutely. But it's more than mere devotion to Janey.

There's some connection with Brown and Harp, though I don't know what.''

"So it's a setup," Chey concluded, "a really heartless one, if you ask me.''

Brodie made a fist and smacked it into the opposite palm. ''Damn Janey! I was so worried that I'd done her harm with the move, because before she had seemed half-aroused, almost irritated, as if she might be gradually coming out of it. Then afterward she seemed deeply unconscious again. The doctors decided I had it all wrong, though. So I accepted that she had sunk back into deep coma, when all along she must have been waking up!''

"And the Shellys must have known it," Chey pointed out. "That's why they moved to New Orleans.''

He shot her an astute look. "You're absolutely right. He didn't so much as call to check on her before he turned up here. Brown must have alerted him that Janey was awake. They probably couldn't decide how best to handle things. Then when they thought I was about to step out of her reach for good by marrying you, they came up with this stupid amnesia thing.''

"But how can they hope to pull it off?" Chey argued. "Surely they realize that your patience will come to an end.''

"That's why Harp has brought in this Dr. Champlain," Brodie said. "He told me that he'd found a specialist he trusted to give us a prognosis on Janey. I'll bet you dollars to doughnuts that Champlain's going to give us all sorts of dire warnings about the consequences of disrupting her fiction.''

"Do they really think you'll agree to this pretense indefinitely?" Chey asked. "Even you have to have your limit.''

"Yes, and they know exactly what it is," Brodie said quietly. He slid his hands into his pants pockets. "Harp's already shown his trump card. They'll sue me for custody of Seth if I don't do what they want.''

That certainly rankled. Chey brought her hands to her hips. "But you have an agreement."

"Agreements are broken every day, sweetheart, and we have very little in writing. All she has to do is say that she's changed her mind, and you must admit she makes a very sympathetic picture."

"But is she physically able to take care of a child?" Chey asked.

"She will be," Brodie assured her, "and she has Brown to thank for it. No nurse was ever more devoted. She exercised and massaged Janey's muscles for hours on end every day. The doctors say that except for some weakness on her left side she'll eventually regain all of her strength and muscle control."

"But still, you are obviously the better parent."

"You're forgetting one thing," he told her. "I'm not Seth's natural father, and they won't hesitate to make it known, believe me."

That, of course, could be a huge problem. "So what are you going to do?" Chey wanted to know.

Brodie rubbed his chin, fingering his neat goatee consideringly. "Well, I'm going to fight, in court, if necessary, but I doubt it will come to that. They'll probably eventually settle out of court."

"For a huge sum of money," she surmised.

"Oh, I expect they'll want it all," he said almost casually, "everything I have or ever will have."

"You can't let that happen," she told him heatedly.

"I don't intend to," he said, snapping his fingers. "It just came to me, the perfect plan. They want me to pander to her fiction, so that's just what I'm going to do, but I'm throwing a spoiler into the mix. That is, if you'll help me."

"Me?" Chey cried in dismay. "Why me?"

"Because you are the threat," he pointed out reasonably. "As long as I have the hope of you, they have no hope of foisting this fiction on me. Don't you see? We can't let them believe they've driven you away. It was the threat of marriage to you that pushed them to show their hand to begin with. That same threat can still work. If you'll help me."

"How?"

"By pretending to love me and to want to marry me." He came to her then, placing both of his hands on her shoulders. "We'll have to pretend to be carrying on a thinly veiled affair right under their noses. Can you do that?"

She knew what her answer should be, what the safe answer was, but standing there looking up into his troubled blue eyes, she couldn't make herself take the safe path. "With very little effort," she admitted.

His hands tightened on her shoulders. "Will you?"

She sighed inwardly and closed her eyes. "You know I will."

He pulled her into his arms, tucking her head beneath his chin. "Thank you," he whispered. "Thank you."

"You would do the same for me," she muttered against his chest.

"Yes, but I love you," he answered softly.

She knew that he was hoping she might repeat those words to him, and they were poised on the tip of her tongue. All it would require was opening her mouth, but she couldn't do it because saying it would move pretense into the realm of reality, and she wasn't sure that she could do that even now.

After a moment he chuckled humorlessly and muttered, "Well, at least you're willing to help me keep my son. I'm grateful for that much."

She closed her hands in the fabric of his shirt at his sides and asked, "What do you want me to do?"

He set her back from him, his grin wide and cagey. "Move in with me."

Chapter Eleven

"It's really very simple," Brodie said to the group assembled in the scantily furnished family room, "we need to finish the house as quickly as possible as I'm expecting an important foreign delegation shortly, so we have decided, Chey and I, that she should move in here to oversee the completion of the work." He smiled at her, and she took up the explanation on cue.

"Often the flaws in design and execution are only recognized by those actually in residence," she began, hoping the lines did not sound as rehearsed as they were, "and while that's to be expected, it usually means returning repeatedly to make small corrections and follow-up. By living here, I'll be able to devote more attention to the details and, I hope, shorten completion time by weeks."

"Besides," Brodie said, holding out a hand to her, "she's such a pleasure to have around."

"My goodness," Chey simpered, slipping her hand into his.

He leaned close and kissed her lightly on the cheek. As if remembering himself, he released her again rather abruptly and cleared his throat.

"All right, then. Kate, I've already carried her suitcases upstairs to the room across from mine. If you'll just make the bed and leave some fresh towels, she'll be comfortably settled, I think."

"I'll take care of it right away," Kate said, getting up from a stiff-backed chair that had been carried in by her husband and hurrying away.

"Well, I think it's a fine idea," Viola said, tying Seth's shoe for the second time in as many minutes. How he managed to untie it repeatedly without using his hands while sitting relatively still on a small settee next to his great-grandmother was a mystery to Chey. He just seemed to move a tiny bit and the laces came undone again no matter how diligently Viola tied them. Chey couldn't help wondering if hook-and-loop fastenings wouldn't be better, not that it was any of her concern, of course.

Marcel leaned forward at the waist and spoke to Chey pointedly. "I must know what your favorite dishes are."

She laughed just because it was a so very *Marcel* thing to say and promised, "We'll talk later."

"I just don't see why it's necessary for her to move in here," Janey said petulantly. She wore a flowing pink gossamer dress and delicate sandals that seemed to interfere somewhat with her rather shambling gait whenever she left the wheelchair in which she now rested. Chey detected a faint droop in the muscles on one side of her face, but the petite strawberry blonde still managed to look radiant and ethereal. Brown, on the other hand, looked as if her stomach was cramping.

"We've explained why," Brodie said with excruciating patience. "To finish the house."

"But it's all going to have to be redone, anyway," Janey insisted, wrinkling her nose. "None of the colors are right, and everything's so old-fashioned."

Brodie rolled his eyes, pinched the bridge of his nose and said tautly, "We aren't redoing anything. It's perfect as it is."

"It's exquisite," Viola agreed, rising and shepherding Seth toward the door. "You've done a magnificent job, Chey dear. I hope you'll stay with us a long time. Now, if you'll excuse us, we are in need of a nap." With that she exited.

"Well, it's my house, too," Janey grumbled. "Don't I have any say about it?"

"You have enough to do just getting well," Brodie told her with clearly forced gaiety. "Speaking of which, Marcel is preparing a feast in celebration of your having the feeding port removed. No more liquid in a tube! That's a milestone worthy of celebration, don't you think? And as a member of the household, Chey will join us, of course."

Chey acknowledged this with a practiced smile, though in truth she did not relish sitting down to table with Janey and Brown. No more, apparently, than Janey, who whined, "Shouldn't it just be family?"

"Everyone in this house is family, Janey," Brodie told her lightly. "Besides, the more the merrier, I always say."

"In that case, I want my father and brother here, too," Janey insisted, and Brodie shrugged in unconcerned acceptance.

"I'll set two extra places at the table," Marcel said, rising.

"Make that three," Brodie said, and Chey assumed that the third was for her. "It'll be a double celebration," Brodie went on, "the removal of Janey's feeding tube and new additions to the household." Janey's face turned an unbecoming red, but she clamped her jaws shut and flashed a commanding look at Brown.

"I'll take you upstairs now for a rest," the burly nurse mumbled, and Janey nodded limply, suddenly the fragile beauty again.

"I'd like a word with you in private, Chey," Brodie said purposefully.

She nodded and followed him out of the room, aware of Brown and Janey following. At the foot of the stairs he halted, and pointedly waited as Brown pushed Janey's chair around the corner toward the elevator. Once the pair disappeared from sight, he slipped both arms around Chey and pulled her close.

"Are you sure this is wise?" Chey whispered, feeling watched.

"Essential," he murmured, and proceeded to kiss her with slow, hot deliberation. After he lifted his head again, he said a little too loudly, "If you want me, darling, you know where to find me."

The implication was obvious. Chey batted her eyelashes, trying not to let him see just how much she did want him while at the same time allowing others to do so. She stood gazing upward adoringly while Brodie climbed the stairs, then turned and strolled toward her makeshift office, pretending not to hear the sound of rubber tires whirring swiftly over hardwood floors. This was going to be even more difficult than she'd feared. Playing the part of Brodie Todd's not-very-clandestine lover felt achingly natural and was all too easy, and that alarmed her. The difficulty came in keeping fantasy and reality apart. That, she knew, would be a constant struggle, but it would be worth it if their ploy somehow caused the Shellys to tip their hand and give Brodie the proof he needed to destroy their scheme.

Chey sensed the tension in the dining room the instant she stepped through the door. The last to arrive, except for Kate and Marcel who would serve before taking their places, she hurried to the table, glancing around as Brodie eased her chair beneath her and took his place at the head, to her immediate right. The two chairs opposite her, on Brodie's right, were occupied by Janey and Brown, in that order. Then came Janey's dullard brother Dude and her father Harp, the latter literally radiating fury. The chair on Harp's right and that at the foot of the table were empty. Seth had been placed next to Chey, at her left, and beside him was Viola. The surprise, and the evident reason for the present consternation, sat next to Viola at the end of the table. A young man with rugged, chiseled features and a thick shock of dark blond hair waving back from his high, intelligent forehead, he was as pretty as he was fit, with bulging biceps and a body builder's chest.

"Chey, dear, I believe you know everyone but Nate Begay," Brodie said, indicating the stranger. "Nate, allow me to introduce Chey Simmons."

"How do you do?" she murmured with a perfunctory nod.

Nate Begay glanced uncertainly around the table, then leaned forward and said politely, "I've heard of you, Ms. Simmons. I worked with Jewel Chancery last year after her accident. I believe you did her house."

"Yes, I did," Chey replied with equal cordiality. "How is Jewel, by the way?"

"Quite well, I think," he answered smoothly.

"I'm glad to hear that." An avid horsewoman, Jewel had taken a bad spill and broken several bones, including vertebrae. She had languished in a coma for a time, then awakened to a difficult prognosis. Uncertain if she would ever walk again, let alone ride, she had apparently descended into a deep depression, emerging only gradually as her physical dexterity had returned. It was interesting that Nate Begay had worked with her. Chey glanced a question at Brodie.

He smiled and confirmed, "Nate is here to assist Janey with her recovery."

"And I was just reminding *my husband,*" Janey said tightly, sieving her sugary voice through her teeth, "that I already have a nurse."

"Oh, but Nate is specially skilled," Brodie argued lightly. "He has a wealth of experience in physical and coma therapies, as well as mental illness. He comes very highly recommended, and I'm confident that he'll soon have you fully recovered.''

''But what about Brown?'' Janey insisted plaintively.

''What about her?'' Brodie returned. ''No one's replacing Brown.''

''And what if I choose not to cooperate?'' Janey demanded, folding her arms beneath a shocking display of bosom.

''Then I'll have no choice but to send you to a special hospital where they can see to your recovery properly,'' Brodie returned mildly.

''You can't send her anywhere!'' Dude bawled, and Harp instantly clamped a hand down on his son's leg so tightly that the younger man winced.

Janey glanced at Harp, swallowed and said sweetly, ''He is my husband, Dude, and he loves me and will do what's best for me. Isn't that right, Brodie?''

''I will definitely do what it takes to make you well again,'' Brodie answered blandly. Kate entered the room just then through the butler's pantry, carrying two trays crowded with small bowls, one in each hand. Brodie shook out his linen napkin, saying, ''Now let's enjoy the fine meal that Marcel has prepared.''

Kate carried the trays to the table and placed one at each end before taking her seat near the foot. Brodie passed a bowl to Chey, who reached across Seth and handed it to Viola, who in turn passed it to Nate. Kate passed a bowl to Dude, who dug into it with his spoon. Harp reached over and snatched away the bowl, which he plunked down in front of Janey, reaching across Brown to do so. Dude, meanwhile, stabbed his loaded spoon into his mouth, made a face and yelled, ''What the hell *is* that?''

''Vichyssoise,'' Brodie answered calmly, a twitch of his lips betraying his amusement, ''potato soup, mild enough for your sister's delicate digestion, cold enough for summertime consumption.''

"I like *hot* potater soup," Dude grumbled, eying the second bowl Kate passed to him with open suspicion.

Harp reached over and snatched it away before Dude could sample this one, too. Plopping it down in front of Brown, he reached across Dude for another, growling, "If you don't like it, don't eat it."

Dude slapped his spoon down on the table and folded his arms. The rest of them ate in near silence. Even after Marcel entered with the main course, poached salmon and greens—which was, as always, sublime—no one seemed to have the heart for conversation, not even Brodie. It was doubly shocking then when Brown rose, immediately following the dessert service, and announced baldly to Janey, "I'll start moving your things now."

"Moving?" Brodie echoed, a spoonful of sherbet halting midway to his mouth. "What do you mean?"

"Oh, darling," Janey said brightly, beaming that angelic smile, "Brown's ruined the surprise. I'm ready to move back into our room now."

"You mean *my* room?" Brodie exclaimed.

"Well, of course, I mean the master bedroom," Janey said coyly. "I've so missed sleeping close to you."

Brodie actually laughed, the sound short and sharp. "Janey, we have never shared a bedroom, and we certainly aren't going to start now."

Janey darted a glance at her father, but her smile and tone remained sweet. "But we're married, a-and I miss you."

A muscle flexed in the hollow of Brodie's clamped jaw. "No," he said flatly.

"It must seem old-fashioned," Viola said, leaping into the conversational breach, "but I assure you that none of the better people actually share a bedroom. I suppose it's a matter of preference, but there are many who consider it quite common behavior, really. I certainly wouldn't want to share."

"Yeah," Seth put in seriously. "I don' want sharin', too."

Everyone laughed at that except Janey, who snapped, "Someone needs to teach him some manners!"

The levity died swiftly as Brodie leveled a warning look at Janey. "His manners are just fine for a three-year-old."

Janey immediately went saccharine again. "I only meant that he needs to learn to share."

"You wouldn't know what he needs," Brodie retorted, and behind her determined smile, Janey colored violently.

"I think we'll go up," Viola said smoothly, rising from her chair. "Seth needs a bath before bed."

Marcel, Nate and Brodie leapt to their feet, but the notion of standing in deference to an elderly lady never seemed to occur to the Shellys. Brodie rose and helped Viola remove Seth from his chair. Once he was free, Viola ushered the boy quickly toward the door.

"I'll be up to help in a few minutes," Brodie called.

"Chey-Chey come," Seth insisted.

Chey glanced at Brodie then at Janey, who was glaring at her from across the table.

"Uh, Ms. Chey has...something else to do," Brodie told the boy, but Chey shook her head and got up, glad for any excuse to escape the hostility directed toward her.

"No, it's all right. I'll be glad to give Viola a hand."

Seth waved happily at this news and allowed his great-grandmother to take him from the room.

"You don't have to do that," Brodie told her. "I'll go up as soon as I've had a private word with Nate."

Chey glanced at Janey, then said softly to Brodie, "I want to do it."

Brodie's eyes warmed significantly, and he took her hand in his. "Thank you. I promise it won't become a habit."

"Don't worry about that," she told him lightly, worried about it.

"Listen," he said, his voice pitched intimately low, "I

have a movie I think you'd enjoy. Join me for that later?''
Chey knew what her part was supposed to be and nodded.

"I would enjoy a movie," Janey purred.

"I want to talk to you, girl," Harp growled, putting an
end to that.

She frowned, then nodded in apparent resignation and
said, "Yes, Daddy."

"Come up when you can," Chey said lightly.

Brodie squeezed her hand, promising, "I'll join you
soon." Then he looked pointedly to Nate Begay. "If you
have a minute, Nate, I'd like to discuss Janey's treatment
with you now."

The other man nodded and rose. "Sure thing."

Chey thanked Marcel for the excellent meal and slipped
from the room. It had been a long, trying day, and she could
only wonder how many more she must endure before she
could return to her simple, solitary life. The larger puzzle
was why that thought didn't bring the comfort she expected.

Her bedroom door opened, and Chey glanced away from
the screen of the computer propped against her knees. Two
bright blue eyes peeped up at her from the edge of the high
tester bed upon which she rested. She squelched the urge
to reach out and ruffle the silky, bright red hair. More and
more often over the past few days, she'd been squelching
similar urges.

"Hasn't anyone ever told you that you should knock first
and wait to be invited inside?" she asked mildly.

The boy shook his head, wide-eyed. Then, at the sound
of footsteps in the hallway, he dropped down onto his belly
and slid under the bed. Chey's mouth fell open and an
unguarded chuckle tumbled out. Setting aside the laptop,
she rolled onto her side, grasped the canopy post with one
hand and leaned down to lift the crocheted bed skirt with
the other, peering beneath it. Seth lay with his hands

clapped over his mouth as if to prevent any unintentional sound.

"Come out from under there," she said. He shook his head. "Why not?"

Just then the door swung open again, and Chey jerked up in time to see Harp Shelly stick his head inside and glance around the room, demanding rudely, "Did that boy come in here?" *That boy,* not *my grandson* or *Seth,* but *that boy.*

Chey sat up and swung her legs over the side of the bed. "I would appreciate it if you'd knock before you open my door again," she said firmly.

Harp smirked and replied, "I'm lookin' for the kid," as if that were excuse enough. "I went in to tell him good-night, an' he said I stunk, jumped outta bed and run off. Someone needs to teach him some proper behavin'."

Chey had stood downwind of Harp on a couple of occasions now, and she could readily attest to the fact that the man did, indeed, smell unpleasantly of stale tobacco, sour alcohol and unwashed sweat. She had noticed, as well, that his breath could peel paint. She could not, however, implicitly condone the boy's behavior, but neither did she mean to turn him over to Harp Shelly.

She folded her arms and glared at the man, saying, "I suggest you leave that to someone who knows better than to barge into a private room without first knocking and being granted permission to enter."

"Whatsa matter? 'Fraid I'll catch you and my son-in-law playin' house?"

"Ex-son-in-law," she corrected firmly, not bothering to deny the accusation.

Harp Shelly narrowed his eyes and growled, "Ain't you got no shame?"

"More than you. Now get out of my room."

He glared, stepped back through the door and yanked it closed behind him. She waited until the count of ten, then bent and lifted the bed skirt again. "You can come out now. He's gone."

After a moment, Seth dragged himself out from under the bed and got to his feet. With a sigh, Chey sat down on the edge of the bed. Uninvited, he crawled up beside her with much pulling and sliding of the covers. She lifted a censorial eyebrow. "It is not polite to tell people they smell bad, even if they do."

He wrinkled his nose and bowed his head, mumbling, "Don't like Grumpa."

"All the more reason to be polite," Chey told him. "It's all right not to like someone, Seth. It's not all right to hurt them and say bad things to them or about them. Do you understand?" He turned up huge, guileless eyes and nodded solemnly. "In that case," she decided, "I won't have to tell your father about any of this." Seth immediately brightened, so she judiciously added a caveat. "But if it happens again, your father will be instantly informed. Is that clear?"

He nodded again and clambered up onto his knees to wind his arms about her neck and squeeze hard. She laughed and hugged him back. Only as he was sliding out of her embrace did it occur to her that she had just done a very mommylike thing. She had offered guidance and safety and comfort and affection to a child about whom she cared a great deal, without even thinking about it. She closed her eyes, ambivalence and affection shivering through her, then quickly set him on his feet.

They moved to the bedroom door. Chey opened it slightly, looked both ways and tiptoed out into the hall, Seth's small hand clasped firmly in hers. He giggled, thinking it an elaborate game and crept along exaggeratedly behind her. They had just reached the nursery door when another opened elsewhere and voices, though lowered, could be clearly heard.

"I still think this is a mistake."

"Look, the longer I'm in that chair the longer Begay will be around."

Recognizing the voices of Brown and Janey, Chey quickly hustled Seth through the door into the nursery, motioning him to silence. He looked up at her curiously while she listened at the crack in the door. She'd lost part of the conversation but quickly picked up on the rest.

"...stay vulnerable. Harp says you can't get well too quick."

"I don't care what Daddy says," Janey snapped. "Begay is too much of a threat, and the only way to get rid of him is for me to get well."

They seemed to stop just past the door, and the next voice was Brown's. "That may be so, but it don't get rid of that Simmons hussy, and until we can find a way to do that, you got to stay sick."

"Oh, it's hopeless, Brown," Janey moaned. "He's in love with her!"

"Don't you say that!" Brown ordered sharply. "You just stay the course, young lady, or Harp will know why, and you know how he gets."

"*I* know better than anyone," Janey hissed, "and you're not my stepmother yet, so don't try to tell me what to do!" With that she flounced off, her footsteps just slightly uneven as she moved down the hall. Brown heaved a sigh and clumped after her, muttering under her breath.

So Brodie was right. Harp was masterminding this whole amnesia ploy, and Brown was helping him, apparently believing he'd marry her, silly woman. Their plan, hers and Brodie's, was definitely beginning to show results. Chey put her back to the door, folding her arms in satisfaction. Only then did she look down and recall that Seth was standing there. He curved his mouth into a big smile and said, "I real quiet."

Smiling, she leaned forward and cupped his face in both her hands. "Yes, you were," she praised. "Thank you very much. Now let's find your great-grandmother to tuck you back into bed. I need to talk to your father."

* * *

She laid her head back against the side of the pool and lifted her hips, allowing her body to float atop the cool water. Brodie had decided it was time to step up the program. Beside her, he peered over the edge of the pool and murmured, "Here she comes." Janey had been moving freely for several days now, resorting to the wheelchair only after a strenuous physical therapy session or whenever she thought it might garner her some sympathy.

Moving back from the edge of the pool, Brodie hooked an arm about Chey's waist and pulled her against him. Aware of a building charge of electricity between them, Chey allowed her feet to sink and lifted her arms around his neck. Brodie grinned, arched a wicked eyebrow, and laid his mouth across hers, his hands smoothing over her back. She moaned as her breasts flattened against his sleek, muscular chest, and his tongue slid into her mouth.

Despite the fact that this was for show, her heart was slamming inside her chest, and her head had started a slow, disorienting spin. He was equally moved, she knew. The evidence rode against her abdomen, hard and long and thick. Everything else gradually faded away, and she hooked a leg around his, craving the heat and weight of him. Dimly, in some part of her mind, she was aware of a grating sound in the distance, but she had forgotten about Janey and the little scene they were staging for her. All she could think about was the man kissing her as if he never meant to let her go.

She didn't recognize the vague clicking noise as heels on cement until those same shoes came to a sliding, hissing halt. Suddenly aware of an audience, Chey felt herself beginning to pull back, but that was precisely when Brodie deepened the kiss, cupping her bottom beneath the water and pulling her hard against him. His palm slid along her thigh, encouraging her to twine a second leg around him. Allowing him and the water to take her weight, she pressed her most private, needy part against the hot ridge throbbing between them and completely forgot about Janey—until

Brodie turned his head slightly, his mouth still pressed to hers, and made a sound of satisfaction deep in his throat.

Memory slid back, and Chey opened her eyes, whispering against his mouth, "Is she gone?"

"Mmm-hmm."

"Did she see us?"

"Mmm."

"We can stop then?"

"Um-um."

He once more deepened the kiss, plundering with exquisite finesse and attention to detail. The lapping water buffeted their bodies, creating delightful frictions and maddening pressures until she was breathless and mindless and desperate. She remembered in lush detail every moment of the night they'd made love, increments of sensation and completion flashing over her, the frightening intensity of satisfaction that so temptingly beckoned her now. When he turned her and carried her two long, heavy steps to the side of the pool, she wrapped herself tighter about him, answering every manipulation of his mouth with an equally fervent one of her own.

He held her there against the side of the pool with the weight of his body and the force of his mouth, his hands roaming where they would. She realized how easy, how wonderful, it would be to make love here in the pool, and her own hands wandered below the surface of the water. It was then that a small voice quite close to her ear calmly said, "Daddy, I whim wif woo?"

Chey knocked both elbows painfully against the edge of the pool even as Brodie jerked away. Widening his eyes at his son, he demanded, "Seth, what are you doing out here? You know you aren't supposed to come inside the gate without an adult."

"Mommy open it," Seth said plaintively.

"Your mother brought you out here?" Brodie asked skeptically. If so, Chey thought, it would be the first time to her knowledge that Janey had given the child the time of day. Seth shrugged in answer to his father's question, and Brodie lifted a censorial brow. "You followed her out here secretly, didn't you?"

Seth shrugged again, then looked at Chey, lifted a finger and pressed it to his lips. Chey disciplined a smile. Obviously the tyke understood more about eavesdropping on his mother than she had assumed. She cleared her throat. Just then another voice lifted.

"Seth! Get away from there! How did you get inside the gate?"

Brodie stepped aside so Viola could see him. "It's all right, Grandmama."

"Oh, Brodie. He scared the fool out of me. I went in to check on him and his bed was empty."

"He followed his mother out here," Brodie told her. "I'll have a talk with her about it. Meanwhile, I'm having a lock put on that gate. But first, I'm going to take Seth upstairs and have a stern conversation with him."

"Da-a-ddy," Seth whined. "I wanna whim!"

"Seth, you disobeyed the rules," Brodie told him calmly. "You know that you aren't supposed to be anywhere near the pool without permission."

"Chey-Chey?" A little hand snaked around her neck, and she gave him a look that let him know he'd be getting no support—but no scolding—from that quarter. At his downcast look, she twisted around, placed her palms on the edge of the pool and propelled herself upward.

"Come on," she said to the boy, reaching for a towel. "I'll go back to the house with you. Okay?" The fact that she was escaping Brodie and the possibility of picking up where they'd left off provided strong incentive, now that her blood had cooled somewhat.

Seth nodded and reached for her hand, blinking against the small shower of water that sluiced from her body. Behind her, Brodie began wading toward the steps. Seth's little hand clasped Chey's as they walked toward the house.

Inside, she was quaking, knowing how very close she had come to surrendering her body to Brodie a second time. Now all she had to worry about was surrendering her heart to his son.

Chapter Twelve

Chey knew the moment that she opened the door that she wasn't alone. Her gaze swept the room and came to rest on the figure standing before the window. She wondered why she was surprised and reflected wryly that the pool gate was not the only portal in this place that needed a lock. Steadying the towel that she'd wrapped around her head, she stepped into the room and closed the door.

"You Shellys have a real problem with privacy issues."

Janey turned awkwardly, a pitying smile curving her mouth. She sighed and reached for the bedpost, leaning dramatically against it, her wispy chiffon skirts floating about her. "I'm not a Shelly," she said. "I'm a Todd, Mrs. Brodie Todd. I understand, of course, why you'd like to forget that. You want my husband for yourself. And I understand that, too."

"Do you?" Chey said with some surprise. "How magnanimous of you."

"Brodie's a very attractive man," Janey went on, her

voice all that was reasonable and calm. "Any woman would want him, but not just any woman would go after him. Don't you feel bad that you're breaking up my marriage and destroying my family?"

Chey felt chilled in the air-conditioned room, her wet swimsuit beginning to cling uncomfortably to her drying skin, but Janey's pretense sent her blood pressure straight through the top of her head. "What family?" she snapped. "The issue of your 'marriage' aside, you hardly seem to know your son exists."

Janey turned away, arms folded, and limped back to the window seat. "You're right. I-I don't really know my son. He was an infant before the accident, after all."

"That's no reason to ignore him now."

Janey whirled. "You don't understand how much things have changed! I'm doing the best I can. If you would just get out of my way, I could have it all back!"

"If you think that," Chey told her dryly, "then you really are delusional."

Janey lifted her pert chin to a mulish angle. "Stay away from Brodie," she ordered, the veneer of reason and supplication stripped away. "He's mine."

Chey tilted her head. "We both know that isn't so."

Suddenly, Janey's pretty face crumpled, and she collapsed against the corner of the bed, sobbing as if her heart was broken. She was good, very good. If all else failed, Chey mused silently, the woman could always go on the stage. Folding her arms, Chey waited for the melodrama to end, shivering a little inside her wet suit. She didn't have to wait long.

Janey lifted eyes starred with wet lashes, the very picture of a broken-hearted angel. "All I want," she wept, "is a chance to win my husband back!"

Chey sighed and decided to be blunt. "In that case," she said, "you ought to reconsider your tactics. The pretense does no one any good, least of all you."

Janey jerked her head up, all stiffened effrontery. "I don't know what you could mean."

"Oh, come on. You seem to forget that Brodie knows the truth."

"Whatever are you suggesting?" Janey demanded, grasping at the bodice of her dress.

Chey rolled her eyes, at the end of her patience. The last thing she needed was a Janey Shelly rendition of Camille. "Fine. Now if you don't mind, I'd like to change."

Recovering instantly, Janey bounced up and screamed, "I want you out of my house!"

"Your house?" Chey repeated skeptically.

Suddenly, the facade slipped away. In an instant, Janey looked older, more tired, desperate. "I can't let you ruin this," she muttered in a low voice.

"There is nothing to ruin, Janey," Chey told her. "That's the whole point."

"You're just after his money," Janey accused, stumbling toward the door.

"That's not true."

"Then what is it?" Janey demanded, throwing up one arm. "Why not go after some other man? Why does it have to be Brodie?"

Chey blinked at her. Then she tilted her head, studying the other woman. What she saw astounded her. "You really don't know, do you? No matter what you said before, you don't have any idea what it is that sets Brodie apart."

"You mean, besides his bank account?" Janey sneered.

Chey shook her head, amazed at the shallowness. "Yes, he's successful, and, yes, I admire that about him, but it goes far deeper than that. Brodie is a strong, confident, accomplished man who squeezes every moment of joy from life, and not only does he lives up to his responsibilities, he goes beyond them because he *cares*. I love that about him," she said, realizing that it was true.

"But he loves me," Janey insisted. "He has to!"

"How can he," Chey asked, "when all you see when

you look at him is dollar signs?" *And all I've seen is the responsibility that comes with him,* she added silently. "My God," she went on, talking as much to herself now as to Janey. "There is so much to love about this man that it boggles the mind. The pride he takes in this old house, the way he laughs when he drives his car too fast with the top down and the vain attention he pays to his appearance and the way he goes after what he wants. How could I not love him?"

"But he's not yours," Janey whined.

That much was true, and Chey had never been so aware of it as now, but he wasn't Janey's either, and Chey would not stand aside and let this predatory creature get her hooks into him again, so she cocked her head and played her part, saying, "Not yet."

"I'm warning you," Janey snarled, all pretense gone now. "Get out of my way!"

"Not on your life," Chey told her.

"Then let it be on yours," Janey snapped, lurching toward the door and then through it.

Chey stood for a moment, alone and shivering, then she calmly walked over and closed the door. Her every doubt about Janey had now been confirmed. Despite the angelic looks, the woman was incapable of love. What Janey felt for Brodie was more akin to greed than anything else, and he deserved better than that, much better. If only, Chey brooded, she could be what he—and his son—needed, she really would give Janey a run for the money.

"Did Janey actually threaten you?" Brodie asked, his hands enfolding both of hers atop the breakfast table. They were alone in the room, but he craved the feel of her, and as he'd reminded her, one never knew who might waltz in and get the appropriate eyeful. Chey shook her head, but he couldn't help feeling that she wasn't telling him everything.

"She just blustered and accused me of being after your money."

"She would think that," he said wryly.

Chey looked down at their entwined hands and whispered, "The thing is, I think she's cracking."

"She's not the only one," Brodie murmured, pitching his voice low. "My attorney has paid a visit to this doctor of Harp's."

He nodded at her look of question. "It seems there was a 'misunderstanding' about the good doctor's prognosis. My attorney is having the 'correct' prognosis put in writing. It falls short of an outright admission, but it means we can stop indulging this fiction of Janey's."

Chey looked down again and then quite softly said, "Does that mean you're ready to call their bluff?"

"No, not yet. We need more, real proof of some kind."

"And more time to find it," she said, melancholy softening her voice.

He tightened his hands around hers, panic slicing through him. "You aren't giving up, are you? You're not leaving?"

She shot him an unreadable look from beneath the fringe of her lashes and shook her head. Relief shimmered through him, and he gave in to the impulse to kiss the top of her head. "Thank you, sweetheart."

"It shouldn't be long now, though," she said, sounding almost morose.

"You're probably right," he conceded quietly, praying that it wasn't so. He wasn't ready to give up this closeness. On the other hand, Harp could be ruthless, and Brodie was in no way willing to gamble with her safety. "I don't want you to worry," he told her. "I'll look out for you, and so will Nate."

She looked up at that. "Why do I wonder if Nate's really a nurse?"

"Oh, he is," Brodie assured her, "a very experienced nurse, but before he changed careers, he was a cop."

She stared, then rolled her eyes. "And just how did you come across him?"

"He was recommended to me by a certain physician of my acquaintance. It seems that Nate has been instrumental in blowing the lid off several bogus medical malpractice suits, as well as tracking down a hospital drug thief. I have him watching Brown, you know."

Her eyes widened appreciatively. "That's a good idea. You'll let me know what he finds out?"

"Of course. You must be in a hurry for this to be over," he said carefully.

She looked away. "Not really."

He smiled and cupped her cheek, turning her face back to his. "I'll never be able to thank you enough for all that you're doing. I know how difficult it must be for you."

He kissed her gently then, wondering how much longer he could get away with such behavior. As badly as he wanted her to be a permanent part of his life, as readily as she accepted his touch and came into his arms, as willing as she seemed to be to help with Seth and as accepting of the boy's affection as she was, Brodie knew that she remained deeply conflicted. The worst part was that he could do nothing about it, for as much as he loved Chey, his relationship with his son was the one nonnegotiable part of his life. And yet without Chey, he might as well be alone.

Chey plumped her pillow, then settled down into it, reaching for the bedside lamp. Before her hand closed around the short, dangling chain, however, a tapping at her door alerted her to a visitor, obviously not one of the Shellys. She dropped her hand and pulled the covers up to her shoulders, calling out, "Yes?"

Brodie's muffled voice came through the door. "It's me, honey."

It was the first time he had come to her room since she'd moved in, for despite the scenes they'd been staging for benefit of the Shellys, they had maintained a certain distance in private. Knowing that something momentous had brought him here now, she immediately pushed up onto one elbow. "Come in."

He opened the door and slipped inside. "You have to hear this," he said, holding up a tiny tape recorder. He walked over to the bed and sat down, placing the box on the bedside table next to her recharging cell phone. "Nate followed Brown to a meeting with Harp and recorded their conversation. The whole thing is pretty incriminating, but this is the part that concerns me most." He started the tape. Harp's voice, though muted and fuzzy, came through clearly.

"Stupid bitch."

"He's talking about Janey," Brodie put in quickly.

"It's all her fault. She was supposed to get knocked up by Brodie himself, but no, she couldn't even manage to get him in bed. If I hadn't been there to tell her to go after the brother, she'd have walked away without a dime!"

"She's doing the best she can," Brown whined.

"What use is that face and body if she's not smart enough to use them?" Harp snapped.

"She's been sick," Brown argued pleadingly.

"Better than two damned years she's cost us!" he ranted. *"I can't marry the man myself, damn it! And she had him! She had him, and she let him go for a puny million!"*

"She's trying to make up for that!"

"She damned well better," Harp growled. *"I'm tired of living hand-to-mouth."*

"We should've took the million and looked for another mark," Brown opined.

"A million don't go far divided up," Harp insisted, *"and single millionaires don't exactly grow on trees. She's too gimpy now to land another sucker, so she damned well better get her hand back in the pocket of this one!"*

"The problem is that Simmons woman," Brown muttered.

"Yeah," Harp agreed. *"We're gonna have to get her out of the way. There has to be something we can use against her, something to make her dump Brodie or vice versa. Maybe she's padded her bills. I'll have Dude look into it."*

"And if that doesn't work?" Brown asked timidly.

Chey could hear the smile in Harp's voice, feel the smugness of it. *"Maybe she'll get into a coma, just like that stupid Janey did,"* he said.

Chey caught her breath as Brodie stopped the recording. "Oh, Brodie, you don't think he had something to do with Janey's accident, do you?"

Brodie tilted his head. "He was the one to find her, and there can be little doubt that he was angry with her about the divorce and the settlement. I'm more concerned with you, however."

"You don't really think he'd try to *hurt* me?"

"He'll try to discredit you first," Brodie said, "but I'm not taking any chances. I don't want you wandering off alone. From here on out, either Nate or I will be keeping a close eye on you. Frankly, I'd rather not let you out of my sight. Meanwhile, we need someone watching your shop, too."

"You think they'll try to break into the shop?"

"It's the logical choice if they're going to get a look at your invoices."

Chey glanced at her cell phone on the bedside table and nodded. "I'll call Georges and have him move into my place temporarily."

"I hope he won't mind," Brodie said, and she chuckled.

"He'll love it. He's coveted my place ever since I bought the building, and believe it or not, even he relishes the hero role once in awhile."

"But do you think he could actually catch someone breaking into the shop?" Brodie asked skeptically.

"Oh, yes. There's a silent alarm set off by a motion detector inside the shop. When activated it calls the police and turns on the television upstairs."

"That's brilliant! The burglar wouldn't know anyone was on to him. He'd just think someone couldn't sleep and turned on the TV."

"One of my nephews set it up," she told him proudly.

"Yet another Simmons prodigy," he quipped. Then he lifted a hand and smoothed it down her bare arm, adding silkily, "Now we only have to worry about you. I meant it when I said I didn't want you out of my sight until this is over."

Awareness spiked through her. She had to swallow in order to ask, "Do you really think that's necessary?"

"It is for my peace of mind," he told her, stroking her arm again. The nightshirt she wore couldn't be called alluring, but it was short and sleeveless and made of a single layer of thin, tropical-weight cotton, and just Brodie's nearness was enough to put her nerve endings on sensual alert, so when he brushed a strand of hair from her shoulder, she shivered. "Cold?" he asked softly.

"No."

"You know what all this means, don't you?" he asked, stroking her again. "We're one giant step closer to ending this nightmare." He looked down, his gaze moving to the buttoned placket of her collared nightshirt. "I should be glad."

She swallowed again. "But you're not?"

He looked deeply into her eyes then and said, "I'd keep Janey here if it meant keeping you, too."

"Brodie," she began, but what could she say, really? She couldn't stay here forever, unless... She closed her eyes against a fresh wave of longing. Could she be all that he—and Seth—needed her to be?

He put his forehead to hers and whispered, "I want to climb into this bed and make love with you."

It was exactly what she wanted too, and she was so very tired of fighting herself and him and the situation. "Brodie," she said again, lifting her mouth tentatively to his.

He cupped her face with both his hands and kissed her

with studied gentleness, passion tightly leashed. She knew she was going to set that passion free. It was doubtless a mistake to give in to this, but it was a mistake she would make without regret. She slid her arms around him and lay back against the pillow. Brodie lifted his head and took a deep breath, nostrils flaring.

"Tell me to stay," he whispered.

"Stay," she said simply, every impulse she might have had to refuse him gone like a puff of smoke in a stiff breeze. One corner of her mouth kicked up in a wry smile.

His smile mirrored hers, then he lowered his head again. The kiss he pressed on her this time was a hot, open-mouthed joining that melted her bones and set fire to her blood. When he sat up to pull his shirt over his head, she slid her hands over his sleek torso in carnal appreciation. He closed his eyes, sucking in his breath, then sighing it out again before beginning to unbutton her nightshirt. He watched his hands at work. She watched his face, her breath pumping deep and slow. When he reached the bed covers he lifted his hips from the bed and swept the covers back. Chey reached for the chain on the bedside lamp, but he quickly intercepted her hand and placed it once more upon the cool sheet.

"Last time, in the dark," he said, going back to her buttons, "it was like a dream, a fantasy. I want it real this time." He locked gazes with her. His irises were wide bands of blue against the black centers. Then he swept back the sides of her nightshirt and dropped his gaze. "Beautiful," he said, spreading his hands at her waist and sliding them upward to cup her breasts.

Her breath seized. The weight and heat of his hands enveloped her as he began to massage. Her eyes rolled shut as sensation wheeled through her body, her breasts growing larger, fuller, more sensitive. She felt as pliant as heated wax by the time he lifted her into a sitting position and pushed the nightshirt from her shoulders and down her arms. Tugging it from beneath her, he tossed it away. She seldom wore panties to bed, especially in the summer, so she lay back before him naked, lifting her long hair from her nape with her hands to spread it across the pillow.

"Incredible," he said, sweeping her with his gaze. Rising to his feet, he stepped out of his shoes and began stripping away his slacks. The length and strength of his arousal had her pushing up onto her elbows again. "Need I say how much I want you?" he asked, sinking back down onto the bed.

Suddenly he lifted a finger as if something forgotten had just occurred. Then he bent and fished a small article from his clothing, placing it on the pillow next to her. She slid a glance at the tiny foil packet and let a smile tweak her lips.

Leaning forward with a hand braced on either side of her, he confessed, "I've been carrying that for weeks."

"Let's put it to good use," she whispered boldly, sliding her arms about him.

He chuckled against her mouth. "Oh, I love an eager woman."

He slid his hands into her hair and covered her mouth with his, easing his weight down on top of her. It felt so right, lying there together, skin to skin, mouths locked. She moved her legs apart, cradling him between her thighs. The heaviness and heat of him where he nestled against her excited her senses, and she moved urgently beneath him, murmuring, "I think I'd like you to hurry."

Pushing up on one arm, he reached for the packet with the other. "I think I'd better, this first time."

She watched him tear into the packet with his teeth, and suddenly she felt like laughing, a strange new joy and lightness filling her. "I take it there are more where that came from?"

"I live in hope," he quipped. She chortled, and he began trying to sheath himself with one hand, quickly losing patience. "Help me with this, will you?"

She did, and within moments he pushed up into her.

Joined, they lay like that for several moments, hearts beating in double time even as a wave of contentment took them. Then Chey felt him pulse inside her. She bent her knees and pressed her feet flat onto the bed, wanting more of that. He didn't stint. Groaning, he pushed again and again, and then she was pushing, too. Time and place spun away. Shortly, she spun after them. When they all came back together again, he was pulling out of her.

"No, don't," she mumbled, still craving the contact.

"I have to, sweetheart," he said, gasping a little. Rolling to her side, he gathered her close. "I'd love to stay inside you and grow hard again, but the condom makes that problematic."

She snuggled against him, murmuring, "Maybe I'll talk to my doctor about the pill."

He went very still, and so did she, realizing suddenly what she'd said, intimated. Well, why not? She hadn't made him any promises, but she wasn't stupid enough to think that she could so easily pull back from him a second time. Besides, he'd said that he meant to keep a very close watch on her, and she felt that was probably a good idea but couldn't imagine actually managing it without giving in to this again. He readjusted their positions, bringing his face close to hers. Stroking her cheek for a long time, he studied her eyes. Then he kissed her, softly, lingeringly, before getting up and going into the bathroom. She pulled up the covers while he was gone, relatively chilled without the heat of his skin against hers. When he returned he slid down beneath the covers with her and pulled her against him.

Stroking her back languidly, he cradled her head in the hollow of his shoulder and said softly, "I can't always be content with just this."

She sighed. "I know."

"But just now," he said, smoothing her hair, "you've made me very happy."

She tilted her head back. "That's the thing about you,"

she said appreciatively. "You know how to enjoy every moment."

He hummed in response to that and slid a little lower. "Let me show you how it's done," he said, wagging a brow suggestively. When his head disappeared beneath the covers, she gasped. She did a lot of gasping after that, and a little happiness in the moment was the least of what he showed her then.

He woke to the dim light of dawn with Chey at his side, her rump shoved against the hollow of his back. She'd commandeered fully three-quarters of the bed, which was not nearly so wide as his own. If he turned the wrong way, he'd find himself on the floor. Easing over onto his back, he stretched out a cramped arm, brushing the silky top of her head as he did so. She murmured and straightened, pushing farther up onto her pillow and expelling a deep, sighing breath. Muttering the word "hot," she shoved at the covers, neatly exposing one luscious breast for his attention. He smiled, despite the suddenly painful throbbing of his morning erection, and rolled onto his side, propping his head on one folded arm. Using the pads of his fingertips, he lightly stroked that plump, creamy breast until her nipple peaked. Her eyelids slitted open, then she reached for him with both languid arms, purring deep in her throat, but just before their mouths met, her eyelids flew wide and she gasped, shoving him away.

"It's daylight! You can't be here. Someone will see!"

Sighing, he settled down onto the corner of the pillow. "Chey, I'm through pandering to Janey's fiction."

"But your grandmother—"

"Wouldn't blink an eye," he assured her.

"Maybe not, but there are other people in this house, including your son!"

"We're not exactly making it on the couch in the family room," he muttered.

"There isn't even a lock on the door," she hissed.

He sighed. "Okay, even in this big house, it would, admittedly, be more private in my room. So tomorrow night we'll sleep there."

She sat straight up in bed. "I can't do that!"

Anger flashed through him. He tossed back the covers and got up, snapping, "Too much commitment for you?"

"You know I'm not into casual affairs. It's just—"

"Casual?" he interrupted sharply. "You're calling this a *casual* affair?"

"No! I'm calling it what it is, less than you want."

"And more than you want!" he accused, stung.

"No!" She stared at him, anguish pulsing in her eyes. "I don't know," she admitted weakly.

"What do you want from me?" he demanded, snatching up his pants. "Do you want me to give up my son, is that what you want?"

"You know I would never ask that of you!"

He did, but he'd been unprepared for the sharpness of the pain he'd felt at her rejection this morning. How could she do this again? Had last night meant nothing? "I thought we reached some sort of understanding last night. You know I love you. You know I want you. Then morning comes, and you throw me out of your bed again!" He leaned toward her, hands braced against the mattress and demanded sharply, "What the hell is the matter with you?"

"I-I'm just so afraid of disappointing you," she whispered, eyes filling.

His anger melted instantly. Plopping down, he cupped her face in both hands. "I love you," he said firmly. "I haven't said that to a woman since I was eighteen years old."

"Oh, Brodie," she said, "if only you knew how much…"

Someone knocked on the door.

"Chey?"

Her gaze flew to the door. "Viola!" Chey gasped, as if Brodie wouldn't recognize his grandmother's voice.

Calmly, he stood, crossed to the door and opened it. "What is it, Grandmama?"

"Oh," she said, "it's you. I woke early and was headed downstairs for a cup of tea when I heard arguing." Wrapped in a silk robe the color of new grass, Viola craned her neck to get a look past the narrow opening of the door.

"I'm sorry if we disturbed you," Brodie said blandly.

"Think nothing of it, dear," Viola replied. "Would you like anything since I'm going down anyway?"

Brodie looked a question at Chey, arching an eyebrow with I-told-you-so finesse. "No, thank you," Chey said weakly, buried to her nose in bedcovers, as her muffled voice attested.

"I'll leave you then," Viola said. "Sorry to intrude."

"No problem," Brodie said, closing the door. Smugly, he turned back to the bed. "Did she sound scandalized or offended to you?"

Mouth flattening, Chey folded her arms atop the covers. "No."

"No," he affirmed, "but you still think I should leave, don't you?" Chey sighed, and he closed his eyes in defeat. "Fine."

As he turned away again, she flipped back the covers and said urgently, "Come back to bed." He stopped where he was, relief shimmering through him. Then he slid beneath the covers, half-clothed, and gathered her close. "This is all so new to me," she said, wrapping her arms around him. "I'm not ashamed of loving you, but in my family this kind of thing isn't well accepted."

"I know," he said, "and I want to fix that—if you'll let me."

She sighed. "I take it that it's a permanent fix?"

"Permanent and licensed," he confirmed softly, "but we can talk about that when this is all over."

She laid her head against his chest, and after a moment she asked, "Do you think I would make a good mother for Seth?"

He smiled to himself and kissed the top of her head. "Yes. Absolutely."

"Would I have to give up my business to do that, do you think?"

"No! Of course you wouldn't. Why should you?"

"What if I can't give him the attention he needs?"

"Honey, Grandmama and I are here, you know. Does Seth seemed neglected to you now?" She shook her head. "Well, then?"

She said nothing for a long while, then she whispered, "He is a really special little boy, isn't he?"

Brodie closed his eyes, a contented, triumphant kind of elation pouring through him. "He's as special as you are," he told her softly. *And you're both mine now,* he said to himself, not daring to think that it might not be that simple.

Chapter Thirteen

An annoying chirp very near his ear pulled Brodie from the depths of peaceful exhaustion. Next to him, Chey moaned and moved restlessly. Groggily, he groped for the light, found a chain and yanked. Levering up onto one elbow, he glanced around him at Chey's familiar room and smiled with replete satisfaction even as he reached for the tweeting cell phone on the bedside table. Studying the tiny buttons for a moment, he picked out the one he wanted and punched it, lifting the little phone to his head.

"Hello?"

An instant of silence made him think he'd caught the call too late. Then a familiar voice drawled, "Brodie?"

Hoping not to disturb Chey, he sat up, bending his knees and balancing his elbows atop them. "Georges?" He yawned. "What's going on?"

"Quite a lot, actually," Georges replied with enough delight to allay Brodie's worst fears. "I'm here at the shop with the police and an idiotic little weasel whom I take to be your ex-brother-in-law.''

Brodie grinned. ''Bingo.''

''Yes, quite,'' Georges went on. ''He isn't saying much yet, our weasel, but we caught him rifling the desk in Chey's office, his pockets stuffed with petty cash and computer diskettes. The police are taking him down to central booking, but they want Chey to come and file formal charges. I take it she is there?''

Brodie glanced at Chey, who was, even then, pushing hair out of her eyes. She looked as well used and utterly satisfied as he felt. Brodie grinned wolfishly and gave her a thumbs-up.

''Yes, she's here,'' he said blithely. ''We'll meet you at the central police station in twenty minutes.''

''Oh, not me,'' Georges refused smoothly. ''I've had all the fun I can stand for one evening, thank you. I'm just going to tidy up here and get back to bed.''

''Very well. Oh, and thank you, Georges. I owe you one.''

''And don't you forget it,'' Georges simpered.

Chuckling, Brodie disconnected, then heaved a huge sigh of satisfaction. Finally. All over but the shouting now, he was sure, and he frankly couldn't wait. What a glorious future he and Chey were going to have!

Thumping Chey on the hip, he exclaimed exuberantly, ''Up , you luscious woman. We've caught ourselves a weasel!''

The glare she sent him could have peeled paint, but he laughed and hopped out of bed.

His time estimate turned out to be rather optimistic, however. First, he had to give Chey a word-for-word recounting of his conversation with Georges, even though she'd been privy to fully half of it. Then she shocked him by complaining that he shouldn't have answered her phone.

''What do you mean, I shouldn't have answered your phone?''

"That could've been my mother," she pointed out dully.

"Well, excuse the hell out of me," he grumbled. "It was on my side of the bed. I didn't think."

"Now Georges knows we're sleeping together," she muttered, padding naked to her closet to pull down jeans and a polo shirt.

He allowed himself to enjoy the view as he slid into his chinos, which he had left crumpled at the side of the bed. "Surely you don't think Georges cares?"

"That's not the point," she said, pulling on her jeans. "I might as well paint a banner and hang it over the front door now."

"So your concern is that he'll gossip to your family?" Brodie said, genuinely wanting to understand the problem.

She turned her back to him as she busily put on her bra, an exercise he found ludicrous considering that she had started out naked. "Not exactly."

"Then what is it?" he wanted to know, stabbing his bare feet into his loafers.

She pulled the shirt over her head and turned to face him. "Look, I'm sorry I brought it up. Can we just go?"

"I have to let Grandmama know we're leaving," he muttered, realizing that it was so.

He left to do that while Chey was brushing out her hair and searching for her shoes. By the time he woke Viola, explained where they were going and why, the twenty minutes had already elapsed. Then, on a hunch, he went quickly to his office, opened the safe there, and removed a certain item, which he slid into his pants pocket. After that, he returned to Chey's room, only to find it vacant. He hurried downstairs and found her waiting at the front door with her handbag and keys.

"I'll drive," she said. "My car's already out front."

"Fine."

It was going on forty minutes by the time they pulled into the municipal parking lot. Ten minutes after that they finally found the right person to report to and began the necessary paperwork. Half an hour after the paperwork was filed, a uniformed policeman came to speak to them.

"We don't have an identification yet," he said to Chey after describing what they had found when they'd entered the shop. "Your assistant seems to think you know the man, however."

"I expect so," Chey replied.

"I'm quite sure we do," Brodie added.

"Well, let's find out," the policeman said, and led them away to a tiny room where they were to await yet another officer. This one wore a cheap pair of shiny pants, a once-white shirt old enough to vote and the ugliest tie upon which Brodie had ever had the misfortune to clap eyes.

"Well, this here is a weird one," he said after introducing himself as a police investigator.

"How so?" Brodie asked.

"All them computer disks," the investigator exclaimed. "What could he be looking for there?"

"Financial records, I would imagine," Brodie answered, then went on to explain as succinctly as possible. "We suspect this is all part of a plot to separate me from Miss Simmons. If we're correct in our assumptions, the burglar is my ex-wife's brother. She has recently recovered from a long coma and has been pretending to have forgotten that we were divorced."

The investigator's bushy brows rose abruptly, but he just shook his head. "Well, you hear a new one every day."

"I know it sounds ludicrous," Brodie said, somewhat abashed, "but I expect our burglar can fill you in—if we can convince him to do so."

"Well, let's give it the old school try," the other man muttered, motioning them through a door that he opened with a key.

"Can I ask you something?" Brodie prodded gently as they moved along a narrow corridor badly in need of paint.

"Might as well."

"Has he called anyone?"

The investigator shook his head. "We usually let 'em have the phone as soon as they're booked, but he wouldn't give us a name, so we had to book him in as a John Doe, and that's another procedure entirely."

"Good."

A moment later, the investigator opened another door and led them into a tiny room crammed with a table and two chairs, one of them occupied by a glum, slumping, all-too-familiar figure. When Brodie entered the room, however, the culprit immediately straightened in his chair and lifted his chin pugnaciously.

"Oh, yes," Brodie said, sliding his hands into his pockets and rocking back on his heels. "My one-time brother-in-law. His name is Dude Shelly."

The investigator jotted the name down on a small pad that he carried in his breast pocket, saying, "We'll run that through the state data base and see what we come up with."

"Chances are you won't find anything," Brodie told him, his gaze targeted Dude. "The Shellys recently came here from Texas. You'll find that he has a long history of petty crimes, everything from shoplifting and purse-snatching to exposing himself."

The policeman looked at Dude. "Terrific. We just love picking up our neighbors' trash around here," he said in a voice that made the opposite clear. "Ever been in jail?" he asked the room in general.

"Dallas county and city lock-ups, I believe," Brodie answered.

"Well, congratulations, then, Mr. Shelly," the policeman said. "You've come up in the world. This time you'll be a guest of the state of Louisiana. The accommodations may be a little rougher than what you're used to, but you'll likely live—whether you want to or not."

For the first time, Dude spoke. "State pen? Uh-uh. Not for sixty bucks!"

"Well now, maybe sixty bucks is more money down here in the bayou than up in Dallas," the investigator said mildly. "Besides, we got you on breaking and entering sure enough, and then there's all those disks you had on you, not to mention some small stuff stacked by the front door that you were trying to steal, all expensive items, no doubt," he added with a significant look at Chey.

"We only carry exclusive antiques in our showroom," Chey said helpfully.

Dude made a strangling sound. "It was just junk, just pretty junk!"

"Actually," Brodie said, "we have reason to believe that the diskettes contain financial records and were the main objective of the burglary. As I told you, they were hoping to drive a wedge between me and Miss Simmons by finding something with which to blackmail her." Dude's eyes nearly popped out of his head when he heard that.

"Oh, really?" The investigator tilted his head in interest. "That ought to add a few years to his stay. But you said, 'they,' I believe."

Brodie nodded, looking at Dude. "Maybe he would like to tell you all about it. Maybe it would help his case if he did?"

The investigator turned a considering gaze on Dude, who whined and licked his lips. "Pop'll kill me," he told Brodie desperately.

"You think he isn't going to anyway?" Brodie asked. "You failed your assignment. The scheme's blown now, and it's all your fault. Save yourself some legal trouble and explain the whole ugly business to this nice man, why don't you? It was your father who masterminded this mess, so let him do the time."

Dude gulped again, eyes gone a little wild. "I-I wanna make a phone call!"

"Sure," the investigator agreed companionably. "I'll get a phone in here for you, but I hope you'll take my advice, son, and call a lawyer. No one else can help you out of this. You might help yourself, though, if you tell us why you went to Miss Simmons' shop and who sent you there."

Dude gulped, tears brimming in his eyes. Brodie felt a little sorry for him. The man barely had the wits to dress himself on a daily basis. No way he could think himself out of this one, and his father wasn't about to help him, either, but a call to him from Dude now would surely give the older man a heads-up. Harp might even decide it was time to leave town, and Brodie would prefer that not happen just yet.

"Listen," he said to the investigator, "Dude was just following orders." He stuck his hand into his pocket and withdrew the tiny tape cassette. "I actually have his father and an individual who works for me on tape plotting this whole thing, and I'll give it to you to help confirm Dude's story—provided he decides to tell you the truth." Brodie was perfectly aware that the tape probably was not admissible in court, but he was hoping that the investigator wouldn't reveal that to Dude.

The investigator's face was as expressionless as a mask, but he said not a word, almost as if he hadn't even heard Brodie. Taking that as a good sign, Brodie turned once more to Dude.

"You know, if you make a clean breast of this, you never have to go back to Harp. We can see to that, Dude."

Dude looked down at his hands, but then he nodded.

"Still want that phone call?" the investigator asked, and Dude looked up again, shaking his head.

"I'll tell," he said softly.

"You won't regret it, Dude, I promise," Brodie said significantly.

He glanced at Chey, telegraphing his relief to her and once more pocketing the tape cassette as the frumpy policeman walked over to a speaker grid on the wall and spoke into it, requesting an escort for Brodie and Chey as well as an interview backup. Then he pulled out a chair, turned it and sat down, folding his arms across the top of the back.

"Now then, son," he said companionably, "who is this

'Pop' of yours and what kind of mess are we talking about?''

Dude was tearfully explaining how his sister had only squeezed a "measly million" from Brodie before she got into a coma and left him and his pop high and dry in Dallas, when two uniformed policemen arrived, one to bear witness that a proper interview was being conducted and the other to escort Brodie and Chey out of the building. They were told that someone would contact them once the investigation was complete, but Brodie personally had little doubt about how it would all turn out. And he still had the tape cassette in his pocket.

On the way home, Brodie told Chey that if Dude managed to stay out of jail over this, he fully intended to set him up in an apartment somewhere and help him find a job. "It probably won't last, but I can't help feeling that Dude never really had a chance to be anything but what he is, you know?''

"I suppose so," Chey murmured. It was a somewhat subdued reply, but he put it down to lack of sleep. He'd kept her up late making love, and now they were running to and from the police station in the wee hours. It was natural, as dawn began to lighten the night sky, that she should be flagging. He, on the other hand, was too excited to sleep.

"It's almost over," he kept saying. "It's almost over." His brain was so busy with plans, surveying and discarding scenarios, putting together others, that he hardly noticed her silence.

By the time they let themselves back into the house and climbed the stairs side by side, he was pretty sure what he was going to do, but he still had the logistics to work out. He left Chey curled up on the bed in her clothes, her shoes kicked off, sleep already overtaking her, and went to inform his grandmother of their return. After that, he closeted himself in his office, where he carefully laid his plans. At the very earliest opportunity, he made two important telephone calls, then kicked back in his chair for a quick nap, confident that all his troubles were behind him and that a wonderful future lay ahead for him and Chey.

He woke almost two hours later, energized and ready for the farce to end so he could truly get on with the rest of his life. The clock on his desk showed him that he just had time to make the final steps in his preparations, catch a cup of coffee, and grab a quick shower before dressing for lunch. Humming happily to himself, he strolled down the hallway to Janey's suite and rapped smartly on the door. After a few moments, Brown answered.

"Yeah?" she asked suspiciously.

He had to laugh. So often her suspicions were baseless; now they were not, and she had no way of knowing that. "Brown, could you tell Janey that her after-lunch therapy session with Nate is canceled?"

The older woman's heavy features bunched together. "How come?"

"Because I've set aside that time to settle some things about our future," he told her with a wide smile.

Brown studied him from beneath a beetled brow. "What's that mean?"

Suddenly Janey shoved past Brown and presented herself to Brodie dressed in a filmy pink peignoir. She batted her long eyelashes at him and gushed breathlessly, "Brodie, darling, you're looking smart this morning."

He grinned down at her, so pleased with the impending denouement that he wanted to laugh aloud. "Well, thank you. You are quite a sight yourself, a veritable angel in pink." No one would ever guess what a witch she actually was, he mused silently.

She practically drooled all over him then, swaying close. "How sweet. Now what was this about our future?"

He could barely keep the chuckle from his voice. "Janey, you know me, I like things set down in black and white, so my lawyer's coming at one-thirty this afternoon, and we're going to lay this all out. I'd like your father to be there this time, if you don't mind.''

She studied him a moment, then purred throatily, ''I'm sure Daddy will welcome the opportunity to settle my future.''

He smiled, and on impulse, just because she was so easily read and still so very much the Janey he'd always known, he leaned down and pegged a kiss right in the center of her forehead. ''I trust you'll call Harp immediately?''

She nodded, glowing with delight. He could see the dollar signs dancing behind her pretty eyes. ''One-thirty,'' she confirmed.

Brodie didn't even try to restrain his smile, but then a movement behind Janey had him glancing over her shoulder at Brown, who still glared suspiciously. ''Oh, Brown,'' he offered magnanimously, ''you're welcome to come along, if you like. In fact, I'd prefer that you join us. After all, if not for you, we wouldn't have this opportunity, would we?''

She narrowed her eyes at him, then nodded and began plucking at the back of Janey's peignoir urgently. Brodie pretended not to see, saying, ''Well, I'll leave you two ladies to make that phone call, and I'll see you both at lunch.'' With that he went downstairs in search of Marcel's fragrant coffee.

Since Chey had not come down yet, he carried a cup of coffee back up the stairs to her, avoiding everyone but Marcel in the process. Placing the coffee mug on the bedside table, he reached over and shook her gently by the shoulder.

''Sweetheart?''

She sat up groggily, rubbed her eyes and asked, ''What time is it?''

''Just after eleven.''

Groaning, she swung both legs over the side of the bed and announced, ''I need to check on the shop.''

"Sure, but could you put it off a little while yet?" He sat down next to her and explained, "We're having company just after lunch, say about one-thirty, and after the meeting I have arranged I expect we'll be at least two short for dinner, which ought to be reason for celebration." He smiled happily and kissed her. "The you-know-what is about to hit the fan."

She smoothed her hair with her hands and reached for the coffee, asking, "What do you need me there for?"

He drew back at that. "Are you kidding? Darling, you play the central role in this little melodrama I'm staging. Besides, don't you understand that this is it? Janey's hold on me ends today."

She sipped the coffee, then smiled, shook her head apologetically and put down the cup again. "Of course. You're right." Slipping off the bed, she wrapped both arms around him and hugged him tightly. "I'm so happy for you. Thanks for the coffee, by the way."

"I'm happy for us both," he said, slightly troubled by her reticent attitude, but of course she was worried about her shop. "Let me explain the plan," he said briskly.

She pushed away, shaking her head. "I really have to get down to the shop. After I've spoken to Georges and taken care of a few things, I'll be back."

He frowned, but it was unreasonable to be so disappointed, so he pushed the feeling aside. "Okay. It might even be better this way. I don't want to let anyone suspect what's going to happen at that meeting, and right now I imagine Janey's thinking that I'm going to cave, offer to buy them off." He chuckled. "She may even think I've decided to take her back, if you can imagine that. Suppose you could be back by a quarter after, though? I want everyone in place before Harp arrives."

"No problem," she told him with a bright smile.

He put aside all doubts and indulged in a long, deep kiss before tearing himself away to head for the shower. Afterward, he went downstairs and quietly gathered the remainder of the household in the kitchen, where he apprised them of all that had happened and all that he expected to happen, assigning them each their roles.

He wanted Seth kept out of sight, so Kate was under strict instructions to keep him happily occupied in his suite throughout the event. At lunch, however, she had another function. Marcel was to station himself near the front door and usher in their guests at the appropriate moment, then stay to serve drinks. Nate took possession of the tape recorder and received instruction concerning when he was to emerge from Viola's office into the back hallway so he could be handy.

Brodie was famished and nervously eager by the time everyone sat down to lunch. Chey's absence did not go unnoticed, but it was Kate who, as assigned, questioned her whereabouts. Brodie explained that "someone" had broken into her shop during the previous night and that she had gone to investigate the damage. Janey and Brown traded surreptitious glances over that, but wisely refrained from commenting. The others made appropriate noises of concern.

"What is this world coming to?"

"I hope the thieves didn't take anything important."

"Is there anything we can do?"

Brodie waved away their questions with apparent unconcern, saying that he felt certain Chez Chey was fully insured and must have experienced similar misfortune in the past. "Besides," he added expansively, "it really shouldn't concern us. The house is, for all intents and purposes, finished. In fact, I've already begun planning its social debut."

He went on to discuss the elaborate reception that he was planning for the Legantine ambassador and, for good measure, explained the exclusive and very lucrative travel program contract.

Janey was positively effervescent after that, bubbling with excited chatter about the planned party and sending Brodie secretive, conspiratorial looks. Apparently she was more than willing to forgive and forget his involvement with Chey. No doubt she was too busy tallying her supposed share of the Middle Eastern profits. Brodie laughed at the very thought, and consequently, lunch was a deceptively lighthearted affair.

Brodie stayed at the table well after finishing his meal to concentrate on Seth, whom he hadn't seen all morning. Picking up on the mood at the table, the boy exercised himself to entertain, and for once even Janey seemed amused by his antics. Finally the Westminster clock on the sideboard chimed the hour, and Brodie excused himself from the table, saying that he had a quick phone call to make and some papers to check. He sent a direct look to Janey, saying, "I'll see you in the family parlor in half an hour."

She laughed and batted her eyelashes at him. He nodded significantly at his mother, kissed his son, and strolled out of the room with his heart slamming hopefully in his chest. He wished suddenly that Chey was in the house. He felt a great need to hold her just then, to reassure himself that all was going as it should. The next instant he shook off these nameless fears and hurried up to the office to fetch his little tape recorder and ring up the police to find out what he could about Dude.

Chey was too busy at first to think much about the pending meeting. Dude had broken the lock on the grille that protected the shop's front door after hours, then had busted a window in the door to get inside. Georges had taken photos and called the appropriate repairmen, but the insurance company had to be notified, forms filled out and the claim verified, which meant dealing with the police again. Once she'd accomplished all that, Georges demanded a word-for-word account of what had transpired at the police station. It was half past twelve by the time they sat down at her desk over sandwiches from the deli around the corner and really talked over the events of the night.

Georges was shocked and quite admittedly titillated. His curiosity over the pending meeting, which would presumably put the Shellys into retreat once and for all, far surpassed Chey's own, and Georges required barely a thought to figure out why. "You're not ready for this, are you?"

She shrugged and said the most patently ridiculous words that had ever come out of her mouth. "It doesn't have anything to do with me."

"Don't give me that. I woke him in your bed last night. That is, I *presume* you were sleeping by then."

She felt her face color revealingly but stubbornly said nothing.

Georges nibbled at his sandwich for a moment and then asked assiduously, "So, you're not going to marry him?"

She bit her lip and gave up any attempt at pretense, replying miserably, "I don't know."

"You love him, don't you?"

She put her head in her hands and said to the desk, "Yes."

"And Seth?"

"Seth's very dear to me," she said softly. "I-I've never felt the biological need to bear a child of my own, but..." She shook her head, unable to explain.

"But Seth is a child who already exists," Georges deduced gently, "and, your personal convictions aside, you've found it impossible not to love him."

She nodded. "Yes, that's it exactly."

"So what's the problem?"

She sighed heavily. "How do I know that I can be a good mother to Seth? I—I think about giving up my career, and I know that if I do, I'll be miserable, and yet, I just don't know if it's fair to try to balance my career and motherhood.''

Georges spread his thick hands. "Well, it certainly wouldn't be fair to *you* to ask you to give up something that's so important to you. Has Brodie said that's what he wants?''

"No.''

"Have you discussed it? Does he know how important your career is to you?''

"I-I think so. I mean, we've discussed it, yes.''

"Then the problem is you and not him," Georges surmised with a lift of an eyebrow.

She sighed. "It's just such an awesome responsibility.''

"Look, Chey," Georges said matter-of-factly, "it's just one little boy, not a houseful. It's not like Brodie has ten kids.''

"I know. I've thought of that, and sometimes I think surely I can handle one little boy, but then I think, what if I ruin him? I don't know anything about being a mother, really.''

Georges barked a shout of laughter. "Honey child, for a smart girl you can be awfully dumb. Of course you don't really know how to be a mother. In case, you haven't heard, it's a do-it-yourself, learn-as-you-go proposition, but in so far as you can be prepared, you've got so many legs up on the competition that you might as well be a spider! How many nieces and nephews have you baby-sat? How many runny noses and wet behinds have you dried?''

"Other people's children aren't the same thing!" she argued.

"No, they're not, and I'm glad to hear that you realize it. Goes to show, along with everything else you've accomplished, how well you will do.''

"Do you really think so?" she asked uncertainly.

He rolled his eyes. "Sugar, have I ever lied to you?''

"No.''

"Well, then. Now, will you just think about it like this? He's one little boy, and you won't be in it alone. Brodie is an experienced father, and there's Viola and me and your whole family."

"You?" she echoed doubtfully, a smile wiggling its way across her mouth.

Georges pretended great offense. "Are you implying that I won't be your favorite baby-sitter? Sister girl, I am crushed."

She laughed, feeling lighter than she had since she'd walked out of the police station and realized that her sweet interlude with Brodie had come to an end. Her doubts were not completely put to rest, however. How much simpler it would be if they could just go on as they were!

Unfortunately, that was not an option. Her excuse for living at Fair Havens was at an end, and her family would start asking questions about her involvement with Brodie soon, questions she was unprepared to answer. Besides, Brodie himself had stated flatly that he couldn't go on as they were indefinitely. No, the time for decision had come, the moment she had known would eventually present itself from the instant she had allowed Brodie back into her bed, not that she regretted what they'd shared.

The past few nights had been filled with so many emotions and sensations and moods that she literally marveled. Had anyone told her that lovemaking could be all at the same time playful and fun and soul-binding and spiritual, she'd have marked it down as so much nonsense. Now she knew better, and in order to have more of the same, her only option was to marry him.

How simple that sounded. Perhaps it would be simple if she was like all those other women who seemed to think nothing of committing themselves to marriage, motherhood and career. Yet, everywhere she turned she saw and heard the hand-wringing and debates. Our children are at risk! Women are in crisis! Only in her own family did everyone seem balanced and happy—and the women of her family did not mix motherhood and career. Brodie and Seth made her believe that she could be the exception, but could she? Could she really? At this point, she could only hope so, because the moment of decision was definitely at hand.

It was time to face the fact that she loved Brodie Todd and his son, to put aside her fears and embrace the possibilities. It was time to commit.

Chapter Fourteen

When Brodie walked into the family room, Janey, Brown and his grandmother were already in place. From her position next to Brown on the comfortable chintz-covered love seat, Janey was regaling Viola, who looked politely bored, with news of her amazing recovery pace. She was giving credit, much to Brown's apparent dissatisfaction, to Nate Begay.

"I'll admit that I was skeptical at first," she said upon spying Brodie, "but as usual my dear husband made a brilliant decision in hiring Nate."

Brodie smiled to himself, trusting that Nate could hear what was being said about him. Of course, Janey had no real inkling about certain areas of Nate's expertise. "That's good of you to say," Brodie told her, taking a seat on the sofa next to his grandmother.

"Oh, I mean it," Janey gushed. "Why it's positively miraculous what that man has wrought! I swear, I'm as fit as a fiddle."

"As fit as you've ever been, I'm sure," Brodie qualified with a straight face.

"Yes, indeed, and more than ready to take up my place in, er, life again."

She glanced at Brown, took a breath, and went off on another subject, specifically, the sad state of her wardrobe. It had been *two years,* after all, since she'd last done any "serious" shopping, except for the few "essentials" that she and Brown had managed to pick up in the past few days. Brodie mused that an expensive pair of ostrich-skin shoes and a matching handbag were not exactly his idea of "essentials," but he considered the cost justifiable, a small price to pay for the hours that she had spent elsewhere.

Before he was required to make another comment in response to Janey's prattle, the doorbell clanged, the sound reverberating throughout the house. Every head turned toward the door, including his own. That should be Chey, according to plan—unless she'd decided that matters at the office were more important than what was going on here. But, no, she wouldn't do that. They had worked too hard together to bring this moment about. She knew how important this was to their future.

Didn't she?

Yes. Yes, of course, she did.

Nevertheless, he wished he'd had a chance to discuss his plan in detail with her, but since circumstances had prevented that, he'd have to trust in her support. He couldn't help feeling anxious as he faced the room once again, however. After quickly checking his wristwatch, he straightened the crease of his slacks. He had not until this moment thought about what he would do if, for some reason, Chey did not show, but how much difference could it make, really? A cold feeling in the pit of his belly told him that it made a great deal of difference, indeed, to him. Still, she must know that he was counting on her. She wouldn't disappoint him.

Within moments, the click of heels could be heard coming down the hall. Brodie secretly heaved a sigh of relief, recognizing the sound of Chey's footsteps. Sure enough, an instant later she walked through the open doorway. Janey frowned and traded a look with Brown, who openly scowled. Brodie leapt up and hurried forward to escort the new arrival to a comfortable armchair only recently installed.

"How is everything?" he asked solicitously. "Anything valuable taken?"

She smiled tiredly, and it occurred to him that she hadn't had much more sleep than he had. "Nothing important, really," she answered, exhaustion lowering her voice. "The broken glass has been cleaned up and replaced, and I've decided to go with a padlock until a new grille can be installed. The repairmen are saying they'll get to it by the end of the week," she finished gamely.

"Not more repairmen!" Janey complained, obviously overhearing only the last part. "I thought we were through with all that."

"These repairmen are working at Chey's shop," Brodie told her. "If you'll recall, there was a break-in of some sort." He looked a mild warning at Chey.

She smiled wanly and said, "No cause for alarm."

"Well, that's good," Viola said heartily.

"But," Janey injected, "I'm sure you'd rather be there than here just now."

"Actually, I asked Chey to be here," Brodie said pointedly.

Janey did not take that news well. Her delicate brows drew together and her plump lips pursed in a pout. "I don't see why we need her for this."

He had known she was going to say that, of course, and had planned exactly how to derail her complaints. "But, Janey, didn't you say that you wanted to make some changes in the house? This is your chance to itemize them."

Janey immediately brightened at that, though Brown's

suspicious nature moved her to pinch her charge in warning, not that it did any good. Janey merely brushed away
Brown's concern with a slap of her hand, then sat forward
eagerly and began speaking again as if the floor was hers
by right anytime she wanted it.

"The main problem is the colors," she told Chey.
"Golds and greens aren't flattering to me. I need pinks and
creams. And well, this furniture is all so *old-fashioned*."

Brodie traded amused glances with Chey and sat down
next to his grandmother once more. Janey happily prattled
on, telling Chey just what she'd like to see changed, from
the paintings to the rugs. When she started talking about
Egyptian artifacts and Danish furniture, Viola made a strangling sound, then covered it by harshly clearing her throat.
Thankfully, the bell rang again.

This time Brodie managed not to look at the door, knowing perfectly well that the new arrival would be either Harp
or his own personal attorney. A few moments later, Harp
appeared, grumbling about having to find his own way
through the house alone.

"Marcel is needed at the door," Brodie told him.

"Well, where's that woman, that skinny housekeeper?"
Harp wanted to know.

"She's with Seth," Brodie answered calmly, then
adroitly changed the subject. "Why don't you take that
comfortable armchair over there, Harp? It's a new addition.
Chey had it brought all the way from Boston."

Harp grunted and swaggered across the floor to drop
down into the chair. "What's this all about?" he wanted
to know.

"All in good time," Brodie assured him and once more
directed the conversation onto safer paths, saying, "Janey,
you may want to rethink your plan to overhaul the house
yet again. Are you aware that twice recently people have
stopped by to ask if they can look around inside? If this
keeps up, we'll have to start charging admission." He

chuckled to show that he was teasing, but, as expected, Janey took him seriously.

"Do you really think so?" she asked eagerly, apparently calculating her share of any such profits. "Do you really think people would pay to see inside?"

"Ah, that's hoo-haw," Harp insisted. "Ain't nobody with a lick o' sense gonna pay to see inside some old house."

"Oh, but they do," Viola told him. "All along the River Road, in the French Quarter and right here in the Garden District, people pay admission to the historic older homes. Many families and organizations support themselves that way."

Janey was enraptured. "You don't say!" Before she could warm to this new subject too obnoxiously, that glorious gong reverberated again, and suddenly Brodie's nerve endings went on alert.

This was it. Finally. He tried to think it all through clearly one more time and found to his horror that his mind was a perfect blank. Instinctively, he looked to Chey and found her looking at him, the softness of her gaze wrapping around him like a warm blanket. Resolve returned. He rose to his feet and was standing at the end of the sofa, one hand resting lightly on its back, the other at his waist, when Marcel appeared, followed by the final player in this farce.

"Mr. Harvey," Marcel announced.

Brodie clapped his hands together and rubbed them vigorously. "Excellent! Now we can begin." Looking at Marcel, he said, "You may serve now, please." Marcel made a little bow and hurried away. Brodie smiled at the man standing before him. "I suppose introductions are in order." He glanced around the room and said, "Allow me to present my personal attorney, Mr. Lionel Harvey."

Harp leapt to his feet at that. Brodie looked from one to the other of them, mentally comparing them in a snap. Both were solidly middle-aged, and together they made a perfect study in opposites. Wary little Harp, his thinning hair plastered across his balding pate with some sort of dressing, stood there in pointy-toed cowboy boots with heels so high that he seemed to be standing on an incline, eyes darting around the room as if he expected an ambush. The tail of his faded T-shirt was cinched into the waistband of his baggy jeans with a cheap vinyl belt stamped to look like snakeskin. Tall, controlled, substantial Harvey, on the other hand, fairly shouted wealth and status, from the distinguished gray at his temples to the cut of his expensive pinstriped suit and the brilliant shine of his Italian shoes. The hang of his burgundy tie against the front of his French blue shirt was as perfect as the slender line of the briefcase at his side. Absolute opposites: snake oil and grease, integrity and substance.

Harp brought his hands to his hips and demanded, "What's this all about? Why've you brought your lawyer in, and how come the old lady and the other one are here?" He pointed an accusing finger at Chey.

"I'll thank you to speak civilly of my grandmother and Ms. Simmons," Brodie told him, taking a firm rein on his temper. "Otherwise, you'll miss the celebration, Harp."

"Celebration?" the small man echoed. "What celebration?"

"Daddy," Janey interrupted anxiously, "I told you. Brodie's going to see to my, er, our future."

"He don't need no lawyer for that. Lawyers is what got you in trouble before!"

Brodie rolled his eyes. "If you'll just shut up and sit down, Harp, all your questions will be answered."

Harp huffed, but he dropped back into his chair. Brodie put the attorney in his own place on the couch next to Viola, the briefcase parked next to his feet. Just then Marcel wheeled a service cart into the room. It was filled with crystal champagne flutes and a silver ice bucket containing a bottle of champagne so recently uncorked that it was still vaporizing. Quickly, the flutes were dispersed and partially filled. Afterward, Marcel parked the cart out of the way and left the room. Armed with the requested prop, Brodie waved his glass airily.

"Now where were we? Oh, yes. Introductions. You already know my grandmother, Lionel, so allow me to present the others. I'd like you to meet my ex-wife, Janey."

Janey caught her breath at that, and Harp started blustering again, but Brodie ignored them.

"Next to her is her faithful nurse, Brown, and as you might have guessed, this is her father, Harp Shelly." He pointed to Harp, then abruptly turned his back on the man, who seemed to be gathering himself for another outburst. "And, finally," he said, smiling at Chey, "Ms. Chey Simmons." She was beautiful, astonishingly so, and the one truly bright spot in the whole room. He stood there looking at her and made a sudden decision. "Or I should say," he went on, "the future Mrs. Brodie Todd."

That announcement carried all the impact of a bomb. Chey gasped. Harp Shelly plunked his glass down on the floor next to his chair and yelped an expletive. Brown screamed hoarsely, while Janey dropped her champagne and keeled over in an apparent faint, even as Viola called delighted congratulations and Lionel calmly saluted Chey with his glass and drank, making it a toast.

Chaos reigned for a moment, with Harp, Lionel and Viola all speaking at once. Brown managed to set her own champagne flute safely aside and cradle Janey against her on the love seat while Brodie stared at Chey. Would she refuse him outright or step into the role? It wasn't as if they hadn't discussed marriage—in a roundabout way. They had even used it, obliquely, as the ultimate threat with the Shellys. Perhaps he shouldn't have made the announcement this way, but the moment had seized him and he had run with it. Now he prayed that she would understand the dual purpose here. This was meant to rout the Shellys, yes, but it was also what he wanted.

His heart in his throat, Brodie held out his free hand to her. After a moment, Chey rose and placed her hand in his.

Elation filled him. He lifted his glass in a silent salutation, inviting her with his eyes to join him in a toast to their future. She looked down at the glass in her hand, then lifted it to her mouth and sipped the sparkling champagne. The chaos receded. A moment of peace wrapped around him.

Then Harp Shelly stuck his face up close to Brodie's and shouted, "Bastard! You can't do this!"

The room and all its chaos came back into focus, along with a fresh sense of purpose. "But of course I can," Brodie replied, calmly stepping aside. "What's to stop me?"

Harp stabbed a finger at Janey, who lay slumped against Brown's lap, and accused Brodie with both tone and words. "Just look what you've done to my girl! A shock like that could kill her! You know what the doctor said!"

Brodie nodded sagely. "Um, yes, that would be the same doctor who so recently gave Lionel here a signed, notarized statement indicating that you *somehow* misunderstood his prognosis for Janey. That is the term he uses, Lionel, isn't it? *Misunderstood.*"

Harp gaped like a landed cod.

"Um, yes, *misunderstood,*" Lionel confirmed in his calm, unruffled way. "The exact term, actually. Concerning the notion that honesty would somehow set back Ms. Shelly-Todd's recovery, especially in reference to the state of your past marriage and subsequent divorce, it was all a big *misunderstanding.*"

Brodie smiled benignly, enjoying himself now. "There you have it. Misunderstandings are so easily arrived at, especially when one thinks one is hearing what one wishes to hear."

Harp drew himself up as tall as he could and made what was for him a cogent reply. "Damn you, Brodie Todd!"

Brodie grinned with obvious relish. "Game's up, Harp. Get over it."

Janey whimpered pathetically and slid off the love seat onto the floor.

"Oh, for heaven's sake," Viola muttered.

Seething with rage, Harp coldly ignored her. Clucking like a mother hen, Brown knelt at her side and alternately chafed Janey's limp wrist and shook her as she might a misbehaving child. Lionel Harvey merely raised an eyebrow, as if to say that he found the whole thing in very poor taste. Viola rolled her eyes, and Brodie chuckled to himself, winking at Chey, who was disciplining a smile. Suddenly, Brodie wanted nothing more than the lot of them gone so he could kiss his bride-to-be.

"Well," Viola commented firmly, it becoming apparent that Janey wasn't going to give up the pretense anytime soon, "I say that's good news for everyone concerned. We can all get on with our lives now."

"You mean *he* can get on with his life!" Harp snapped. "How's that good for anybody else? It sure ain't good for my girl or me, far as I can see!"

"Yes, I understand why you would think that," Brodie mused, studying the bubbles rising through his champagne. He switched his gaze to Harp's face, feeling a fierce satisfaction. It was time to end this. "I know you were hoping that Janey could get more out of me than she already has, and your last supposedly private conversation with Brown proves it."

Harp went very still, but then he carefully blanked his face. "I don't know what you're talking about!"

"Allow me to jog your memory, then," Brodie said affably. He called out for Nate Begay. The male nurse opened the door that led into the back hall and stepped inside, the tape recorder in one hand. "Janey was very right earlier to laud Nate's expertise," Brodie went on. "Nate, you see, is a very interesting person. Why, did you know that before Nate decided his heart lay in nursing, he was one of New Orleans' most highly decorated police officers?"

"He's a cop!" Brown brayed at Harp. "I told you! I told you both!"

Janey opened her eyes then, staring up accusingly at Nate. Harp suddenly looked hunted. "Now, see here," he began, "there ain't nothing illegal about looking out for your own!"

"No?" Brodie turned a cold smile at Nate and instructed, "Turn the volume all the way up."

"Yes, sir." With that, Begay switched on the recorder.

A few seconds into the tape, Viola began to tsk and Harp to bluster. After hearing enough to know that the scam really was blown, Janey suddenly sat up and glared at her father. "You old fool!"

True to form, the Shellys neatly turned on one another. "Don't you talk to me like that, you stupid bitch!"

"Stupid!" Janey shrieked, and Brodie signaled Nate to turn off the recorder, which he did immediately, while Janey pecked herself repeatedly in the chest with her thumb. "I lived right here in the same house with him for weeks pretending to be in a coma," she bawled, "and got away with it! You waltz into town and get yourself recorded!" Realizing suddenly what she'd said, she flew a glance at Brodie and immediately changed tactics. "It wasn't my idea. None of it was my idea! Brown bullied me into going along. From the moment I opened my eyes in that ambulance, she—"

"Ambulance?!" Brodie echoed disbelievingly, bringing his hand to his hip as Chey slipped free of him then. "You came out of the coma in the ambulance on the way to New Orleans? You've been pretending this whole time?"

Janey glanced at Brown, then lurched to her knees and quickly climbed to her feet. "Now, Brodie," she said placatingly, "please remember that you're speaking to the mother of your child."

"There's the mother of my child!" he bawled, pointing his finger at Chey. "She's already been more mother to Seth than you could ever be, and she'll be the mother of *all* my children! So get that nonsense right out of your head! It won't play with me. I know you too well, Janey. All Seth has ever been to you is a meal ticket. You're just as greedy as Harp!"

"You don't understand!" she told him desperately. "For myself, I'm quite satisfied with our original agreement. But I was afraid!" She pointed a finger at her father. "He pushed me in the pool, you see, flung me down there and cracked my skull! Just because I couldn't get you to give me more money!"

"You traitorous bitch!" Harp howled. "Don't you put this off on me! You were the one who said a million didn't leave you enough to even share with your old man! If you'd done what I'd told you at the beginning, none of this would've happened!"

"Oh, dear God," Viola said softly.

"As to that original agreement," Lionel Harvey said, pulling his briefcase up onto his lap while obviously trying to inject a note of calm into the proceedings, "I believe, in light of this new information, that the changes we've made are most appropriate, even generous." Flipping the latch open, he reached inside and extracted several papers.

"What changes?" Janey asked warily, signaling her sputtering father to silence with a slicing motion of her hand.

"It's simple," Brodie answered sharply, forcing himself to reign in his temper as best he could. "The money, the original million, has been held in trust for you from the beginning. Anyone else could live comfortably on the interest, but whether you can or not is another matter entirely, one in which I have no concern. I agreed to give you the money, and I'll hold to that, but before I release it, I'm going to require your signature to an addendum to the original agreement."

"All right," she said. Satisfied that she was going to get the money, she folded her arms. Obviously it made no difference to her what she had to say or do for it, but Brodie couldn't leave her uninformed.

"By signing," he told her, "you release all claim on Seth, even visitation. That goes for you *and* your family."

Janey nodded her head sharply. Harp, however, as if suddenly recalling his trump card, quickly intervened.

"Oh, no, you don't! I got as much right to that boy as you, more even, 'cause you ain't even his father!" When that announcement failed to elicit the reaction he expected, he tried again, sneering, "You're just his uncle." Silence ensued. Harp looked around in bewilderment and bawled, "His brother knocked up Janey!"

The women looked away at his indelicate phrasing, and Harvey laid a finger alongside his nose as if cleaning something from the inside corner of his eye. Brodie just knocked back the remainder of his champagne and set aside the glass, placing it on a nearby side table. Chey had moved away and now sank down into the chair she had earlier vacated, sipping from her glass thoughtfully. Brodie felt a spurt of unease, but it was quickly sublimated.

"You're not telling anyone here anything they don't already know, Harp."

Harp frowned and changed tack. "Just 'cause the secret's out don't mean I can't still take you to court! I'm that boy's grandfather. I got just as much right to him as you do, and I ain't letting you get away with this!"

"Oh, put a sock in it, Daddy!" Janey yelled shrilly.

"You shut up and let me handle this!" he shouted back.

"Actually," Lionel Harvey said, again the voice of reason, "you might want to rethink that."

"Really?" Harp sneered. "And why would I do that?"

"Well, for one thing, this type of litigation is quite expensive. You, sir, cannot afford to fight my client in court—unless your daughter is willing to bankroll the litigation, and even then, I daresay, Mr. Todd's pockets are much deeper than hers."

At that, Janey sat down and folded her arms once more, seemingly oblivious to the wet champagne stain trailing down the front of her dress. "Not a penny," she told her father bluntly.

"Damn you, Janey!" he began, then broke off. "We'll discuss this later," he said through his teeth.

"Then there is, of course, the matter of your record," the attorney went on smoothly.

Harp shifted his weight from foot to foot, sneering. "I ain't got no record in Louisiana!"

"Strictly speaking," Brodie said blithely, "that may not be so. You see, we know you masterminded Dude's little break-in at Chez Chey last night, and more importantly, the authorities know." Brown groaned, Janey rolled her eyes, and Harp literally paled at that, but Brodie pressed on. "In fact, I have it on good authority that, even as we speak, Dude is spilling his guts to the District Attorney. It appears he's been most forthcoming, detailing every scam you ever ran, and I understand that the state of Louisiana will be delighted to forward you and that information right back to Texas."

"Oh, Harp!" Brown gasped, heaving herself up from the floor. "They'll revoke your probation!"

"At the very least," the attorney confirmed dryly.

"And if they don't, I'll tell them what you did to me," Janey promised maliciously.

Howling obscenities, Harp bolted. Brodie stepped aside and let him flee. Brown, however, pounded after him, calling, "Harp! Harp! Wait for me!" She caught him just as he reached the door to the hall, latching onto his scrawny arm with her much beefier ones.

"Get away from me, you useless old cow!" Harp yelled, pulling forward and shoving her back at the same time. They struggled for a moment, her demanding to be taken along, him intent on ridding himself of her.

"But you need me, Harp!" she begged.

"Why would I need a frumpy, ugly old fright like you now?" he shouted, finally ripping his arm free of her grasp. "I don't need you, and I sure don't want you!" With that he reeled out the door and ran.

Clinging to the door frame, she stared after him, tears

rolling from her flat little eyes. "But Harp," she whispered, "I love you."

The entire room seemed moved by that faint declaration. Brodie looked at Chey, who bit her lip and, after a moment, looked away. Janey sighed and got up to walk over to Brown, sliding a supportive arm around the older woman's heaving shoulders.

"It's all right," Janey said. "I need you. I always have." Brown looked up at that, then began to sob against Janey's shoulder. Janey patted the other woman awkwardly.

Brodie cleared his throat and said, not unkindly, "I've reserved a suite for you at a good hotel and paid for a week's stay. Marcel and Kate will help you pack, and Nate will drive you over. I'll transfer the money and let you know how to access it." Janey nodded, and he went on. "I'd appreciate it if you'd go now."

"Of course," she said, and turned Brown toward the door, but then she stopped and looked back over her shoulder. "Thank you," she said, and dropped her gaze as if acknowledging that such simple words could never balance the scales, not that she would ever turn down the cash for any reason. He nodded as she moved her sobbing nurse toward the door.

Lionel Harvey got up then, papers in hand, and reached inside his coat for an ink pen, saying, "I'll get these papers signed before Ms. Shelly leaves the premises." He looked down at Viola and asked, "Would you mind witnessing the signature, ma'am?"

"Not at all," she said, rising regally to take his arm. As the pair strolled past Brodie, they stopped so Viola could press a cheek to his. "It's all over now, dear. It's finally over." With that she glanced toward Chey, then turned and allowed Lionel Harvey to escort her from the room.

"I'll let the authorities know that Harp Shelly's on the move," Nate said.

"Thank you," Brodie told him, lifting a hand to his forehead.

Nate left the room, and Brodie closed his eyes, sighing deeply. He felt rather as if he'd been dragged behind a fast-moving train. For a moment, he was lost, wondering what catastrophe or crisis required his energies next, but then he remembered that this was a moment of triumph. He ought to be happy, and so he would be.

Turning on his heel, he opened his arms to Chey, but she just stood there, staring down at the champagne flute swinging gently from her fingertips. The bottom fell out of his stomach. He lowered his arms, pasting a smile on his face.

"We did it, sweetheart," he said hopefully. "The Shellys are history."

She looked up, but her smile was a wan, wasted thing. "Yes. They won't bother you anymore. I'm glad I was able to help."

A cold breeze shivered through him where none could blow. "But?"

She shook her head slightly, and it felt as if a fist clamped around his lungs. "Nothing," she said after a moment.

Thoughts, words, ideas whirled through his mind, but it was all chaos, all but one idea. "You're upset because I didn't warn you about the announcement."

She looked up sharply again, and after a moment said, "Not really."

He didn't quite believe that, couldn't, didn't dare, believe that, so obviously explanations were in order. "I didn't know I was going to do it. I only decided at the last moment. You have to admit that it was an appropriate way to burst the Shellys' bubble."

She nodded, as if understanding perfectly. "We agreed that I was to play the spoiler. I understand. It's only…your grandmother won't be disappointed, will she?"

He shifted his weight warily. "About what?"

She flipped her hand back and forth between them. "About us."

It felt as if he'd swallowed a rock the size of his fist. "Why should she be disappointed about us?"

"I mean, when we don't get married."

That rock suddenly weighed a ton. He staggered beneath the weight of it. "B-But...I know I didn't make a proper proposal, but I thought...y-you're the one who said your family wouldn't approve of us...as we have been. Marriage is the only logical conclusion, then. Isn't it?"

Apparently, it wasn't. She walked over to the table where he had earlier set his glass and placed her own next to it, so close that the crystal hummed elegantly with the friction. "I can't marry you, Brodie," she said so softly that he could barely hear.

"I don't understand. We discussed this. I-I'll even hire a nanny. With two parents it won't be as if the nanny's raising him, and Grandmama is here. She's devoted to Seth, you know."

"It isn't Seth," she whispered.

But if it wasn't Seth, he thought, what was it? Then it hit him. It must be him! He remembered then with painfully acute clarity that she had never once actually said that she loved him. "I-I thought...that is, I assumed.... My God, Chey, we've been sleeping together, sharing a room!"

"And that was a mistake," she said, tears thickening her voice.

"Why?"

She turned suddenly, exclaiming, "I'm not the woman for you, Brodie! You need a normal woman who wants all the normal things, like children of her own." She looked away, murmuring, "Yours and hers."

Seth again. Anger was building behind the hurt now because what Chey said made no sense to him. Clearly, she was avoiding the truth. She didn't love him, and she didn't care for Seth, either. In some dispassionate corner of his brain, he knew that he was in too much pain to think rationally. Instinctively he sought to remove the source of the pain.

"I don't understand," he told her coldly, "but if that's how you feel, then you'd better go."

"All right," she said, folding an arm around her middle. "I'll leave as soon as Janey's gone." With that she wrenched around and headed for the door.

Momentarily frozen, he watched her walk away, unable quite to grasp what had happened. She was wiping tears from her face as she left him, and that struck him as very wrong, but he was too hurt and angry to really analyze it at the moment. All he could think as he stood there alone in that lovely room she had made for him was that he could not bear to go on living in this house without her.

It was only later that he came to the conclusion that he'd missed something, that there must be more here than he had seen and heard. All right, she hadn't said that she loved him, but she'd allowed him back into her bed, and he'd have bet his last cold cent that she wouldn't have done that if she didn't love him. So what was really going on here? If her tears were any indication, she hadn't wanted to leave him, and yet she'd insisted she wasn't the woman for him, and at the same time she'd claimed Seth had nothing to do with it! Was this simply Chey reverting to type? Was she running now just because that was what she always did when he got too close? He felt sure that was the answer.

Okay, so she had run. Again. He could bring her home. He had done so before, and he could do it once more because, by golly, that woman belonged here with him. He was going to require help this time, though. Luckily, he knew just where to get it.

Chapter Fifteen

Chey looked down at the tastefully embossed invitation in her hand, an intense longing knotting her insides into painful contortions. She had looked at it often over the past week, unable to make herself toss it into the trash. The party was only two days away, and she couldn't possibly go even if she wanted to. She just couldn't trust herself to see him again.

"So that's it?" Georges asked drolly. "You go your way, he goes his, and never the Fair Havens and the Chez Chey shall meet?"

"That's about the size of it," she said, trying for flippant and achieving only morose.

Georges rolled her a skeptical look over one shoulder as he helped himself to coffee from the pot in the corner of her office, adding, "In this city? I don't think so. Even if you turn down his invitation to this reception, you can't avoid him forever."

He was right, of course, she realized with a pang. She

and Brodie were bound to cross each other's paths at some point. She had hoped that, given enough time, she could manage. Three weeks obviously wasn't enough time, though it had seemed like an eternity to her.

"Besides, it isn't very business-friendly, you know," Georges went on doggedly. "This is the official debut of the restored, refurbished and redecorated Fair Havens. Any other architectural designer would be there with bells on and business card in hand. It's even been suggested that you could give a short tour and talk about what you've accomplished there. We'd have to hire help to keep up with the workload if you did."

Right again. Chey parked an elbow on the desktop and propped her forehead in one upturned palm, still staring at the neat white card with its slim, elegant black script. She was perversely aware that the business could go hang for all she cared these days. Somehow, without Brodie, not even the most precious things in her life seemed to mean anything anymore. All she wanted to do, all she kept dreaming about, was throwing herself into his arms and begging him to take her back, but she knew where that would lead. He had said it himself that day.

The mother of my children. The mother of all my children.

He hadn't been speaking of one child, of Seth. He'd been speaking of future children, more children. Something defiant and desperate in her demanded, *Well, why not, if that's what he wants, if that would make him happy?*

It wasn't as if she hated children, after all. She loved cute, cuddly babies as much as the next woman—especially when she could give them back to their mothers and go on about her business. Yet, she knew she'd naturally love a child of her own, just as she loved every child within her permanent orbit, all her nieces and nephews. Seth. She closed her eyes. How had she come to miss his bright little face so? Did he miss her, too? Did he ask for her? Wonder about her?

"Of course," Georges went on, needling her deliberately, "you might get there and find that you're already replaced."

Unwittingly she lifted her head at that, spearing him with an entirely too telling look. He pretended to be mulling the thought over.

"Still," he murmured, "it would be better to find out in a controlled environment, don't you think? I mean, what if you should just run into him about town with some luscious thing hanging on his arm?"

The idea was staggering for her. The pangs of jealousy she had suffered about Janey before she'd known the truth of that situation paled in comparison.

"Even if you accept the fact that a man like Brodie Todd will always have a woman within reach," Georges went on blithely, "it's never easy to stumble upon your own replacement. I should know." He smirked at that, explaining with self-mocking sarcasm, "I divorced my second wife for incompatibility. We were complete opposites. Couldn't wait to get rid of her. Six months later I walked into a little diner down on Royal and spotted her cuddling with another man in a booth, and...well, the dyspepsia had nothing to do with the food because I didn't stay to eat. In fact," he murmured, almost to himself, "I haven't ever been back."

Chey swallowed painfully. Even knowing that Brodie had been married to Janey, even thinking that they might once have been in love, she had never allowed herself to picture them *together,* certainly not as she and Brodie had been together, not making love, not joined in body and soul. When she'd found out how wrong she'd been about him and Janey, the depth of her own relief had frightened her. Could she be wrong about this? Might there not be room for negotiation? Surely, if he really wanted to be with her, Brodie would take her desires into consideration—as she must do with his.

Oh, God. Oh, God, what had she done? Perhaps it wasn't too late. It had only been three weeks, after all. He couldn't have found anyone else so quickly, not if he loved her. Then again, what self-respecting man in his right mind would languish indefinitely for a woman, any woman? Of course Brodie would move on. Eventually.

But not yet. Please. Not yet.

Eventually, some day in the distant future, without any doubt, he would fall in love again, laugh with someone else, dance with someone else, make love with someone else. She couldn't let that happen. She put her hand over her mouth, afraid she might sob aloud otherwise. Georges suddenly sounded worried.

"Chey?"

She just shook her head.

"Oh, honey, I didn't mean to make you cry. He hasn't—"

"Go," she managed to gasp. He stood there looking like a puppy that had stained the carpet. "Please." Georges set his coffee cup on the counter and left the room quickly, silently.

She laid the invitation on the blotter and smoothed it with the fingertips of both hands, tears slipping down her cheeks. What a fool she was. Her worries and convictions about parenthood didn't matter anymore. She still believed wholeheartedly that resignation was not the correct attitude in which to bring a child into the world, but if that's what it took to make the man she loved happy, then that was what she would do. If she could be a mommy to Seth, and she felt that she could, what difference did another child make?

An insidious little voice inside her head asked, *And if you should come to resent such a child?*

Well, she'd just have to see that she didn't. She'd stay aware of the possibility, guard against it, and she'd have Brodie and her family and Viola to help her. Even if she did find herself resenting having her world turned upside down by the demands and needs of an infant she had never expected or dreamed of or planned to have, the child would never know. Surely. But perhaps it wouldn't come to that. She had often been told that pregnancy was wondrous, a time of miracles. She could be worried for nothing. She could even turn out to be the most obnoxiously adoring mother ever! In fact, she planned on it. If it wasn't too late.

Please, God, do not let it be too late.

Resolved, she removed the RSVP card and tiny, corresponding envelope from the larger one on her blotter. An ink pen lay close to hand. She picked it up and quickly signed the card before slipping it into the stamped, self-addressed envelope and sealing it. After that, she dried her eyes, calmly stood, picked up the sealed envelope by one corner and carried it into the show room. She walked up to Georges, who was dusting a display of Victorian chandeliers, and held out the card.

"It's too late to mail it. Think you could take it over to Fair Havens for me?"

He put down the feather duster, glanced at the address on the envelope and smiled hugely. "Yes, indeed!" But then his smile faltered. "It isn't just business considerations, is it? Because if it is, you better rethink."

Smiling wryly, she shook her head. "No. It's not just business considerations." She met his gaze and said flatly, "I love him."

Georges laughed, immediately taking on an I-knew-it air. "Hallelujah! The light finally shines!" He started for the door, but his footsteps slowed again almost at once. "Uh, Chey, what I said earlier about him replacing you..."

She waved that concern away with an airy sweep of one arm, but inside her chest, her heart was pounding painfully. "I've already removed Brodie Todd from the clutches of one woman. I think I can do it again if I have to."

"You won't," Georges blurted. "He's barely left the house since you walked out on him. Viola's been worried about him, and frankly so have I. I just said that about another woman to get to you."

Chey smiled and admitted, "Well, it worked."

He slumped in relief. "You aren't mad?"

"No."

"You're doing the right thing, Chey. That man loves you."

"I hope so."

"I know so." He waved the envelope at her. "Sure you don't want to deliver this yourself?"

She considered, then shook her head. "I'm not quite ready for that. I think a social situation might ease the way a bit."

He nodded. "Okay. And for what it's worth, girlfriend, I think you're right."

She widened her eyes in mock surprise. "Well, that's a first."

He widened his right back at her and retorted cheekily, "Ain't it just." She was laughing when the door closed behind him.

Her heart pounded like a big bass drum as she slipped from the car and handed the keys to the white-coated valet hired for the occasion. She knew she was doing the right thing, so why this sudden heart-pounding? It made no difference, however. There could be no going back now. Her decision was made, all the ramifications reconciled. She only hoped that Georges was right and Brodie would be as glad to see her as she would be to see him.

"Enjoy your evening, Miss Simmons," the valet said deferentially, nodding at the doorman stationed on the front steps.

She hadn't given him her name, but obviously he had been told to look out for her. He'd probably received a description of her and her car and alerted the house the moment she'd turned into the drive. Sweeping around the end of the car, the satin edges of her stiff, black petticoats swishing about her knees, Chey walked across the drive, black beaded high heels crunching across the gravel. Squaring her shoulders, chin high, she climbed the front steps.

The dress was strapless and fitted to the waist, with a full skirt that had made her think of ballerinas when she'd seen it in the shop window. A dark royal blue, not quite navy, the dress seemed to bring out her eyes, or so Georges had told her. She had coiled her hair into a sleek cornucopia twist that curved from her nape to her crown. A pair of antique sapphire clips at her earlobes and a matching bracelet on her wrist comprised the total of her jewelry. Dark, berry-red lipstick and a subtle stroke of dark blue eyeliner and mascara completed her makeup.

She'd taken great care with her appearance, so much so that she was running quite late. Knowing that she was looking her best, she had been satisfied with the reflection in the mirror at home, but now, as the doorman moved to admit her, she felt sudden doubts. Her appearance could not undo what she had done. She had walked away from the man who loved her. He was bound to be angry and hurt and wary.

The door swung open, and her heart turned over. Brodie stood at the foot of the stairs, resplendent in a black tuxedo, white shirt and bow tie. He stared at her, his hands in pockets, and she had the distinct impression that he had been waiting there, pacing, even. Hope fluttered inside her chest. Resisting the urge to pick up her pace, she walked toward him, taking in every detail of his appearance. Both the slacks and the jacket were pleated, loose and yet fitted. The shirt, conversely, was smooth-fronted and tailored to a breath. The gleam of his black hair rivaled that of his patent shoes and belt, while his goatee and mustache had been ruthlessly clipped and his jaws so closely shaved that the skin looked new. The very sight of him brought tears to her eyes. Opening her lids a little wider, she willed them away.

He turned to meet her and rocked back on his heels as she came to a stop in front of him. Staring down at her, he stood so very still that he might have been a handsome mannequin, except for the pronounced rise and fall of his chest. Then suddenly he pulled his hands from his pockets and fixed them about her wrists.

"I was in terror that you would not really come."

Something tight and fearful within her gave way, and she blurted, "I couldn't stay away. I've been so unhappy without you!"

He closed his eyes briefly, then pulled her against him, wrapping her arms about his waist. " You won't go again." His voice held a double edge, that of an order, that of a plea.

"I won't go again," she vowed.

"Thank God!" He wrapped his arms around her, rocking her gently side to side. Then he cupped her face, turning it up to his. "But I need to understand why you left. Just tell me why."

"Brodie, I'm a coward," she admitted, sliding her hands over his. "A few of the ramifications of loving you have taken some getting used to. I had a safe little life all planned out for myself, then you turned it all upside down."

"Likewise," he retorted, and she knew suddenly that he needed more than explanations. She gave it to him.

"I love you, Brodie. I love you with all my heart, you and Seth."

He closed his eyes, and whispered, "I love you, too." He lowered his mouth toward hers.

Suddenly heels clacked on the hardwood floor behind him. "Meestair Bro-dee, I ask yew, please."

Brodie moaned softly, then lifted his head, dropped his hands and turned. A short, dark, plump woman encased in heavy, yellow-gold, figure-hugging brocade silk from her chin to her ankles descended upon them. The hem of the sheer veil, which was draped over her head and fixed there with a band of jet beading, fluttered about her shoulders. One corner of the veil had been caught up in front of her face, shadowing full, red lips and calling abrupt attention to the large, kohl-darkened eyes above.

"Highness," Brodie said, bowing slightly. "How may I help you?"

"I beg pardon," the woman said in heavily accented English, nodding regally at Chey.

"Princess, allow me to introduce Miss Chey Simmons. Darling, the Princess Liana Sadhoturan, wife of the Legantine ambassador, daughter of the Shah of Legan."

The princess tilted her head in that regal manner again, and Chey found herself dipping in a slight curtsy. The princess smiled, her teeth flashing white behind her veil. Then she lifted a hennaed, heavily jeweled hand, gold-tipped fingers uncurling about a small object cradled in her palm.

"I must ask, Meester Bro-dee, what is this so tasting good?"

Brodie didn't blink so much as an eyelash at the oddly phrased question or the half-eaten candy in the woman's palm. "That, Princess, is a New Orleans speciality, a praline."

"Prah-leen," the woman repeated with a nod. "I must know this. Tell me, please."

Brodie smiled. "I'm afraid I cannot, but my chef will be delighted to give you his recipe, I'm sure."

"Ah, the dark one," the princess said knowingly. "You take me there, please." It was little less than a command.

"Delighted to," Brodie answered, glancing apologetically at Chey as he offered the princess his arm. The princess deftly pirouetted, kicking the small train of her skirt behind her, and laid her hand on his. Brodie looked to Chey apologetically. "Will you join us, darling, or go on out to the garden? They're all anxious to see you."

"I'll go out," she said, suddenly anxious to see everyone.

"We won't be long," he promised, and she nodded as he led the princess toward the kitchen.

Chey walked through the oddly quiet house, wondering what it was that swelled within her as she did so. Pride, certainly, but also something more. As she stepped out into the garden, she knew an instant of intense clarity. Home. That's what she was feeling. She had come home. Smiling, she walked with growing confidence and delight toward the guests milling about the pool.

A great many people were gathered there, perhaps two hundred. Extra tables and chairs had been set up outside the pool fence, all gates of which were standing open. Two long buffet tables had been set up at angles to an elaborate champagne fountain at which guests could serve themselves. Behind it, using the fully opened pool house as a stage, a string quartet played a lilting, funky, jazzy tune. Chey eagerly looked for familiar faces, a wide smile upon her face, when suddenly she stumbled to a halt. Could that be? Surely not! And yet.... Dear heavens! Hurrying forward, she automatically lifted a hand.

"Mary Kay?" The redheaded woman in the simple beige sheath turned, champagne flute in hand. The two men flanking her turned as well. One of them wore a gold-embroidered scarf draped over his head and held in place with a gold cord. He held a tall glass of iced coffee in one hand. The other had on his good blue suit, a nice white shirt and a striped bow tie. In his hand was a champagne flute. "Sylvester!"

"Hello, sis-in-law!" he boomed. "Wow! Looking good."

Chey stood there and gaped until her sister stepped to her side and kissed her cheek. "You really do look marvelous, sweetie. Here, let me introduce you to this nice gentleman. Some sort of prince, I think. The nephew of a shah, is that right?" she asked the man.

Grinning, the gentleman in question executed a deep bow, fixed Chey with a languid gaze and gave her his name, "Fahoud Mohammed Leganza."

She dipped another perfunctory curtsey, murmured, "How do you do?" and immediately asked her sister, "What are you doing here?"

Mary Kay beamed. "We were all invited, you know, for

all the work the guys did on the house. Looks great, by the way. But there are only about twenty-one of us here, I think, all the brothers and sisters and the older nieces and nephews, oh, except Fay and Carter. She is *so* very pregnant," Mary Kay confided to Fahoud Leganza, who merely lifted an eyebrow. "Anyway, Mom's over there by the pool with Brodie's grandmother. Isn't Viola a dear?"

Chey nodded absently, too astounded to speak.

"Old Brodie sure knows how to give a party," Sylvester commented in his usual near-shout. "I could use a beer, though. Champagne's a little rich for my taste." He winced as Mary Kay elbowed him sharply in the ribs. "What?"

Chey was already moving toward the pool again, searching for her mother.

Mary Louise was not hard to find. She reclined on a chaise next to Viola, chatting amiably. She'd had her hair done in an elaborate French braid and had bought a new dress. The sensible plum silk featured a simple shirtwaist and slender, ankle-length skirt that buttoned up the front. The antique amethyst brooch Chey had given her one Christmas adorned the bodice, and the matching ear bobs were clipped to her dainty lobes. Most amazing of all were the gold wedge sandals on feet. The effect was most becoming, even elegant.

"Mama?"

Louise Simmons looked up and smiled, raising one arm. "Hello, sweetheart. My, how lovely you look." Chey bent dutifully and accepted her mother's embrace, kissing her lightly on the cheek.

"Indeed, you do," Viola agreed. "Come and sit with us for a minute. I haven't seen you in far too long." Viola wore her usual green, almost an olive this time, with elegant silver accessories that brought out the silver of her hair.

Chey sank down on the little table next to her mother, saying, "I can't believe Brodie invited everyone for this! You look wonderful, by the way, Mama. You, too, Viola."

"Hello, Aunt Mary," called one of her nieces, hurrying toward the buffet with a young man wearing a tuxedo coat, string tie, blue jeans, boots and a black cowboy hat. Chey recognized the dress that the girl wore as one she'd bought for the prom.

"I can't believe this," Chey murmured, looking around her. She spied Anthony looking breathtaking in a double-breasted tux, Frank uncomfortably adjusting a new black suit, Bay strutting in his more trendy one. Thomas, bless him, looked like a waiter, and Matt looked like exactly what he was, a redneck who wouldn't be caught dead wearing a tie even if he did have to put up with a collar and a dark blue suit. She gaped at Mary May giggling like a school girl with Frank's wife, Genevive, and a young woman veiled and draped in scarlet. Simmonses were mingling and chatting with turbaned Legantine royalty and New Orleans's elite. She realized with a shock that Johnny and Dana were talking to the mayor! And one of her nieces was flirting shamelessly with a fascinatingly handsome Arab wearing enough gold to warrant armed guards. Unbelievable.

She laughed. What else was there to do? Leave it to Brodie Todd to put together the Simmonses and the Legantines. And why not? He'd put himself, a dedicated single father, together with her, a determinedly childless and, she now realized, slightly neurotic, career-oriented businesswoman. Her heart felt as if it would burst right out of her chest for a moment. He had put together more than that, bless him. He had put together her life. Finally. Melded it into one lovely, rich collage. She looked at her mother, with whom she had so often been irritated with absolutely no good reason, and picked up her hand.

"I love you, Mama," she said softly, "and I'm glad you're here."

Mary Louise squeezed her hand. "That's nice to hear."

Suddenly something barreled into Chey and nearly knocked her off her perch. "Chey-Chey!"

She caught her balance and looked down. Seth grinned up at her. Dressed in a suit with short pants and an adorable bow tie beneath a white Peter Pan collar, he looked utterly sweet, and she was surprised by how delighted she was to see him.

"Hello, sweetie!" She opened her arms, and he climbed all over her, arms locking around her neck, to kiss her three times on the cheek. She laughed again, completely uncaring that her skirts were crushed or her makeup undoubtedly smeared. "How are you?"

"I not go sleep now," he said solemnly, shaking his head to emphasize his abhorrence for the idea. Chey smiled, knowing she was being both charmed and used. She couldn't have been more pleased. It meant that the child trusted her. Chey looked at Kate, who obviously had been assigned to watch over him.

"It's past nine o'clock," Kate told the boy gently.

"I not go sleep!" he insisted.

"You promised your father you wouldn't argue," Viola reminded him firmly.

"Tell you what," Chey said, setting Seth on his feet again, "you go up to your room now and get all ready for bed, but you won't have to go to sleep until I come up to say goodnight, okay?" He considered that skeptically. Any moment now, he'd see the flaw in her plan. Once in that bed, he would undoubtedly slip off to sleep. She quickly amended. "Better yet, you won't have to go to sleep until you're ready. You can play in bed until you're tired. How's that?" Obviously feeling he'd won a great concession, he nodded vigorously. She bent forward and kissed him. "All right then, sweetheart. I'll see you later. Go with Kate now."

He stuck out his bottom lip mulishly.

"Hmm, I believe I see Brodie headed this way," Viola said.

"Oh, we'd better hurry," Kate whispered urgently, and

Seth immediately grabbed her hand. The two of them hurried off together. Chey laughed.

"He's an adorable little boy," Louise said fondly.

"Yes, completely adorable," Chey said with a proud smile. She glanced at Viola. "Thank you for that inspired assistance, by the way."

"Actually," Viola drawled, "Brodie is—"

"Here," he said. Chey glanced over her shoulder and smiled.

"It's about time," Viola said tartly, then she swung her long legs off the chaise and stood.

"Uh, Grandmama," he began, as Viola pulled a lace hanky from her bodice and began waving it over her head. Chey rose, too, then, and took the hand Brodie offered her. To her surprise, it was trembling slightly. "We never seem to get the timing right," he muttered.

"Brodie, are you okay?" Chey felt compelled to ask.

"Yes, I think so," he said, tugging at his collar. "I'm sorry that took so long. I meant to speak to you in private."

"Attention!" Viola called. "Attention everyone!"

Brodie glanced at Chey apologetically. Then he took a deep breath and said, "What the hell."

The music died, and the crowd began to hush. Viola looked pointedly at Brodie. "I believe you have the floor." With that, she sat down again.

Brodie cleared his throat and glanced around, clutching Chey's hand so tightly she feared that he might break something.

"If I could have your attention," he said quite needlessly. "I'd, um, like to take this opportunity to do three things. First, I'd like to thank you all for coming. You honor all of us here at Fair Havens with your presence on this very special night. Among other things, this is a sort of unveiling, and you're welcome to look around the first floor of the newly redone house at your leisure."

He paused, then went on. "Second, I want to extend my personal welcome to Ambassador Sadhoturan and his family and staff. The mayor will have more to say on that officially a little later. However, Ambassador, I want you to know that I consider your presence here on this particular evening a very fortuitous event. Which brings us to the third reason I'm standing here.''

He looked down briefly, sucked in a fresh breath and said, ''Most of you know Chey Simmons. Actually, most of you are family,'' he quipped, and laughter ruffled lightly through the crowd at that. ''Many others of you know her as the most talented, brilliant architect in our fair city, a true expert on restoration and historical detail, as we here at Fair Havens can bear witness.'' Chey felt her face heat slightly at the effusive praise, and she couldn't help wondering what was going on. ''She's also the unofficial general of a formidable army of artisans and builders and suppliers and, well, the list is endless,'' he said, his voice dwindling into intimacy. Then he cleared his throat and raised his voice again, adding, ''But she's even more than that.'' He looked down at Chey and stated quite clearly, ''She is the woman I love.''

Suddenly she knew exactly what was going on, exactly why he'd invited her family here. Oh, this man did like grand gestures! His past efforts paled miserably in comparison. Looking down at her, he took both her hands in his now. She saw the pounding of his pulse at his temples, the working of his throat as he swallowed. Her own pulse fluttered dangerously.

''Shall I get down on one knee?'' he asked softly.

The sound that came out of her was half laugh and half sob. She shook her head, saying shakily, ''You're doing just fine.''

''Okay, then here's the part I skipped before.'' He took a deep breath and asked in a clear, loud voice, ''Will you marry me, sweetheart?''

It was all laughter now. ''Yes!'' He let go of her hands, and she threw her arms around him, felt him folding her close.

"Finally!" he said, as applause swelled around them.

She was lifting her mouth to his when a hand clapped him on the shoulder and a familiar voice said, "I believe you've forgotten something." Chey glared at Georges, who stood behind Brodie, resplendent in a white dinner jacket and black bow tie. "Congratulations, by the way."

"Oh!" Suddenly Brodie was cramming a hand into the inside pocket of his coat. "I hope you like it," he said, coming up with an antique filigreed platinum ring bearing an enormous emerald-cut diamond solitaire. "Because if you don't," he hurried on, "we can both blame Georges and get something else."

Georges took one look at her face and chuckled. "It's not going back, Brodie. Trust me."

"Oh, my gosh! It's fabulous!"

Brodie was trying to get it on her finger, but her hand was trembling so badly that she had to help him, and then it was safely in place and he was kissing her as ardently as the circumstances allowed. When she looked up again, they were surrounded by family and other well-wishers. She hugged her mother, who was weeping, and Frank, also suspiciously wet of eye, and all the rest of them. For several minutes they were trapped by the excitement of her family and his guests. Then the music started again, and Brodie took control.

"If you'll excuse us," he said firmly, pulling her after him as he pushed his way through the crowd, "I'd like a moment alone with my future wife."

They practically ran for the house and didn't stop until they were at the foot of the stairs again. "My head's swimming," he exclaimed, pulling her to him, "and it's not the wine."

She laughed, hopping up and down on her toes, blood percolating frantically. "I love you!"

"I love you, too. How do you want to do it? *When* can we do it?"

"Get married, you mean? I—I don't know. What did you have in mind?"

He narrowed his eyes. "I've had this picture of you in my head, coming down these stairs in an, oh, Audrey Hepburnish gown."

She clapped her hands together at that. "I like that!"

"Then when?" he demanded.

"Well, how many people are we talking about?" she had to know. "Do you want a big wedding or just family?"

He laughed at that. "Sweetheart, with your family, it's the same thing."

She put a hand to one cheek. "It is, isn't it?"

"Look," he said, "if it's going to take more than a month, I want a civil ceremony right now and then a formal one."

"Would you settle for six weeks?" she asked hopefully.

"If you're moving in here tonight, I will. I'm taking no chances on losing you again."

She slid her arms around his waist. "I'm home, and I'm home to stay."

A slow, sensual smile grew across his face. "We'll save the master bedroom for our wedding night. What do you think of Legan for a honeymoon?"

"Perfect." She was thinking of her old room upstairs and all that had taken place there, when she remembered with a sudden catch of her breath that a certain family member remained uninformed. "Let's go tell Seth!"

"Good idea."

Catching her hand, he practically hauled her up the stairs. They reached the top. He swung her around the newel post and into his arms for a long, deep kiss, at the end of which his expression became solemn.

"You still haven't told me why you left before? What happened that day to drive you away?"

"It doesn't matter," she said evasively.

"It matters to me," he told her softly, fervently. She

sighed inside, hoping he wouldn't think ill of her but knowing that she had to clear the air between them.

"It's not Seth," she began. "I can't imagine a world
without Seth. I love him, I've missed him, and I'm looking
forward to being his mommy. It's the idea of *other* children
that I had to get used to."

"What other children?" he asked, brows drawing together.

She pressed herself against him once more, lifting her
chin. "*Our* children."

His eyebrows went straight up to his hairline. "*Our*…?"
He backed up a step, tilting his head. "Chey, do you want
children, I mean, babies? I—I thought you had decided
long ago that you don't, ah, didn't."

"I can change my mind, can't I?" she asked softly.

"Sure. Yeah. I suppose. I mean, if you really want to."

"I want to," she said carefully, "if you do."

"Well, I just thought we agreed about this, that's all,"
he murmured.

She pulled back, looking up at him in confusion. "But,
Brodie, you're the one who said you wanted more children.
Sort of. I mean, you sort of said it."

He goggled at her. "When did I say that? I don't remember saying anything like that!"

"That day, that last day," she reminded him. "You told
Janey that *I* would be the mother of your children, *all* your
children. Those were your exact words!"

He stared at her in pure bewilderment for a moment, then
he exclaimed, "I didn't mean it that way! I only meant
that, in my mind, in my heart, you are more Seth's mother
than she has ever been and that should I ever, by some wild
quirk of fate, have another child it would most assuredly
be with you and no one else!"

Of course he had meant that. Of course he had. She saw
it clearly. Now. "It didn't sound like that at the time," she
muttered.

"Chey," he told her, impatience tinging his voice, "we

talked about this at the very beginning. I told you then that I understand your decision not to have children. It's one I shared. I never saw myself as a father until Seth came along, and believe me, any latent tendencies to fatherhood that I might have had, he has more than fulfilled.'' He closed his eyes and seemed to be struggling to make her understand. ''I love Seth,'' he said. ''I wouldn't trade one moment of his life for anything or anyone, not even you. I'd kill to keep him safe. He's an integral part of me.'' He looked her straight in the eye then and added, ''But I wouldn't go through another baby unless I had absolutely no other choice. Again.''

Chey looked at him, standing there with his hands at his hips, and bit her lip, appalled by her own stupidity. Hadn't her heart always known that this man was perfect for her? That was something else he'd taught her, to listen to her heart. But she still needed a little reassurance.

''You, um, you don't think we're being selfish, do you?''

''Selfish?'' he echoed, then he shook his head. ''More like self-aware, I think. We know ourselves, Chey, especially in this. And we don't owe it to the world to produce children, Chey. We do owe it to the world to take care of the child it has already brought to us.''

She smiled, sure for the first time who and what and how she really was. Because of him. Because of this incredible man.

''I should have known,'' she said. ''I'm sorry.''

''For having misunderstood?'' he asked dismissively.

''For not knowing that you are the one man in the world who truly understands and accepts me as I am.''

He smiled with great satisfaction. ''You were willing to turn yourself inside out for me, willing to set aside your convictions and misgivings to give me what you thought I wanted. There is nothing to forgive in that.'' His smile slewed to one side. ''If it took you a little longer than I would've liked to figure out that you want me that much, well, I think I can devise a suitably delicious penance.''

She blushed, just thinking about it, excitement beginning to simmer in her veins. "Do your worst," she pleaded.

"My best," he promised, "at the earliest opportunity."

"I can hardly wait," she whispered, leaning into him. "But now let's go tell our son the news." She straightened and held out her hand. He took it and pulled it through his arm.

His eyes said it all, everything that she now knew without any doubt. Oh, how good life was going to be with this man! Together, they walked down the hallway of the grand old home they had resurrected from the past and into a future as bright as dawn.

* * * * *

SILHOUETTE®
SPECIAL EDITION™

AVAILABLE FROM 19TH DECEMBER 2003

SEAN'S RECKONING Sherryl Woods

The Devaneys

Fireman Sean Devaney knew love never lasted—so he refused to chance it. Until he met vulnerable single mum Deanna Blackwell. But could Sean risk his heart and build a family?

COMPLETELY SMITTEN Susan Mallery

Hometown Heartbreakers

Lawman Kevin Harmon longed to teach virginal Haley Foster the art of lovemaking. But his integrity—and a fear of commitment— kept him in check. Then his resolve was put to the test…

THE FAMILY PLAN Gina Wilkins

The McClouds of Mississippi

Caitlin was a lawyer with a plan—and it didn't include falling for gorgeous single dad Nathan McCloud. But when Nate's smile melted her heart, she was tempted to revise her schedule…and reach for the stars.

THE TROUBLE WITH JOSH Marilyn Pappano

Rugged Josh Rawlins never wanted to settle down. Then he met reformed 'bad-girl' Candace Thompson whose past was unforgivable to Josh's family. So what could he do except deny the hunger he felt for the one woman who should never be his?

JUST A SMALL-TOWN GIRL Patricia Kay

Callahans & Kin

Bumping into old flame Zach Tate—now a single dad and desirable sheriff—again made Maggie Callahan's hopes sparkle anew. But would Zach propose this time and make her a happy wife and mum?

THERE GOES THE BRIDE Crystal Green

Kane's Crossing

When Daisy Cox fled from her wedding with the help of loner Rick Shane, the last thing she expected was for passion to flare between them. So would Daisy actually walk all the way down the aisle one of these days?

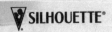

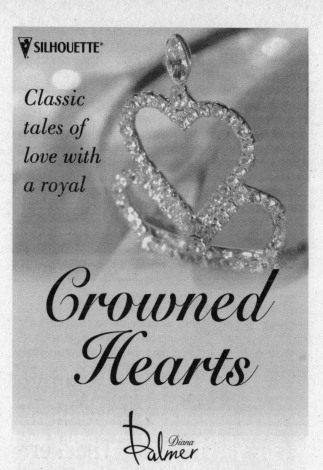

SILHOUETTE

DORANNA DURGIN

VIRGINIA KANTRA

MEREDITH FLETCHER

Femme Fatale

Under orders to get their man...

Available from 19th December 2003

0104/055/SH71

▼ SILHOUETTE®
DESIRE™

are proud to introduce

DYNASTIES:
THE BARONES

Meet the wealthy Barones—caught in a web of danger, deceit and…desire!

Twelve exciting stories in six 2-in-1 volumes:

0104/SH/LC78

FREE

4 BOOKS
AND A SURPRISE GIFT!

We would like to take this opportunity to thank you for reading this Silhouette® book by offering you the chance to take FOUR more specially selected titles from the Special Edition™ series absolutely FREE! We're also making this offer to introduce you to the benefits of the Reader Service™—

- ★ FREE home delivery
- ★ FREE monthly Newsletter
- ★ FREE gifts and competitions
- ★ Exclusive Reader Service discount
- ★ Books available before they're in the shops

Accepting these FREE books and gift places you under no obligation to buy; you may cancel at any time, even after receiving your free shipment. Simply complete your details below and return the entire page to the address below. ***You don't even need a stamp!***

YES! Please send me 4 free Special Edition books and a surprise gift. I understand that unless you hear from me, I will receive 6 superb new titles every month for just £2.90 each, postage and packing free. I am under no obligation to purchase any books and may cancel my subscription at any time. The free books and gift will be mine to keep in any case.

E3ZED

Ms/Mrs/Miss/Mr ....Initials.......................................

BLOCK CAPITALS PLEASE

Surname...

Address..

....

....Postcode ....

Send this whole page to:
UK: FREEPOST CN81, Croydon, CR9 3WZ
EIRE: PO Box 4546, Kilcock, County Kildare (stamp required)